translating WOMEN

translating WOMEN

BILL STENSON

thistledown press

Library and Archives Canada Cataloguing in Publication

Stenson, Bill, 1949-
        Translating women / written by Bill Stenson.

ISBN 1-894345-77-0

        I. Title.

PS8637.T46T73 2004   C813'.6   C2004-904341-2

Cover and book design by Jackie Forrie
Typeset by Thistledown Press
Printed and bound in Canada on acid-free paper

Thistledown Press Ltd.
633 Main Street, Saskatoon, Saskatchewan, S7H 0J8
www.thistledown.sk.ca

 **Canada Council
for the Arts**   **Conseil des Arts
du Canada**   Canadian   Patrimoine
Heritage   canadien

Thistledown Press gratefully acknowledges the financial assistance of the Canada
Council for the Arts, the Saskatchewan Arts Board, and the Government of Canada
through the Book Publishing Industry Development Program for its publishing program.

ACKNOWLEDGEMENTS

Some of the stories in this book have been previously published as follows:

"Nadine Needs Time To Think", "Lonnie and the Man With an Even Keel" and "Elvira's Thirtieth Birthday" in *Grain*; "CLICK: a girl with two pails" and "Oil Paint" in the *Malahat Review*; "No One Can Fish Forever" in the *Antigonish Review*; "Translating Women" in *filling station*; "Simple" in *Storyteller*; "The Only Sign of Fire" in *Love and Pomegranates* (Sono Nis Press); "The Short Life of Carmelita" in *Blood & Aphorisms*; "Hope" in *echolocation*; "Hot Wheels" in the *Wascana Review*; "Horse Sense" in *Prairie Fire*; and "John Lennon's Car" in the *Toronto Star*. "Wise Men Don't Have Speaking Parts" was originally published as "Bad Men Who Love Jesus" in *The New Quarterly*.

Gratitude goes out to all those working at Thistledown Press who graciously welcomed my agent-less manuscript with open arms.

Writers work in solitude but they are never alone. A long list of people contributed to the evolution of the stories in this book through their editorial suggestions and support. The list includes: Larry Cohen, Bill Gaston, John Gould, Michael Kenyon, Kimberly Lemieux, Mike Matthews, Janice McCachen, Linda Rogers, Leon Rooke, Jay Ruzesky, Patricia Young and Terence Young. The author has been inspired by a long list of students he has taught over the years and would particularly like to thank the editors of the literary magazines listed for publishing some of these stories.

A special thanks to John Lent for his superb edit of the manuscript and for caring about these stories as much as the author did, and to Susan Stenson who was brave enough to give all of these stories a first read.

Contents

for Devin, James, Cole and Yvonne

Elvira's Thirtieth Birthday

EDMUND DID EVERYTHING IN HIS POWER to make Elvira's thirtieth birthday picture perfect. There was something about reaching a decade, something in the way it marked one's progression through life like pencil marks on a door jamb. He could tell Elvira was ruffled at the thought of reaching such a milestone and Elvira was the kind of wife who told him everything.

As far as Elvira knew, a couple of friends and her mother were popping over later in the evening to celebrate her birthday, but Edmund had arranged a surprise party spread out over the two floors of their house and into the backyard. Edmond had rented three large tables for the yard, which was decorated with streamers and balloons and, for later in the evening, lanterns in the fruit trees. Twenty-eight guests had been invited and with the two of them, that would make thirty. Edmund had never completed his English degree but he'd always felt comfortable with the Romantics. At eight o'clock a three-piece band called the Emory Brothers was to arrive and they could play rock and roll, swing music, reggae, even country music if there was a request. Only two of them were brothers, apparently, but they came highly recommended.

The guests were to come at five for cocktails, and shortly after, Elvira would arrive with her mother after their annual trek to Butchart Gardens. Elvira's mother treated her to Butchart Gardens for her birthday present in a tradition that spanned eleven years. Edmund felt there was a difference between tradition and routine, but he never said anything. He was addicted to kind thoughts.

With his mother-in-law's help, he had pictures tracing twenty-nine of Elvira's thirty years cut and laminated to fit under half of their glass coffee table. The only picture he could get his hands on of Elvira at twenty-one was of her in the arms of Eddy Funk, whom she'd considered marrying, so Edmund inserted instead a picture of their cat, Tickles, even though the cat wasn't around when Elvira was twenty-one. If Elvira liked the coffee table, it could remain as a conversation piece, and if she cared to, she could do the same for him when he turned thirty. She had four years to consider the matter.

The caterer was doing a Greek dinner and it didn't come cheap. When Edmund's best friend, Lucious, found out how much Edmund had committed to, he gave him two hundred dollars to take the sting out. Lucious was a lawyer and could afford it. That's the only reason Edmund accepted.

"You've done a wonderful job," Lucious said. "Elvira is going to be one happy lady."

Lucious graciously offered to help Edmund with the last minute decorations. It took two of them to string the lights between the trees, and then, with a wink and a thumbs up, Lucious was on his way out the door and Edmund was left to shower, get dressed and fret about what might have been forgotten.

The invitations read "gifts not requested" to remove any sense of obligation. Edmund wanted the party to be a celebration, not a mourning, and he'd been quite specific when asked what one might bring if one were to bring an unrequested gift. Nothing, he said, that would underline the time span of thirty years. Things like dildo soap on a rope, hair dye, coke bottle glasses, shirts that read *Over the hill and underpaid getting there*, a Donny and Marie Osmond eight track tape. Edmund was hoping for things like personalized cards, milk bath, scented candles.

Edmund had found the perfect gift. His wife loved to swing and he'd found a two-seater, handmade, that could be moved to the front porch once the weather changed. Right now it sat under the plum tree with a pink bow and the latest Maeve Binchy novel. He was excited just thinking about it.

By three o'clock he was showered, clean-shaven, and had all the cashews put into bowls. Elvira loved cashews. When the phone rang, Edmund washed the salt off his hands before answering.

"Hello."

"Edmund, is that you?"

"Oh, it's me all right. I'm the only one home except the cat and she refuses to answer the phone." Edmund remembered that the cat hadn't been fed in all the confusion. He tucked the phone under his chin and headed for the cat food.

"Edmund, this is Muriel, your mother-in-law."

"Yes, Muriel. I recognized your voice. You phone here quite often, remember?"

"Has Elvira turned up?"

"No, of course not. She's coming here at six with you. How are the gardens this year? Did you enjoy lunch?"

"That's what I'm trying to tell you, Edmund. She's not with me. We walked around the gardens for about an hour and we were standing there watching the stage band when she started talking to this man. She knew him from work I think. She introduced him to me but I can't remember his name."

"Tickles," Edmund said.

"No, that's not it," Muriel said. "I think it began with an L."

"I'm trying to get the cat's attention. I think she forgot she didn't eat breakfast."

"Edmund, I can't find Elvira anywhere. What am I going to do?"

Edmund could see his mother-in-law on the other end of the phone, her fingers spread and pushed into one of her many wigs. She complained her hair was thin, but being out in the wind made her nervous and he couldn't see that the trade-off was a good one.

"I wouldn't worry about Elvira. She won't have gone too far. Check the washroom. The dining room. She'll show up. Phone me back when you find her."

Tickles was hiding under the couch and chewing on something, possibly a mouse. Some cats required more patience than others. People who hated cats were lacking in patience, in Edmund's experience.

Thinking it might be a good idea to have some background music before the band showed up, Edmund started sorting through the CDs. He had them spread out all over the living room carpet when the phone rang again.

"Edmund, has Mother phoned?"

"As a matter of fact she has. She's more than a little stirred up. You know as well as I do it doesn't take much to homogenize your mother. Leonard Cohen or Bob Dylan for background music tonight. What do you think?"

"I don't know. Maybe something lighter. I know Mother won't care. Speaking of Mother, did she say where she was?"

"Not precisely. She's at Butchart Gardens looking for you as far as I know. Where are you, anyway?"

Edmond spotted the sound track to *When Harry Met Sally* under his left foot. It would be perfect. A romantic mixture. Something for everyone.

"I'm in the dining room of the Sidney Hotel. The waitress was downright snippy in my opinion and I don't think I'm particularly picky. Do you think I'm picky?"

"No, Elvira, I think you're very tolerant."

"I think so. Anyway, I ran into Lenny when I was out with Mother. He's the man from work I was telling you was having trouble. I did mention him, didn't I?"

"Lenny . . . Lenny. I don't recall."

"Well, let me tell you, he's been having trouble lately. He's right on the edge, Edmund. Right on the edge. Anyway, I could see he was in big trouble so I offered to step out with him. He suggested the Sidney Hotel because it was the first place in Canada he'd ordered a beer. Imagine that. Anyway, we're not in the beer parlour, we're in the dining room."

"What did you order?"

"Just an appetizer. And a small martini. I could see Miss Snippy was going to be a while, so I phoned you."

"I'm glad you did. I was wondering where you were. What about your mother?"

"Oh, don't worry about Mother. We came in her car, remember? She can find her way home. If she phones, tell her I'll meet her at the party, will you?"

"Sure, I can do that. So . . . you'll be home about what time?"

"Well, I'm not sure. Lenny looks pretty shaky right now. I'm working on him."

"It's your thirtieth birthday, Elvira. I want it to be special."

"Please, Edmund. Enough about birthdays. I'll phone you if I'm going to be long."

Elvira hung up before he could run the idea of playing soundtracks by her. Soundtracks would be perfect. He was surprised he hadn't thought of it before.

Lucious and his wife, Manny, arrived at five o'clock and the rest of the invitees were in place by six, except for Elvira's mother, Muriel. She phoned and was in a fluster because she didn't have

Elvira with her. Muriel said she thought her role was transportation, so Edmund told her that was precisely why she should transport herself over to the party, *pronto*. She finally arrived after six o'clock, somewhat teary-eyed, and Edmund had to take her aside and settle her down with a glass of white wine.

The wine Lucious brought was some he'd made six months earlier, just for Elvira's party. There were thirty bottles and he had them specially labelled: *Gently aged and full-bodied*. Edmund's friend from high school, Lou Honish, was in the trucking business and brought two kegs of beer from Alberta. People were milling around and seemed to be having a good time with the cashews. Finally, someone yelled, "Hey, where's Elvira? It's nearly six thirty." Edmund shot Muriel a look that successfully conveyed she was to say nothing. Then the phone rang again. Edmund ran up the stairs off the balcony and took the call from the kitchen.

"Hello, Elvira?"

"It's me again. Edmund, I swear you're intuitive. I've always said you have a special talent."

"How's Lenny progressing?"

"Slowly. Don't get me wrong, he's coming along. The reason I'm phoning is because we're on the ferry. These phones don't work too well once you get out in the middle of the strait."

"What are you doing on the ferry?"

"We're going to Vancouver. Lenny said he couldn't spend another minute on the Island because of this problem he's having. Everything here reminds him of her."

"I see."

"I've heard of that happening, Edmund, I really have. For some people it's a song, for others it's Chinese food. For Lenny, everything about Vancouver Island brings him down. It's sad but outstanding at the same time. He's acting very strange, Edmund. He says things like, I bet the ocean is cold. Of course it's cold, everyone knows that. That's why I'm here on the ferry. I'm afraid he might try to jump ship. I've got my eye on him right now, Edmund. He's sitting down reading a *Popular Mechanics* magazine."

"Elvira, I hope you don't mind me saying so, but that sounds pretty normal to me."

"The magazine's upside down, Edmund. That's how bad he is. I'm just going to see him over to the other side, get his feet safely on the ground. Then I'll be home."

"I'd really like you home here, Elvira. It's your birthday. What ferry will you be catching?"

"Well I just caught the six. We barely made it, too. We were the second to last car. So that means we get over there about eight. If I feel he's safe, I might get back on the nine. Otherwise, it'll be the ten. I told him *I'm* driving off the ferry. He was doing this jerky thing with the wheel on our way here that I didn't particularly care for. We don't have guests yet, do we? It's awfully early."

"No, why?"

"I just thought I heard something in the background. Let me guess, you're watching the golf channel? It's amazing to me you watch the golf channel and you don't even play golf. Lenny has his face against the window so I'd better go. This connection is fading. Maybe you'd better phone Mother and tell her I'm okay. I wouldn't want her to worry."

When he got off the phone, he found Tickles up on the kitchen table poking his paw into the birthday cake. The cake read: *Happy Birthday Elvira*. No mention of it being her thirtieth, only a small replica of Tickles in the corner, now sporting a paw print. Elvira loved Tickles.

"That was the birthday girl," Edmund said, when he came down the stairs. "She'll be along in a while. We'll just carry on with the party until then."

The catering company arrived and quickly set up. Edmund poured Muriel another glass of wine and put on a CD. "See if anyone can guess the movie this one came from," he said.

"Food is ready," the caterer said. He was a round man with unnaturally black hair and a ridiculously thin mustache. Edmund couldn't see why anyone would shave a mustache down to a thin line. He sensed the caterer wasn't Greek. Just a man who acted like a Greek.

"That's fine. We'll start. Grab a seat, everybody. Let's eat it while it's hot."

"What about Elvira?" someone said.

"She'll be along. She wouldn't want us to wait. We'll warm hers up later."

Edmund sat at the end of the table near the large bouquet of flowers. There was a hint of a sunset and no wind. He was thankful there was no wind.

"*Shirley Valentine,*" Manny said. "The music. I'd know it anywhere."

"Woman go to Greece," the caterer said. "I watch this movie. Independent woman."

"The calamari is very good," Edmund said. The caterer crossed his arms over his stomach and grunted.

The dinner was a big hit. Bonnie, a young girl Elvira had taken a shine to at work, said she'd written a special tribute for Elvira and what was she going to do with Elvira not here for her own birthday. Edmund insisted she read it anyway and he would summarize later. It was a generous tribute and he realized Bonnie hadn't known Elvira all that long.

The Emory Brothers arrived with their instruments so Edmund made room for them at the end of the table. The wine and the band were a good combination; liquor and rock and roll made the backyard thick with celebration. The caterer didn't seem to be in a hurry to go anywhere and he joined the party. He soon had everyone doing a Greek circle dance and once in a while he'd yell out, "Perikles," which was the name of his restaurant. Muriel got into the swing of things and seemed to have her eye on the caterer. Edmund considered warning her he was an artificial Greek but thought better of it. Three sets of uninvited neighbours, two with kids and one with their dog, were somehow in the middle of it all. People started in with requests but they couldn't stump the band, hard as they tried, and Edmund overheard someone say the Emory Brothers had a second cousin who'd won a Grammy. They slowed things down with "Moon River" and it made Edmund look up and thank the sky for a perfect night, hanging with stars and a half moon.

"Hey, Edmund," Lucious yelled from up on the deck. "Elvira's on the phone. She's calling collect from somewhere."

If anyone had heard what Lucious said, they didn't let on. When Edmund took the phone from his friend, Lucious looked at him with complete understanding or no understanding at all, Edmund couldn't decide which.

"Elvira?"

"Elvira speaking."

"Elvira, what time is it?"

"I've got 10:15. This is the best watch I've ever owned. You bought it for me, remember? It actually says 9:15 because it's standard time but I just add an hour."

"Where are you? It's getting late."

"At the Quaker Inn. Believe me, it's nothing fancy. No pool or anything."

"In Vancouver?"

"Abbotsford, actually. I'm a bit nervous about driving in the big city. Lenny seems much better, Edmund. He really does. I think getting him off the Island was a stroke of genius."

"How are you getting home?"

17

"I'm assuming by ferry first thing in the morning. We're a long way from the airport out here. But don't worry, Lenny is paying for everything. He ordered us both room service from a restaurant down the street. My god, but that man can eat. You'd think it was The Last Supper. He ordered cabbage rolls because it was the one thing *you know who* refused to cook."

Edmund held his hand over the receiver and smiled as someone he didn't recognize trudged through to use the washroom. If she was a neighbour, she must have just moved in.

"So you're not going to make it home for your birthday?"

"I would if I could, Edmund, you know that. If you had a chance to celebrate your birthday or save a man's life, which would you choose? Tell our friends I'm sorry things worked out this way. Did you buy me anything?"

"Listen, Elvira, there's something you must do for me. I want you to phone back in half an hour exactly. OK?"

"I'm at a phone booth in the lobby, Edmund. The rooms don't even have a phone. No TV either. Just a radio and a bible and the radio doesn't work."

"Use your cell phone and call my cell number."

"Edmund, you're a wizard. I forgot I had one. It's now 10:18 Seiko time. Let's make it 11:15, OK? I've got to tuck Lenny in properly. My guess is he'll sleep like a log."

The birthday party began to develop pockets of eccentricity. It didn't seem to matter what music was playing, Muriel was content to slow dance with the caterer, an intimate slow dance in Edmund's opinion. The courtesy dancers had fulfilled their obligation and were sitting on lawn chairs having detailed conversations and serious drinks. Many of the guests were still dancing, however, because the music was so damn good, and under the lanterns the neighbourhood kids were playing boccie ball for money with Elvira's boss. The kids were making a killing. The party now had a momentum of its own except that Manny, who occasionally suffered from narcolepsy, was beginning to nod off in a lawn chair, and Lucious was leaning toward taking his wife home early. Edmund made a decision to fetch the cake even though it wasn't yet 11:15.

The cake had three large candles, each representing a decade, and when Edmund came down the stairs with it, the band started playing "Happy Birthday" and people joined in.

"I don't see Elvira. Where is the birthday girl?"

"Elvira has had an emergency to contend with," Edmund said. "I didn't think it would be fair for anyone to leave without sampling a piece of the birthday cake. It's a carrot cake ordered from the Swedish bakery."

No one said anything for a while. They just stood there and looked at the three candles burning into the night.

"I guess we should blow out the candles," Edmund started to say, when Bonnie pushed her way forward.

"I'll blow them out for her. Elvira and I are soul sisters."

The neighbourhood kids had grown in number. They kicked the boccie balls under the hedge and loitered around the cake. Tickles ran under the table with a mouse and, with help from the kids, Edmund retrieved the mouse and threw it in the garbage.

The cake was cut and served. The crowd shifted to the table covered with gifts and began speculating on what Elvira would be opening if Elvira were here. Once it was clear that guessing was futile, people started explaining what they had brought. A Japanese foot massager that didn't require batteries, *A Lover's Guide To the Best One Hundred Places In the World To Kiss*, a colour your own lipstick kit that was completely barium free. When the phone rang, Edmund was prepared.

"Listen up, everybody. This is going to be Elvira on the phone. Let's sing 'Happy Birthday' so she'll know what she's missing."

Edmund held the phone up high so the full force of the choir could be heard. It was more like yelling the song, really, and in the time it took, most of the neighbourhood kids had helped themselves to a second piece of cake.

"Happy birthday, beautiful," Edmund said, then covered the phone with his hand. "She's crying," Edmund said. "I knew she'd like that. Thanks you guys. You were great. Elvira, we all wish you were here with us. I think this is the first birthday celebration I've ever been to where the guest of honor wasn't present. Elvira?" The band started up again so Edmund walked around the side of the house with the phone.

"Edmund . . . he's dead."

"What?"

"I was tucking him in, like I said I would, and he kind of got twisted up in a knot and when he relaxed he wasn't breathing. Edmund, what am I going to do?"

"Are you sure? There's no heart beat?"

"He's dead, Edmund, I'm telling you. I've never seen a dead person before but you know one when you see one. He even looks funny. Kind of limp or something. He was all worked up and I was reading from the Book of Job to calm him down."

"Is anyone else there?"

"Not a soul. I don't think anyone else is staying here. What do I do now? I can't just leave him."

"You have to phone the police. Elvira, do you hear me? You must phone for help."

Elvira started crying again. "I can't do that, Edmund. What are the police going to say when they find someone my age in a room with a man who's supposed to be asleep by now, not dead? I'm thirty years old, Edmund. *Thirty years old.*"

Edmund was patient. He had to be. Elvira was like a punctured tire when she got this way. Eventually she would run flat.

"Everything is going to work out, Elvira. There are some things we can't do anything about. I can't help you. I can't help you one bit."

❖❖❖

By the time the band had packed up, most of the guests were gone. There was a little corner of the birthday cake untouched and Edmund took it upstairs and put it in the fridge for the next day. He helped Lucious load the empty wine bottles into his Volvo and slowly walked around to the back of the house. The yard was a mess as he knew it would be. He would wait until tomorrow to put things back in order. He just didn't have it in him tonight.

The caterer and Muriel were wrapped in a blanket, borrowed without permission, enjoying the swing Edmund had bought for Elvira. Muriel's auburn wig was slightly off kilter, but neither of them seemed to notice. Tickles was up an oak tree and meowing pitifully. Edmund got out his extension ladder and climbed nervously until his head was hidden in the branches. Without actually climbing out on a limb, it would be impossible to reach the cat.

"Put mouse on ground," the caterer said, watching him the whole time but not offering to lend a hand. "Cat come down to mouse."

Edmund slowly made his way down the ladder. When he got his feet back on the ground, the world seemed a more comfortable place. The guy wasn't a Greek, of that Edmund was certain, but it didn't matter. Retrieving the dead mouse from the garbage can just might work and the way things were, there was nothing else to be done.

John Lennon's Car

MARRIAGES HAPPEN ALL THE TIME. Emilia and Franz married in a DeHavilland Beaver and said their vows flying over Mt. Baker. The service was small, but when they returned to earth they had a hanger reserved in Richmond where the reception ran until 2:00 in the morning. Their friends, John and Nancy, married on an Indian Reserve for spiritual reasons. Elvira and Edmund were married in a Catholic church even though no one in either family was Catholic. This wasn't easy to arrange, but Elvira had her ways. Ed proposed to Lorraine under water during their scuba lesson, and they were later married in the desert because Ed felt it important to balance yin and yang. When Penelope married Jerry she went the conventional route: an invitation list longer than Wilt Chamberlain was tall, thousands of dollars in flowers, a twenty-one day cruise for a honeymoon. People lost touch with Penelope for a while, but clearly something had happened. Penelope said Jerry died but never gave any details. People had the feeling she was speaking metaphorically and Jerry had moved on to greener pastures.

These marriages spurned a new generation of Canadians with names like Wednesday, Sunshine, Dakota, Ulysses, Morningstar, Yoda and Carnation. Elvira and Edmund only had one child, a girl, and as yet she didn't have a name. Technically she was called Blank, but that was only because her parents refused to fill in the blank. They were trying names on as she grew older, thinking her eventual name ought to in some way reflect the person she was to become. When Elvira and Edmund took her places, there was always an element of expectation while people waited for "Blank" to be introduced. At various gatherings she had been referred to as Stubborn, Passion, Finicky and Recalcitrant. Her parents were making a list of all of them and had agreed to let their daughter pick one if they couldn't agree on an ideal name, once she turned thirteen. Teenage years were hard enough on a child, even with an identity.

People were always on the lookout for change, for something spectacular to deal with. That, according to Franz, was why people were fascinated with the weather. At least once a month you could comment on a terrific wind storm, a severe snowfall or a pending water shortage. Franz believed he'd never seen as many happy people in Victoria as during the dreadful winter known as the blizzard of '96. Three feet of snow in two days and only skidoos on the road. You'd swear they were on drugs, Franz said, harkening back to an earlier time. Emilia wasn't sure if she agreed with Franz on this point, though she agreed with most of his ideas. It wasn't healthy to agree with your spouse on everything, so at least for now she'd decided to reject his boredom theory.

Franz was waiting for Emilia to pour the wine before starting in on the mail. They got a lot of mail and enjoyed opening it together over a glass of wine after work. They always divided the fat envelopes and the skinny envelopes equally between them, but anything with the least bit of flare became instantly communal.

"Oh, boy," Franz said. That was all he said.

"What?" Emilia was in the middle of considering a *Chatelaine* renewal and was only half listening, her "what?" obviously made to fill a gap.

"Edmund and Elvira are having a party on the date of their anniversary. The party's at their house."

"We should do that sometime," Emilia said. "I've always found it funny how people celebrate their wedding with friends and then every year after that it's like they're in a cocoon."

Franz thought about what his wife said. Then he thought about butterflies, how they miraculously developed out of a cocoon that looked like it would never change. "This isn't a regular party," Franz said. "It's a divorce party."

They read and re-read it, but it didn't make a difference. Edmund and Elvira were getting divorced and holding a party to mark the occasion. It said absolutely no gifts for obvious reasons. Come between 7:00 and 12:00 and stay as long as you want.

"What do you make of that?" Emilia said.

"I think it's some kind of joke," Franz said. "It must be."

"No way. Some people can laugh about a divorce after the fact, but no one jokes about it. I wonder what will happen to . . . "

Franz knew his wife was trying to remember what Blank had been called the last time they saw her. He couldn't remember either.

Emilia and Franz weren't the only ones to labor over what to wear to a divorce party. No one in their circle of friends had ever heard of such a thing, at least not when both parties were involved. Nancy had run into Elvira down at Value Village the week before. Nancy was doing an article on thrifty shoppers for *Monday Magazine* and Elvira was looking for something to wear to the party that was completely new. The styles in Value Village sometimes dated back to the sixties. Nancy asked if this was for a real party and Elvira said it would be for real if people showed up and if they didn't, she and Edmund would call it an early night. Either way, she'd said, it didn't matter.

Emilia had to work to convince Franz that wearing black wasn't the thing to do. They obviously don't see this as a bleak experience, she explained. Emilia's idea was to wear what they were wearing when they first met up with Elvira and Edmund, but Franz was now three sizes larger so he settled on a new pair of black jeans and a sweater that floated over his middle. They both figured they'd see eight to ten people there, but when they turned down Denman Street it was obvious that Edmund and Elvira had accumulated more friends over the years than they'd been able to keep track of.

"That looks like John Lennon's car," Emilia said. "It couldn't be."

"Of course not. That car's in a museum in Victoria under lock and key. Someone's just trying to be a clever copy cat."

"But how do you know that?"

"I just know."

"It sure looks like John Lennon's car," Emilia said.

When they got to the door they were greeted by the daughter who explained that she'd been Charity for two months now and it was beginning to stick. She curtsied and offered to take their coats even though neither of them was wearing one.

"I guess we could have brought coats in case we're outside later," Emilia said. "I never thought of it."

"If you do need a coat," Charity said, "just let me know. My parents have all kinds of coats they won't be needing after tonight."

Emilia looked inside and grabbed Franz's arm. "There's a lot of people here. People I don't know. I don't think I'm going to like this."

"If they had a fire alarm I'd pull it for you," Franz said. "Here, let me get you something to drink. There's Penelope out on the back porch. *She's* smiling. *She's* having a good time."

"Of course she is. She's single. She needs to meet new . . . you don't think Penelope is after Edmund?"

"Don't be silly," Franz said. "Penelope's a Leo. She married a Virgo once and look where that got her."

Franz felt ill at ease when he finally ran into Edmund. He couldn't explain why but he did. "You've invited a lot of people," he said. "I was beginning to think you weren't here. Where's Elvira?"

"Someone in her office has decided being an alcoholic isn't a good idea and she takes organic brown sugar in her coffee. Elvira's gone to get some."

Franz said life was full of surprises. He knew it was a cowardly way of surrounding controversy, but it was the best he could do.

"We talked about it for three days in a row," Edmund said. "We set aside an hour each night and made a list of what was and wasn't working. It was a pretty lopsided list."

Franz had an image of the lists being recorded on two long scrolls that rolled around on the floor like free spirits. Logic suggested they would be on sheets of paper, 8 1/2 by 11, but the idea of scrolls wouldn't go away. He considered asking for clarification when Edmund pulled a cigarillo out of his shirt pocket and nodded toward the balcony.

"And Elvira's comfortable with all this?"

"Elvira's completely comfortable. She's ecstatic in fact. Do you want one of these? You're welcome."

"No thanks, I don't smoke."

"I just started. It's not fashionable these days and I think that's part of the appeal. Both my parents died before I got around to rebelling. Do you want to shoot some pool? A guy's coming to pick the table up tomorrow so it will be your last chance."

❖❖❖

There were so many people at the divorce party it was an hour later before Franz spotted Emilia. She emerged from a bedroom and had apparently been talking to Elvira. Emilia's mascara was running, but Elvira, whose hair had been in a bun but now danced on her shoulders, was somewhere in the plateau period of inebriation — the part where your senses appear to be stimulated and the heavy head hasn't yet arrived.

Just after ten o'clock Edmund rang a bell and he and Elvira stood beside the fireplace while as many people as were able gathered around. They shared in their explanation that anything they owned and wanted had been stored in the garage and everything else in the house was up for grabs. Edmund brought out a package of Post-it notes that were sealed in plastic wrap. Elvira said people who wanted something only had to put their name and what they were willing to pay for it on the Post-it note and attach it to the item. She said she knew the kind of friends they had would make reasonable offers, and if they saw something they liked and were willing to pay a higher price just to put a note on top of the original. It's not a silent auction, more of a whispering auction, she said, then added that if anyone saw something going they'd given them as a wedding present, they shouldn't be offended. They were both entering a phase of materialistic cleansing was what it amounted to.

There was amazing stuff sitting around the house and Emilia and Franz weren't the only ones who knew it. Charity wanted to stay over at her friend's house, so Edmund and Elvira decided they'd both walk her there. If there is such a thing as a silent *h-m-m-m*, that's what was left in the room.

People who were outside on the porch and balcony wormed their way in to see what all the fuss was about. Slowly, the plan Elvira and Edmund had outlined was repeated over and over until it almost seemed practical.

Ed said, "Well, I'm only going to bid on one thing. If they're going to sell it anyway it might as well be me who buys it. I've always wanted one of these."

When anything happens, someone has to go first. He struggled to open the Post-it notes and pens from their packaging, then wrote something small and placed a note on the black vibrating chair. Everyone who'd ever come to visit had tried the chair. It looked just like an expensive lazy-boy, but when you pressed a button on the side it sent a delicious, vibrating chill down your spine.

Soon the house looked like an ant hill, people grabbing notes and discussing prices. Huddling with their spouse and arguing over what they'd be willing to pay. Penelope waltzed around the living room with an invisible partner, stopping from time to time to snuff out candles lit around the room. Edmund and Elvira returned from delivering Charity and announced that all bids were final come eleven o'clock.

"I can't believe what I'm witnessing," Franz said. Emilia wanted to say something, he could tell, but she couldn't think what. "It seems almost disgraceful, people pouring over their personal possessions. They look like scavengers."

"I saw $75.00 on the wicker picnic basket we bought them. I'm sure we never paid that much."

"Prices do go up," Franz said. "I can't think of anything here I'd want to buy. Can you?"

"Absolutely not. Unless they're accepting bids on some of their art. I've always adored that black and white marble statue in the entranceway."

❖❖❖

It was close to midnight and the house was almost gutted. Ed and Lorraine were still there, as were Franz and Emilia. Penelope was there too, but she'd passed out on the couch hugging a teddy bear. All the small stuff had been carted out, and people said they would return for things like beds and couches in the morning.

"Thanks for coming," Elvira said. Franz looked at his watch. It was five minutes before midnight. "We really appreciate seeing you all again. This is our last night together so we don't want to waste it, if you know what I mean. We're going to retire."

If Edmund had anything to say he didn't, he just followed Elvira into the bedroom and shut the door. Ed and Franz argued over who should get Penelope home and in the end they left her sleeping on the couch. Lorraine said she'd look after the lights and the party was over.

A whole section of the city was without street lights. Driving home felt eerie, almost like they were out in the country or driving through a city devastated by war.

"I feel like I'm caught in a dream," Emilia said, peering out the window, trying to find definition in the landscape. "I can't believe what happened happened. Edmund's been studying Greek, did you know that?" Franz said he didn't know that. "He's going to work on a freighter and travel around the world. Elvira is off to volunteer in India for two years. By herself. Charity is going to a boarding school in Shawnigan Lake. It all started with a list they made. Did you know that?"

Franz did know that, but he let Emilia tell it all over again. It was one of those things that might come clearer if he heard it one more time.

"Elvira said she thought every couple should sit down and make up lists. I don't think that's a good idea. Do you?"

Franz didn't say anything, just kept his eyes on the immediate future, hoping he wouldn't run into a road block. With the lights out they were probably busy with other things.

Some things you knew for *certain* and other things you just knew. He knew Emilia was pleased with the marble statue that lay like it was passed out on the back seat, and he was pleased with what he'd paid for Edmund's brand new set of Ping irons. That was enough to know for one night.

No One Can Fish Forever

MOVING TO A NEW PLACE ISN'T EASY and Uncle Roscoe says you can stuff your suitcase all you want and still never remember everything you need. Uncle Roscoe came to Canada years before us and he's still not settled. Learning to be a good speaker is a big thing and I'm doing my best. I'm not the first one to do grade eight twice and I get to stare at a bunch of new girls. I like girls and I like to collect things.

I was seven when we moved. Canada is a big place on the map but I only know this valley where we live. It's small with a lot of trees and a lot of rain. First it was pine cones. I used to keep them in the woodshed, barrels and barrels of them. Then I collected bottle caps. I had seventy-three different caps and some people said I was a genius but most thought I was stupid. Collecting can be lonely. That's why I moved on to stamps. The best way to get stamps is to buy them cheap off someone who used to think stamps were worth collecting but found out they weren't. I went to my stamp collecting club every Friday night for a whole year. Stamp collectors may look different but they are the same in a strange way. If you went to a stamp collector's meeting you'd know what I mean. Stamp collectors are what my Uncle Roscoe calls "over the moon."

I gave up on stamps after the fire. My brother Brucy used to like my stamps and I'd get mad at him for licking them. I would beat him up and I'd take it all back if I could but you can't. A beat person's been beat and there's not a damn thing you can do about it. Mom says not to sit around and feel sorry for things in the past. There's only one point to go on living from and it's right now. Mom's a survivor. Tough like a mean fist.

There were books of stamps from different countries all over my shelf and then the fire came like a big tongue and licked them off the earth. People tried to give me stamps to get me going again but I just couldn't do it. When you lose some things you never recover. It was time to move on and now I collect suicide notes.

> *I haven't been on earth for a long time. I've been floating and I feel so close to heaven I can taste it. I don't want anyone to feel sad tomorrow. I'll be watching you and I don't want sadness. Think of my safety. Think of me being pulled somewhere better. Think of me finally going to a place I belong.*

> *your son, Trevor*

I collect notes but mostly I don't have the real notes. Sometimes I get lucky, like with Trevor. I went to school with Bonnie and Trevor was her older brother. He got to be seventeen and no more. They moved away somewhere but Bonnie gave me his note without her mother knowing because I was the kind of person who understood someone like Trevor. I hear about notes or read about them and copy them down. I listen closely to what each one says and I try to write it down just like the real person would. I don't know how close I come but I think I come close. My teacher, Mr. Maxwell, says I have intuition for a guy who doesn't read much. I asked him is it true what the newspaper said about American suicide notes being written full of poor English and he laughed and said he would not be surprised. I don't always know the big things about language but I learn a lot by studying the little things. I haven't thought about my stamp collection for a long time.

One thing different now is my private life. Stamp collectors want more stamps or better stamps or stamps no one has seen for a long time. I keep my collection in a metal box under my bed and wear a silver key around my neck.

If people saw my collection they'd be sad. You can't help but be sad when you read them but sadness is only on the top. You've got to look underneath. This guy in school, Bradley, has his locker next to mine. His parents have big problems but they've got money. He tells me about his visits to a shrink called Dr. John Skull. I thought it was a joke at first but his name is in the phone book with a red box around it. I think Dr. Skull would be an all right guy if you went fishing with him, but Bradley has to sit there each week and let him chip away. I think I could do that. Sometimes I think I already do.

Boys are four times more successful at suicide than girls and most of my notes are boy notes. When I get a girl note it almost tastes funny. I get this creepy feeling and I don't know why. Girls should be protected, Uncle Roscoe says. Women and children first. I think about Mom sometimes and how tough her life is. I read my notes over and over and learn more each time. I've been reading Marsha's note a lot lately.

It must be hard for a mother to stand up when she's needed. Mother, I know you know what's going on. I know it. You never stopped him. You pretend everything is just fine, as if this kind of thing happens in every family. He's still after me, like last Wednesday when you went to your book club. If you want to do one thing right in this world, Mother, you'll take this note to your book club in June. Discuss it with other women. Pretend it's a novel. Learn something.

Shana, I love you. The last thoughts of Marsha T.

Even if the name is Turner I only put down T. because I know people are in a lot of pain. Statistics say it happens every seventeen minutes and more often in the spring. When I read about Marsha it makes me mad. I think about the torture she's suffered and it makes me want to be mean. I don't get that way with boy notes. Boy notes are clean and straight. Or angry.

My dad was a good man. He'd get mad sometimes, but mostly he was in a good mood. He used to play tricks on me and my brother. They were all in fun, like when he'd stick his finger in the peanut butter and grab Brucy's teddy and say the bear had had an accident. My brother didn't play with his bear for weeks and he never ate peanut butter again. Dad laughed for months. Mom says she wishes he hadn't played so much poker with Uncle Roscoe until the sun came up. Uncle Roscoe's coming in one week and I'm looking forward to that. When he's here I feel strong and alive.

The world changed after the fire. We had to move and rent again. After a house fire things you miss aren't the ones you'd think. My stamp collection got really big, mostly foreign stamps, but I got over it. What I wish I had was the trophy my grade three teacher, Mrs. Dearholme, gave me for having the best disposition. I didn't know what it meant then, but I do now. I would go without shoes to have it back again.

Last week Mom suggested I sign up for baseball. Every month it's something new because she thinks I need to be involved. I spend too much time in my room with my thinking she says and she doesn't like my silence. I don't want to stand in right field two times a week and listen to parents yell about how to play the game right. In my room it's not my thoughts I'm thinking.

Some people try to kill themselves and if they don't get it right they keep trying. Jarett from Oklahoma was one of them. He tried to starve himself and was in the hospital on intravenous tubes, then he took sleeping pills but his brother found him and the doctor pumped his stomach out. I don't know if Jarett wrote a note the first time. He might have written more than one.

> *Mom and Dad, I don't want to write this. The last time was hard on you and I'm sorry. I want to stay but I can't. I was born stupid. God says there's a special place for me. I don't know what happens now. It has to be better. You always said third time lucky. I'm not afraid.*
>
> J.

I think about Jarett right after he tried starving himself to death. It's hard to make what's wrong go right. When you're born you want to live but not all ideas seem worth it. Some ideas aren't very bright, like killing yourself being against the law. Stupid as skunk cabbage. That's what Uncle Roscoe would say.

My dad was arrested drunk one night downtown. It was after the fire and they kept him behind bars all night. Mom went down to the police station and told them how my dad was hurting and they told her to go home. The things you don't want to know about can hurt so bad. That's how I felt that night, and I felt sorry for Mom.

After that night my dad didn't get mad or drunk ever again. Mostly he got quiet. He used to watch European soccer on TV but he lost interest. It was the TV that caught fire and most TV's never catch fire. My dad was mad because he thought he should've rescued my brother and he tried but the firemen wouldn't let him go back in. Everyone got out but my brother and they said it was the smoke that got him and he didn't feel a thing but we heard him screaming for help. The TV isn't used any more and Dad doesn't collect anything. It's bad when people don't want something.

My collection tells me how different people are. I use a scale of one to ten to judge if people would kill themselves. Some people I don't think would do it. I think Uncle Roscoe would only be a one. Everything that happens to him is an adventure. He has owned seventy-two different cars since he came to this country and he has thirteen cars in his collection right now. Last year he rolled over twice in his sports car and got his picture in the paper holding onto the bar that saved him. He told people he wouldn't be in the news if he didn't roll over two times. No one I know is a zero, not even Uncle Roscoe. Something could easily push them up the scale. Uncle Roscoe will have new stories to tell when he comes this time and they will be good. Maybe the two of us will go fishing.

I apply my scale to people I meet at school. Most teachers are five. They're not happy but their show keeps them going. They make me work with Mr. McDermott an hour every day for English. I thought it was a stupid idea at first but now Mr. McDermott is the best part of school and my English is getting better. I talk with an Irish accent sometimes. Mr. McDermott moves around and he's always busy. He'll ask me an innocent question like what's my favourite hockey team and when I tell him he says, "Don't tell me. For the love of Pete, don't tell me that." If I say my favourite drink is orange juice he says the same thing. Sometimes we go outside and shoot on net with the road hockey equipment. "Holy St. Francis," he'll say, "he picks the top corner, with his backhand nonetheless." The two of us are out in the sunshine while the rest are inside facing the blackboard. He says I read some words backwards and because of this we read *The Three Little Pigs* starting at the end. It makes us both laugh. On Fridays he makes up stories in Gaelic and tells them with a twinkle in his eye.

Sadness can be the opposite of laughing but sometimes it's anger. There was anger in the note Molly left when she found her husband.

Ron when you read this I hope you get the message you are a complete fucking asshole your life is a big infected sore and you are the puss Ron and I'm not the first to tell you you're whole life stinks I'm glad Amy died at birth because I wouldn't want anyone to grow up and call you their dad you've fucked more women since you got out of the navy than you did when you were in and you don't care about anyone but your own fucking self you're the worst kind of Catholic there is just show up on Sunday and your slate is clean you could start saying your Hail Mary's and not stop until you die and God wouldn't listen look in the mirror and imagine what other people see and you'll take a gun to your ugly head fuck you fuck you fuck you

M.

Molly's note is full of hatred and I feel sorry for her. I also think about Ron. He's got problems and I wonder what he does with them. If you don't love a lot you leave room for hate. It doesn't stop there. Molly left Ron and drove to her twin sister's house and shot a hole in the roof of her mouth with Ron's gun. Seven days later, her sister did the same thing. A girl has to be pretty mad to use a gun.

Sometimes I think girls don't like me. Rebecca has beautiful long hair and I walk behind her on the way home. Every day I'd walk closer and closer but one day she turned around before her driveway and called me a bohunk. Then her older brother started kicking me. Mr. McDermott will know what bohunk means but I already know it's not good. Now I'm careful not to follow too close.

Mom's quiet most of the time but she can stand up to anything. She got mad at me because I tried to help with the dusting and I broke a picture on the mantle. The glass broke and cut my dad's picture across his face and arm. It was the one picture she had of us four she got from Uncle Roscoe after the fire. When she gets angry she throws things, but this time she just held the picture against her chest and cried. Pictures should be covered in plastic. That's a good idea. I like it better when Mom throws things. That's the saddest she's been since Dad left us.

I was the one who found him in the basement. I don't think he thought about it much except for the hanging part. Leather boot laces are strong things. You get to the basement from outside the house. He didn't mean for me to find him. He didn't know he'd be hanging there turning first one way then the other. A dead body doesn't know which way to turn. Uncle Roscoe came and held Mom through the night. I cooked breakfast.

So many things come to mind when you collect notes. I think of so many reasons and I ask people about suicide. Some say it's okay if you're in big pain and you're going to die anyway, but most people in pain can be fixed like cars. My dad didn't think he could be fixed so he hung himself. If my dad was still alive and our neighbour was hurting, my dad would say fix him up. That's what I think. I think people have had enough. When I go fishing I go by myself and I can fish for hours. If I don't catch anything, after a while I've had enough. No one can fish forever.

There's a dance at our school and Mom says I should go. I told her most people ask someone to go with them and then you don't feel alone. I already asked two people and I still don't have a date. I'd like to ask Rebecca but I'm afraid.

Mom reads romance novels and it takes her a week to read a whole one. Reading a whole one I can't do yet so she reads me parts of hers. These people meet in places like the Eiffel Tower and the Leaning Tower of Pisa. So many towers. Last night she says Uncle Roscoe isn't coming for a visit because he met a woman on a big boat cruise. That's good for Uncle Roscoe and I can see his smile from here but now I'm sad he won't be at our house. Uncle Roscoe make us laugh around here. Mom says she doesn't want to talk about it.

The news about Uncle Roscoe makes me miss my dad again. I asked Mom if we should have done things differently. She says it's better not to talk about it but I want to know. Sabrena killed herself in Pittsburgh after she left notes for her mom and step dad every day for a whole month. Leon had eleven overdue library books because he was trying to figure out how to make a gas stove leak into the house. Willie R. from Goose Bay made a New Year's promise he would die within a year and then ate rat poison on Christmas Day. Did my dad plan like that?

Oil Paint

"WHISTLER, YOU TEND TO THAT CHAMBER POT or I'll ask Maggie to do it when she gets home. And don't think I'm kidding."

Mom knows how to pull me away from my painting. She knows I don't like going down there three times a day, but somebody's got to do it. Mom uses two canes now and hasn't been down to the basement for almost a year. And it's no secret how much I love Maggie.

I fell in love at thirteen when Maggie won a blue ribbon for her caramel fudge at the Fall Fair. There were four judges that year: Dr. Abernathy, family doctor to half the town; Miss Nicholson, the grade three teacher who should have been retired years before but kept working because she lied about her age; Jan Paige who wrote a food article in our weekly paper, and me. For the life of me I don't know how I got to be a judge but my mom had something to do with it. Probably my credentials were I loved sweets. Maggie was the only junior who baked fudge that year so they put her up against all the sweet-toothed, recipe-harbouring homemakers who baked with a passion that must have pleased our local dentist, Dr. Qually. None of us knew who we were voting for: Maggie just made the best fudge, that's all there was to it. When they gave her the blue ribbon and the miniature gold trophy, she shook the judges' hands and curtsied. When it came my turn she wrapped her arms around me and kissed me on the cheek. I hadn't given much thought to what a girl was good for that Labour Day weekend, but I now know a fudge kiss can last a lifetime. Five years later I married Maggie under the apple tree in her back yard.

Uncle Bob was always taking me places as a kid, and I wouldn't have been interested in the Fall Fair if it wasn't for him. "Uncle Bob," I say, "if it weren't for you I wouldn't have met Maggie." Even when I say it now you can see a twinkle in his eye, and Uncle Bob doesn't react to much anymore.

My dad changed too, but not before my mom married him and stayed with him long enough to have me. After a drinking spell he'd be gone for months, although not far, and there were always a few people in town who'd take turns looking out for him. Eventually they'd turf him out, and he'd settle under the Connie Mack baseball grandstand. People took pity on him and left him food. Even the friends who couldn't stand him any more felt sorry for him and dropped off a mickey from time to time. Mom had no use for him. She'd walk me to school in grade one and make me say things about him as we walked down the sidewalk: "My daddy is lazy," she'd say, and I'd repeat, *My daddy is lazy. My daddy's a drunken fool. My daddy can't hold down a job. My daddy's useless.* By the time my mom was finished, I was never caught short if teachers asked about my family.

Four times Mom let him back into the house, and he'd get a job and stay dry as long as he could, sometimes for a couple of months, once for a whole year. He was a carpenter and built the house we still live in, although I know it wasn't what Mom had in mind, and the house got bigger every time he came home to live. One section has shingles on the side, one has cedar siding, another orange stucco. The last time he lived with us he added our living room and what I use as an artist's studio, and he covered the outside with tar paper and cedar strips and it's been that way ever since. It's a huge house with five bedrooms, two bathrooms and a basement that works best for short people and, although we've had a few problems with the roof leaking, my guess is this house will be here as long as we care to live in it.

Uncle Bob is my dad's brother, and because of that you'd think my mom wouldn't want to have a thing to do with him. But it was my uncle who stood up to Dad when he got out of hand, and that's when I started doing things with Uncle Bob. He took me creek fishing, helped me build a car with lawnmower wheels, taught me how to swim on my back and how to tell when a penny was worth more than a penny. If you pack a lunch when you go fishing, he said, never take salmon sandwiches. He delivered vegetables and came every Sunday for dinner and always brought a box full of vegetables he said they were going to throw out. Growing up, we ate a lot of cabbage rolls, and we went to church every Sunday where Mom would pray that Dad would never be seen again. She'd say these prayers out loud in the church, and for eight years in a row her prayers were answered. Uncle Bob started to go soft after that, and one Sunday we came home from church and found him sitting on our front porch, blubbering into his hands that the Russians were going to drop a bomb and could he come in to take cover. Mom said yes, and he's been living in our cellar ever since.

"Whistler, you heard me!"

"I heard you, Mom. I'm just cleaning up here. I'm on my way down."

I've been painting for six years, and I try to do a painting a week but sometimes it takes longer. It's been interesting to watch my art evolve over time because I started painting faces, then I moved on to fruit, but my most successful phase has been nudes, and the most money I've ever got for a painting was one of my Maggie staring into a handful of cards. One card, the ace of spades, is turned away from her, and the look on her face is one of uncertain expectancy; her beautiful long legs are crossed tastefully as if to suggest playing cards in the nude is routine. Lately I've been toying with nature in some extraordinary ways, trees with blossoms that don't normally blossom, houses growing branches and roots. Some of them are quite striking, and every spring I take everything I've painted down to the agricultural hall for the annual art show. But I'm an artist who's committed to change, and anything that doesn't sell I bring back home and paint over. That's what I like about oil paint — the canvases last forever and I can feel the difference in weight between a new canvas and one I've done over a gazillion times.

The chamber pot was outside the cellar door With no bathroom downstairs I have to pack it up to the main floor, which I try to do surreptitiously because I know it's the one thing about living in the cellar that Uncle Bob wishes wasn't necessary. That and his weekly bath. On Sunday evenings I take a bucket of warm water and a washcloth and towel and leave them outside his door; then before bed I pick everything back up, and that seems to be clean enough for Uncle Bob. He owns two pairs of long johns, and I set a clean pair by the door with his bathwater.

Maggie is the only one who works, my mom is never afraid to remind me; she delivers fish around town in the morning, and Mr. Owens, who owns the truck, lets her use it all the time. She cleans houses in the afternoon, even on Saturdays, and she takes our daughter with her wherever she goes. Starla-Fawn goes to school next year, but she can read already, and she reads to Maggie while she drives the truck. I worked on construction myself for a while, but Maggie believes in my art and says someone with my talent needs to devote time to living the life of an artist. I know it would be a lot easier on all of us if more of my paintings sold but, like Maggie says, some artists like Van Gogh took a long time to become famous. Nobody to this point has had to sell any vital organs. Mom cooks dinner for us most nights, and all she asks in return is that I take care of Uncle Bob and drive her to church on Sunday, which I can do because Maggie gets to use Mr. Owen's fish truck.

"Take these magazines down for Uncle Bob when you go. We're going to try roast beef and baked potato tonight. Maggie won't be home till late."

"He won't eat it," I said.

"We'll see," Mom said — *we'll see* from a woman whose eyes are failing to the point where she can't tell one of my paintings from another. I'm not sure this phrase will work for her much longer. Every few weeks she tries giving Uncle Bob what we eat, but it never works. He has toast and jam and orange juice for breakfast, then Red River cereal and plain hot water in a stainless steel cup for supper. Every time Mom tries one of her experiments I end up bringing it back untouched, cooking the usual and taking it down. Uncle Bob never eats lunch.

I flipped through the magazines before I put them outside the cellar door with the chamber pot. Uncle Bob reads nature books mostly, and magazines are a luxury he looks forward to, so Maggie picks them up from the houses she cleans. We have to be careful there are no articles on politics, war or anything to do with the Russians, because such topics will set him off and he can take weeks to pull out of it, and while Mom's usually pretty careful I always double-check. If Uncle Bob wants someone to talk to he leaves his door open a crack, but his door was closed so I went upstairs to help with dinner.

I heard Maggie pull into the driveway, and I'd heard her coming a block away because the pickup's muffler is barely hanging on. Mr. Owen's theory is that it's more economical if you only fix a vehicle when something breaks, and he claims to have statistics to back it up. Sometime in the next couple of weeks Maggie will finish her deliveries without a muffler and have to take the truck in. Mr. Owen is one of those people who can be kind and temperamental at the same time.

"How was art today?" Maggie asks the same question every day she comes home from work. Her smile is like a sunflower.

"Good," I said. "Good but not great. What I'm painting lacks inspiration, you know. Everything I paint feels like an exercise."

"My bet is the inspiration you're looking for is right under your nose. Be patient. It will come. Mother, I brought a couple of fish home. When there's only two Mr. Owen doesn't bother to freeze them."

"Thank you, Maggie," Mom said. "If Whistler sold as many paintings as you sold fish we'd all be rich."

When she says things like that it's mostly to thank Maggie for being who she is; it's a sadly understated fact Mom's had a hard time accepting she has an artist for a son.

I took the plate of roast beef down for Uncle Bob and put the water on for the Red River cereal. The meal was delicious. I sometimes wonder what Maggie, Starla-Fawn and I would do if Mom wasn't around to cook for us.

After supper I took the cereal downstairs, and the cellar door was slightly ajar. He's always relieved when he gets his real supper, so I sat down on the only chair and watched him dig in. Meticulous is the best way to describe him because he never wastes a thing. The first few times I ventured into his little den I thought his life hideous, but I've gotten used to it now, and when I look around at the stacks of nature books, the lamp on a small end table, and the magazines neatly stacked underneath, I'm convinced Uncle Bob is completely content, his world uninterrupted by decisions. While he was eating he pointed to the single package of spare light bulbs beside the lamp.

"I'll bring down some extras," I said, and he smiled in appreciation. He finished eating and put his bowl beside his cot and stretched out, hands like butterfly wings behind his head, and I knew from experience it was best to let Uncle Bob pick the topic for the day. He's not what you'd call a talkative man, but he'll save up for months, then get this look on his face like he has gas and only one idea of how to get rid of it.

"The two of us built a raft out of logs washed up on the beach, and the Russians weren't a threat in them days, you could be out in the open, so we got big spikes and built a platform to stand on, and we put a flag up, a white flag to show we meant peace, but we didn't care where the raft ended up so long as we landed in a foreign country. Trouble was when we were finished it was too heavy to drag into the ocean, so we pestered our father for weeks to help us, and one night when he'd had more than enough to drink he took us down to the beach, stole an outboard and pulled our raft out onto the water, and I remember we were amazed that it floated. Well, he towed us out past the dock, and it occurred to me it was already deep water, and we thanked him, but if he heard us he didn't let on, he kept pulling the raft farther and farther into the bay, all the way out to the narrows, and we were screaming for him to stop, but he was laughing above the sound of the motor and paid no attention, then he finally let the towrope fly and powered his way back to the dock, and I think he figured he was rid of us for good. After a while we noticed we were drifting out of the bay, and then it got dark and your dad started crying, so I started telling him stories about how we were going to be all right. They were good stories, and I think I half believed them myself, but it took hours for us to drift close enough to land so we could swim to shore. The water was cold, and it was the middle of the night, and then we scrambled up the beach and found the road and flagged down a car. When we got back there was no one home because when your grandfather went on a tear your grandmother went after him—he was always getting into fights, and she was afraid he was going to kill someone. So nobody knew what happened to us that night, and the raft was never mentioned again. Even our father had no recollection."

Mom had tried over the years to get Uncle Bob out of the cellar. She had Dr. Abernathy make a house call, but Uncle Bob clung harder to the sides of his cot because he was terrified back then, not the complacent soul he is today.

When it was clear he had finished his story I told him how happy Maggie was and how Starla-Fawn was reading all by herself, but he just stared at the ceiling, and I imagined him reliving the hours he'd spent on the raft with my dad. I thanked him for his visit, and when I left I realized Maggie was right: the inspiration for my painting was right here in the house.

By the time I got upstairs, the dishes were done and put away, something Mom doesn't mind in the least if I'm doing something to help Uncle Bob. I read to Starla-Fawn and tucked her into bed, and I asked her what she would do if she were stranded on a raft on the ocean and it got dark and she had no idea where she was going, and she said she would look up at the stars and use them to guide her to California so she could visit Disneyland. Starla-Fawn knows there's a man called Uncle Bob who lives in the basement, but she's never met him. Maggie once suggested I take her down to meet him, but I worry about what she might think of a man dressed in long johns living in a root cellar, because Starla-Fawn is the kind of kid who can turn fearful when you least expect it, like the time she saw a pirate on the back of a Shreddies box and didn't want a thing to do with that cereal until she got a pair of scissors and cut the pirate out of the box and threw him in the garbage. I wish Uncle Bob could see solutions to things the way a five-year-old does.

That night in bed I told Maggie the story of Uncle Bob and my dad out on the raft, and Maggie went silent on me, almost like she was dreaming with her eyes open, then when she did speak she said she didn't know who to feel most sorry for, my dad who was living under the grandstand or Uncle Bob who was living in the cellar. Maggie and I always fall asleep holding hands, and that night Maggie fell asleep long before I did.

When I woke up it was four in the morning and I could see my way into the painting. By the time Maggie was ready for work I had an outline of a fabulous log raft with just enough moonlight to find my dad hunched over in fear and my uncle with one hand on his back and the other on the flagpole, staring hopefully at a small light that could be a cabin onshore or one of the many stars in the sky, it's not clear. I embellished the ocean, making it wild. Maggie stared at it a long time and never said anything; she just gave my hand a squeeze and left. That day I worked until I had it just right. It was the first painting I'd done I felt compelled to finish, driven by something outside.

❖❖❖

I didn't paint a thing for almost a week. I was exhausted, and the painting had cast a spell over me. I was hoping to show the painting to Uncle Bob, but his door remained closed for the next three days so I had to wait. His door was eventually left open a crack, and I felt giddy and nervous taking the painting to show him. When I walked in he looked at me oddly, as if I had unsettled his universe, but when I turned the painting toward his cot he sat there, dumfounded. His reaction was the same as when he first heard the Russians were threatening to drop a nuclear bomb — emotion without sound, and he kept wanting to touch the painting. That night Uncle Bob didn't say a word, and every time I'd try to leave with the painting he would reach out and grab hold of a corner. He finally lay back and fell into a deep sleep, and I took the painting upstairs.

❖❖❖

I don't leave the house much as a rule, except on Saturdays when Mom looks after Starla-Fawn and Maggie and I go to town to do the grocery shopping. When we're finished, Maggie visits her parents, unless she has a cleaning job that can't wait, and she drops me off at the ballpark. Dad's been living underneath the grandstand at the baseball park for almost four years this last stretch, and the city seems to accept his presence like a weed in a gravel driveway. He even has his own mailbox hanging on the outside, and any mail he gets, including his monthly assistance cheque, comes addressed #1 Connie Mack Grandstand. Being a carpenter by trade, he's managed over the years to build himself a regular apartment under the bleachers by snitching materials from construction sites around town. He's a hard man to track down in the summer because he's never around if there's a ball game on — the kids drive him nuts, he says. But the rest of the year he looks forward to my Saturday visits, and I always bring him a burger, onion rings and a large coffee with two sugar and one cream from the Dog House.

I never know what state he'll be in on Saturday mornings, and if he's suffering from a fight with the bottle he makes a brave attempt not to show it. I know he looks forward to my visits, and never once have I found him drunk on a Saturday, which I take as consideration on his part. He has a padlock on both sides of his door, and he knows it's me by our secret knock, one that follows the beat of "The Russians are coming, the Russians are coming!" Dad knows all about Uncle Bob living in our basement, and I think he appreciates someone looking out for his brother.

"Morning, Dad. I brought you a hamburger. Thought you might be hungry."

I always say something stupid like that even though we both know I routinely bring him a hamburger and onion rings. He's always liked surprises, and I think it's his way of holding out hope that some day his life will turn around.

"Thank you, son. You're always so kind to your old man." He never calls me Whistler. "Son" is his way of underlining our genetic relationship. I like to think he still remembers my name.

Our usual conversation covers the health and well-being of Maggie, Uncle Bob, Starla-Fawn and my mom. He always asks about Mom, and I don't mention that her eyes are going and that her arthritis has to be monitored with painkillers most days. He only met Starla-Fawn once when she was still a baby, but I bring pictures of her that he has hanging up. Dad says Starla-Fawn will break a thousand boys' hearts before she's through.

"How's your painting coming along?" he asked.

"Great. I think I've made a breakthrough. I did a painting with you in it."

My dad went quiet and curled into a ball. He remained quiet while I told him about the story Uncle Bob gave me about the raft and how the two of them were left to drift toward the brink of death. He always asks about Uncle Bob, but he never wants to know anything other than he's still alive. When I finished telling him about the painting he sat still, like someone had hit him over the head with a sledgehammer and he was trying to decide which way to keel over.

"The story about the raft," I said. "It's a true story?"

"As true as a story can get," he said.

If he's feeling up to it, we often go for a walk along the river. The river holds a myriad of memories of fishing with Uncle Bob, but I've lazily walked along its banks so often with Dad that it no longer seems like a place to take anything out of. I'm able to measure Dad's health by the pace he wants to keep and how far he wants to walk. This Saturday had a nervous energy that walking couldn't seem to use up, and he uncharacteristically began to tell me a story.

"Your Uncle Bob was the oldest, and he had too much to worry about when we were kids. He always knew when things were about to turn sour, but he wasn't able to do much. If he tried to stick up for our mother he'd get the back of the hand if the old man was in a hurry or the belt across his bare ass if there was time to kill. I was completely useless. I'd hide behind the sofa or under the bed and save my crying until it was all over. Your Uncle Bob would look out for me if I was in trouble but he'd make me pay if I didn't do what he said. Don't borrow my bike today, he'd say, then wait until I couldn't resist temptation and pounce on me and slug me in the stomach, give me a pepper belly until I'd cry out for mercy. I think he figured if he practiced on me long enough he'd be able to whip the old man.

"One night in the spring, right after the time change, we came home late. Dad hadn't been home for three days, and Mom worried, thinking the phone was going to ring and she'd have to go down and bail him out of the clink. It was almost nine-thirty and we were supposed to be in by eight o'clock and asleep by eight-thirty. All the way home we'd made plans to sneak in through the bedroom window and pretend we'd been there all along, but when we got close to the house we could tell something was wrong. There was yelling and laughing and the sound of a bottle hitting the floor. Bob opened the door to the kitchen, and there was our mother standing on the table without a stitch of clothes, surrounded by our dad and four of his drunken buddies, taunting her to turn around, arguing over whose turn it was. When we opened the door, something in the room escaped. No one moved. Everything was silent. Our mother stepped off the table, grabbed her dress and said something threatening to our dad, who sensed his public violation of our mother had travelled where it didn't belong. We both ran after her, and she barricaded us in her bedroom by shoving the dresser against the door. She needn't have bothered. The place cleared out, and our dad yelled something abusive from the kitchen before he left. None of us ever saw him again.

"After our dad left and enough time passed to make Mother believe he was never coming back, she started telling people we were illegitimate, that she had no idea who our father was. Looking at it from her perspective, I think she was right."

When we got back to the grandstand he thanked me again for the hamburger. I said I'd see him next Saturday, and he said it depended on ball season. I realized I might not see him again for several months.

❖❖❖

Sunday was a miserable day. I had my dad's story on my mind and no way to expiate it until the following day. Sunday was a day we all took off because Mom wouldn't have it any other way. That week my painting flowed so easily I felt I was an observer to the process, and by Wednesday I had two paintings completed that captured the scenes my dad had described. When I took Maggie into my studio, she started to cry. She didn't need to ask where the ideas came from.

"Are you going to show him?" she asked.

"I think I owe it to him," I said.

❖❖❖

Saturday, baseball had started up. Dad was nowhere to be found. On Sunday, Maggie helped me load the paintings into the truck, and we drove them to the grandstand late at night, after Mom and Starla-Fawn were asleep. He was inside because the padlock was off the door, but he was obviously in no shape to receive visitors. Monday and Tuesday evening it rained, so we tried again Wednesday, arriving just as daylight was fading. Maggie stayed in the truck.

He seemed to be sober enough, so I fetched the paintings and brought them to the door. He looked at them a long time, glancing at me and then back at the paintings.

"My son is an artist," he said. That was all he said.

❖❖❖

I was prolific for the early part of the summer, producing two paintings a week, many based on one-sided conversations I had with Uncle Bob, and then a new and remarkable source of inspiration unveiled itself.

It was almost ten o'clock on a Saturday night. Maggie was off to a show with two of her lifelong friends, and Starla-Fawn was pretending she was asleep and reading in bed. I was sitting on a sofa I keep in my studio, contemplating the work ahead of me. It was beginning to feel like I would grow old and die before I had a chance to paint all that was swirling in my head, when Mom came in and sat on the couch beside me. The lights were off. The see-through curtains strained the creamy light from the street so that I could see well enough, but Mom stopped at the door and stared into the room until her failing eyes adjusted before she followed her canes to the couch.

"Can't get to sleep?" I asked.

"Could, but I don't want to," she said.

I didn't say anything. She'd had trouble sleeping lately, but I begrudged the time I'd set aside for thinking. Shared silence is not a silence for contemplation.

"You know," she started in, "your Uncle Bob has been a big part of your life."

"I know, Mom. He's done a lot for me, and if it wasn't for him I wouldn't have Maggie."

"I've known Bob a long time, Whistler. Longer than you think. I'm telling you this now because I realize time is running out. Your Uncle Bob is three years older than your dad, and when I moved to town they were both on the wild side. Your dad quit school and took up his hammer, and Bob was driving truck by then. It's probably hard for you to imagine, but I was quite an attraction when I was twenty-one. The Maxwell brothers both took a shine to your mom, and they knew how to have a good time. We went to dances at the curling rink. I told them straight off I would go out with them but only one at a time. It didn't seem to matter where I went with one brother, the other would show up eventually. I think it was like a contest between the two. It was up to me to draw a line in the sand or all hell would break loose.

"Your Uncle Bob, being older, had an advantage over your dad, and then one fall he left town to work the oil rigs in Alberta. When he left, I carried on with your dad. It was what Bob would have expected — no different from a weekend when they were both around. That's when I found out I was pregnant. Your dad insisted we get married. When your Uncle Bob came back for the wedding he tried to be brave about it, but you could see as plain as the nose on your face it wasn't the way he'd hoped things would turn out. I was going to tell him at first, but if you could have seen the look in his eyes. I loved them both, Whistler. I really did. Maybe your dad knew he'd been duped. Maybe that's why he turned out so raw. I think the reason your Uncle Bob was so good to you all those years is because something told him he wasn't your uncle."

We sat on the couch for a long time before we heard Maggie come home in the fish truck. Mom pulled herself off the couch and used her canes to guide herself as far as the door.

"If you've got a story to tell, Whistler, it's best to tell it straight off. I don't imagine you wanted to hear any of this.

54

What you do with it is your business. They were both good men, Whistler. Both good."

Maggie made herself a hot chocolate and found me in the den. She wanted to share her evening, but I wasn't in the mood. I wasn't in the mood to talk about anything.

❖❖❖

It took until Tuesday for me to figure out Mom deserved my sympathy. On Sunday after church she cooked dinner as usual but took hers upstairs. She stayed there and didn't cook another meal. I was too scattered to think of painting so I made sure dinner was ready before Maggie and Starla-Fawn got home each night. For the better part of a month, despite Maggie's insistence I get back to my calling, I found myself housekeeping for Mom upstairs and Uncle Bob in the cellar. "What you do with it is your business," she'd said, but of course it was her business as much as mine. It felt like the three of us were caught in purgatory.

Then came the first hot Saturday in July.

Maggie had her day full with three houses to clean. She'd been working harder than ever, and her insistence on my rekindling my art was slowly edging toward frustration with the life we were living. I couldn't blame her for feeling trapped. Starla-Fawn was definitely ready to start school in September, and it was all I could do to keep her occupied. The two of us were playing chess when we heard a knock at the door. Starla-Fawn liked to answer, and it was my move anyway.

"Daddy, there's a grandpa at the door."

That's how my dad introduced himself to Starla-Fawn. He was wearing a clean pair of pants and shirt, and he'd shaved his scruffy beard. At first I didn't recognize him.

"Dad," I said, while thinking, What are you doing here? You look great. Does this mean you're not drinking?

He seemed to understand my thoughts. He put a small duffel bag inside and closed the door.

"I'm back, son. This time it'll be different. I'm going to help out around here. God, but it's hot as Hades out there."

I explained to Starla-Fawn that the man standing before her was her grandfather, and I did so because I figured it was what Mom would want me to say. Starla-Fawn looked interested but not convinced. I knew she would wait for her mother to come home to confirm such a bizarre possibility. To compensate for giving up on our chess game, I allowed her to watch TV, a trade-off she accepted since her one hour of Saturday television had already been spent.

Dad walked around the main floor, inspecting the door frames, the wallpaper I'd put up poorly in the living room, listening for squeaks in the floor joist but finding none. While the place wasn't terribly run down, I knew he was plotting his future. We sat down in the kitchen and I made coffee. I started in with an explanation of what had happened, Mom's self-imposed seclusion upstairs, the routine I had with Uncle Bob downstairs and how, for now, my painting had hit a dry spell. With every detail his demeanor changed — his posture, the glint in his eye, the way he listened hungrily. Starla-Fawn joined us while we made dinner. Dad pulled a picture of her out of his wallet but she still wasn't persuaded. It was going to take time before any of us would be.

❖❖❖

August the first I gave up living in the house I'd called home for twenty-eight years. Maggie's parents offered us their basement suite, which was smaller than what we were used to but virtually free. They said they didn't want any rent, but of course Maggie and I wouldn't hear of it. Dad seemed determined to make a go of it at last, and Maggie said giving him total responsibility was the only way he'd see his way through it. He kept himself busy looking after Mom upstairs and Uncle Bob in the basement. One day we had a summer monsoon, and he was up in the attic checking for leaks. Maggie and Starla-Fawn moved the twenty-second of July, but I stayed on an extra week to make sure Dad could handle the routine.

The first thing he did was buy Uncle Bob a John Deere hat, and Uncle Bob liked that. Next Dad left a plaid work shirt and blue jeans at Uncle Bob's door in place of his long johns. He never touched them for a week and then started dressing like a normal person. Dad's influence was remarkable. Mom was less receptive to his intervention. She kept to herself upstairs, responded to his entreaties with cursory replies and was often critical of the meals he cooked. I had to bite my tongue, and Dad had to bide his time. He kept buying her flowers and exotic plants, and she told him not to waste his money, then proceeded to fuss over them, keeping them watered just so and out of direct sun.

I decided to take Maggie's advice and leave them alone. I'd drop over on Saturday, just like when Dad was living under the grandstand, take my time and visit the three of them in their separate quarters. Uncle Bob was more talkative than ever, and his passion found a home in jigsaw puzzles. He could concentrate for hours on a four-thousand-piece puzzle until it was complete, then go through a mild depression until he got a new one. Mom had the old stereo console moved upstairs, and she'd listen to Mantivani and water her flowers. Besides looking after the two of them, Dad found time to fix the rotting stairs at the back of the house, and he was repainting the inside, one room at a time.

Thursday night was hot and muggy, and the thought of trying to sleep was depressing, so I told Maggie I was going for a walk and went over to see if they were still up. I got as far as the front porch. The door was open and so were the windows to the living room. If the heat was bothering them it wasn't apparent. The three of them were sitting on the couch watching *Gone With the Wind*. Mom was between Uncle Bob and my dad, who were taking turns describing the minute details that are so important if a person is to understand the whole picture. I wasn't sure if I was watching a beginning or an end. Mom's eyesight wasn't what it used to be, and it was difficult to say how much she was able to take in.

Translating Women

YOU CAN BORROW MY JACK IF YOU WANT TO, but it's an old one. That's what I told Lloyd when he was out in the yard one Saturday, trying to pry his Chevrolet up with four two-by-fours he'd nailed together. I could see he'd never get the front end up that way, that's why I offered. Offered out of compassion is what it amounts to.

First off, I'm not fond of Lloyd. Last year he dug up the fence between our two yards, posts and everything, and moved it over our way six inches. This after months of searching for metal pegs in the ground and calling the municipal crew out to inspect the property line. Six inches. I told him at the time he could come over and mow a strip down the fence line if he thought it would make a difference, but no, he had to go into this big production and move the fence over. Six inches by not more than thirty feet: what does that give you? "A bigger lot," Lloyd said. "If I'm going to be taxed on it I want to own it." He even said it like it was the kind of thing a normal person would say.

You can look back on some days that change your life. That's how I look back on the Saturday I offered to loan Lloyd my car jack. Hindsight's a bugger sometimes. It's exactly like in the Robby Burns poem about the mouse whose house is turned ass over tea kettle and he doesn't get all in a flap or anything, just rebuilds his house and goes about his business. "The present only toucheth thee." I remember that line because of Muriel, my roommate. She studies poetry at the university off and on, and she insists on reading me the poems she likes, and she seems to like nearly all of them. I don't mind really, and it makes her day lighter. Muriel and I aren't sexual or anything, just cooking partners, although there have been times I've hoped for more. That's how my appreciation for poetry got started, but it doesn't seem to have made any difference.

The jack was old, and he knew that when he took it. Even an old jack is better than two-by-fours. I asked him if he needed a hand but he said no, he figured he could handle it himself. Lloyd's funny that way. He'll spend a whole day changing his spark plugs and then go into the back yard and whistle like he's just climbed Mount Everest. So I left him to it and went back to planting the two big azaleas that Muriel brought home that didn't cost her a dime because they were digging up for underground wiring. Then I heard this ungodly yell from Lloyd, and when I got over to see what had happened, there he was pinned under the front end of his car with his hips turned sideways. He didn't need to carry on the way he did — any fool could see he was in a lot of pain.

I grabbed the two-by-fours he had nailed together and propped them under the fender and against a block of firewood, and the leverage was enough to lift the weight off him. His wife Laura had come out by this time, still in her housecoat, and pulled him out from under the car. There was soap in her hair from the shower, but she didn't seem to care.

It didn't take the ambulance long in my opinion. Lloyd's opinion was different. When they showed up he was cursing them like they were the ones responsible for his misery. They loaded him onto a stretcher and secured him inside, and just before they closed the door he looked at me and said, "*God damn useless jack.*" To think I could have been anyone's neighbour.

I wasn't going to visit Lloyd in the hospital, but Muriel figured I'd better or else. Muriel says this all the time and I've never pressed her to find out what else there is. Her instructions were specific: I was to buy him a photography magazine (nothing too racy, she said) and take one of her poetry books and read to him. His hip was broken, and they were having trouble getting it set right. He was pretty well drugged the night I went to visit, and it was hard to tell if he was in a bad mood or not. He seemed to like the photography magazine, and I flipped through it with him; then I took a chance and read him Robert Frost's poem "Good Fences Make Good Neighbours". I guess Frost had a neighbour out in the country just like Lloyd. I wish Muriel had come with me; I don't read poetry out loud all that well.

He loved taking pictures of flowers and trees and fences, it didn't seem to matter. That's how I first got to know Lloyd. Every day after work he'd be out there chasing down ladybugs or rabbits with his 35mm and I've always marveled at great photographs. He offered to loan me some of his books, and the next thing you know I'm out buying a second hand camera with Lloyd as my advisor, and I'm spending half my paycheck on film developing. Muriel says some day she and I could work together on a book of photographs that are reflections of some of the great poems she's found. Like a lot of ideas, it looks good from a distance. If I'm going to work closely with someone on a project like that, some other things have to come first.

After going to one of those slide shows down at the McPhearson Theatre featuring Freeman Patterson, Lloyd decided he'd do the same kind of thing in his living room. It was gloomy night in the middle of winter, and he'd been planning his gala event for over a month. It was supposed to start at eight o'clock, and by nine fifteen, Muriel and I were the only guests sitting on the couch. Some people don't take to Lloyd that easily.

Some of his pictures were pretty damn good, to my eyes anyway. Muriel said she liked them herself, but couldn't stop laughing when we got back to the house. Right in the middle of his series on bovines and flowering trees, up on the screen pops a nudie of his wife, Laura. She had her face turned away from the camera and her arms and legs were twined around the branches of a sprawling arbutus tree, but you could tell it was Laura all right. After a while you get pretty good at translating women.

Lloyd was all in a panic and pressed the back button on the slide projector which meant we all got another look at Laura on our way to his river study. Muriel contained herself pretty well at the time, but when we got home the laughter spilled out of her, and as far as I know Muriel and Laura haven't shared a word since. Some things about women I'll never understand.

Could be another eight to ten days, the doctor said. That's a long time for any man to be flat out, and I felt sorry the whole thing had happened even though I'd made it clear the jack was past its prime. I offered to help out around the house, of course. I would have even if Muriel hadn't insisted. I mowed his lawn, even the extra six inches he'd gained last year, and looked after getting his front shocks changed down at Scotia Automotive. Damned if I was going to climb under that car after what had happened to Lloyd. Saturday afternoon I looked after Daniel, who's two now, while Laura went to have her hair done. I'm not much for babysitting, especially when you consider the attention span of a two-year-old who keeps calling you Daddy and insists on throwing his food all over the kitchen. I would have thought two year olds would be over that.

I met Muriel at a garage sale. Some guy was selling begonias at a pretty fair price and I've always loved begonias. I didn't have anywhere to plant them at the time, but Muriel did. She'd just bought a house on the edge of town with money she'd won from a scratch and win. You'd think someone that fortunate would buy a dozen a week, but Muriel hasn't bought one since, and although I didn't know it at the time, there was something about the shade of her personality that kind of pulled me in. I helped her plant thirty-nine begonias out front of her place. Three baker's dozens. Muriel is good at negotiating, and you can tell she's in the mood when she licks her lips. She needed a roommate to help with the mortgage and I moved in the next day. I was technically living with Felicity Underwood when I ran into Muriel, but Felicity had gone backpacking around Europe, and I hadn't heard from her for almost two years. When opportunity knocks, a man has to answer.

Not every man would find Muriel a real looker. That's where the power of translation comes in. Muriel's not the kind of woman you approach aesthetically straight on. It's the way she flips her hair, the turn of her cheek, the pause she's perfected before important sentences. You don't live in the same house with someone and not have a towel, on its way out of the shower, obey gravity once or twice. There's substance behind the veil most people see, I can tell you.

Turns out they had to reset the whole hip again and insert stainless steel. I told Lloyd he'd never get through an airport again, but he didn't find it funny. I guess pain can dampen your sense of humour. Lloyd was home for almost a week, and we didn't as much as hear a peep. The grass, of course, kept on growing, and Muriel and I thought we'd better head over with a care package. Muriel took some homemade soup, and I took over a picture of him in the hospital when his face was all scrunched up. They both enjoyed the soup.

A portable physiotherapist came every second day to visit him while we were at work, but Lloyd didn't like her. She was Scottish and Lloyd doesn't take well to dialects because, he says people like that throw things into a sentence you know nothing about. Muriel's mostly into poetry, but she goes to a massage therapist once a week — has for years. She offered to ease him out of his pain and I'm thinking, go for it Muriel, anything to shut him up about the Scottish lady. It turns out Muriel has more than a green thumb, she has the magic fingers, and I'm wondering why I didn't know that. The next day Lloyd phones in and cancels the physiotherapist and Muriel takes over. For the first week, she went over every night after supper, and I'd tag along once and a while to do their yard work. Sometimes you can't help the thoughts that creep into your skull, and I've got to admit that when I was out there mowing Lloyd's lawn and Muriel's inside soothing his aches and pains, a small revelation slipped in that told me Lloyd had this planned all along. It was an old jack, I admit, but the damn thing still worked. Lloyd may have even felt bad himself, because he offered to let me use his camera filters any time I wanted.

Eventually, he became somewhat mobile. I fertilized our lawn, but damned if I was going to fertilize his. It was about the time I had it down to mowing our lawn once a week and his every two weeks that he started limping over to our house for his treatments. I'd never heard a word between the two of them cloud the skies, but personally I think Laura was instrumental in shipping him over. Lloyd was in a bad way, no doubt about it, but he was milking it for all it was worth. Laura may be someone you can convince to lie spread eagle over the smooth skin of an arbutus tree, but she knows her limits.

There were some nights when Lloyd's treatments seemed to take longer than others. Laura would invite me in for tea, and I'd say yes even though I drink coffee as a rule. I'm not used to kids much, and I guess they're prone to slobber. Daniel usually went to bed after the second cup of tea, which gave Laura and I a chance to do some talking. When she was sixteen she hitchhiked from Victoria up to Campbell River with a friend, and when her mother found out she wired money up and made her come back on the bus. That's the only time she'd done any travelling. I said you must have at least gone on the ferry to Vancouver, and she said once, to visit a specialist. Lloyd had promised to take her in the Chevy to Moose Jaw to visit relatives, but I guess when you have a kid in a quick nine months it can tame your spirit for adventure.

I've never met anyone that didn't have at least one outstanding quality I could admire. Bert the barber, for example, absolutely charms you with his wit, and his customers always say, Just take a little off, Bert, knowing they can come back in three weeks for more. There's a fellow who sold me a suitcase down at Sears a while back who's got a whole other life running his own computer business, air miles, the whole schlimazel, yet every week he works one or two days selling suitcases with a six month warranty. Sometimes people get all fogged up, but if you scratch the surface, it's amazing what you'll find.

Laura, she's honest. There's something natural and open about her. After a few evenings drinking tea and talking the general talk, she starts bringing out her photo albums and her liqueurs. She's proud of everything she's done, but in a calm way, as if she never had a choice in the matter. One thing you can say about Lloyd, he honored her passionately with his camera. I would have never imagined a body could be examined from so many angles, in such extraordinary lighting. An artist has to know what they're doing, but it doesn't hurt when the subject is so cooperative. Immersed in the leaves of her photo albums, sipping tea out of one of those thin-handled teacups was an act of great concentration.

People around here complain it never gets hot until it does. The second Saturday in July was one such night, and I'd spent most of the afternoon building a rabbit hutch for Laura because Daniel wanted rabbits. I said one would be a good idea but was told to prepare a hutch for two. Lloyd couldn't yet bend over without pain so, of course, I marched in as the urban handyman.

It turned out better than expected: it had two floors and a sliding screen at the bottom for the inevitable. I didn't bother painting it. Most people who get rabbits only keep them a month or two.

When I finished, Laura asked me if I wanted to stay for supper. I hesitated briefly and she told me to wash up in the hall bathroom. I asked where Lloyd was, and she said he was over at my place for the final phase of his treatments. It was a great dinner, but I did think it a bit odd to serve rabbit the same week she planned to get one (or two) for Daniel. I guess that's just the way it is.

After dinner I offered to clean up the kitchen, and Laura suggested I give Daniel a bath and she would clean up. Something different. I can understand now why the rubber ducky is such a big thing, because if I didn't keep him occupied with some kind of toy he was forever playing with himself. For the uninitiated, reading a bedtime story to a two-year-old is an experience that requires proper enunciation.

It wasn't long before the phone rang and Laura answered it, saying, "Hello, Lloyd." Not "Hello" but "Hello, Lloyd." She talked to him for less than a minute and came to join me in the living room.

"Lloyd's staying at your place tonight. He said if it's not all right, to phone back. Something about deep massage therapy treatment which needs to be delivered every two hours or it won't work." Laura sat at the end of the couch, removed her sandals, and tucked her legs underneath her.

My mind quickly scanned the situation as it related to me. Where exactly, were these treatments being administered? I was never there when they took place and the smell of liniment was undifferentiated and everywhere. The last thing in the world I wanted was to risk crawling back to my room on a hot night and find myself lying down beside an anal retentive with a pin in his hip.

Laura is such a natural. She's enough to make any man take a serious interest in photography. As the evening wore on, I suggested I sleep on the couch for the night. She smiled in an unassuming kind of way and said it was too hot to sleep on this side of the house. She didn't need another man in the house in need of physio, and in case I didn't know, a night on the couch can deliver a nasty kink. Where would truth be without women?

Lloyd and I don't wear the same size, not even close, so over the next few days Laura and Muriel helped out with a series of clothing exchanges at the property line. He never did return the jack after the accident, so I guess I get to keep it. The damn thing works if you know what you're doing. Thumper and Thumbelina have lived up to their names, and soon enough I'll have a slew of rabbits on my hands, which should cut down on the meat bill. I see Lloyd from time to time limping around the back yard, surveying the new property line. If he thinks he's going to get me to lend a hand moving that fence back he's got more wrong with him that a sore hip, but I'm hoping it never comes down to that. For now, I'm just glad to have my jack back.

CLICK: *A girl with two pails*

THERE IS A LOT OF GREEN SURROUNDING OUR BACK FIELD.
Green that stays all year long. The grey, matted grass at my feet
is full of lime green shoots coming from the ooze of spring mud.
Soon the thick green will be filled with a jungle of still more
green, woven together so tightly that the wind squeaks passing
through.

I'm taking Paddy for a walk. That's my job every day. He's
not much trouble really and we're very close. Sometimes people
don't seem to notice Paddy. He's a part of the world people don't
want to see. I like to take pictures with my Brownie camera and
Paddy likes to trail along behind me, smelling the air from the
farms. Paddy can be a lot of fun. He's twelve years old, but most
people wouldn't guess that. They just look at him and call him
five or twenty-one. There goes Paddy, playing with himself
again, right hand dug down into the woolen cub scout shorts
he wears all the time. And those itchy socks: I know how he
feels. Why is it Paddy must wear those silly pants, Mama asks
me. I tell her I don't know why. CLICK. I shouldn't do that, I
know. Mama was disgusted when she saw some of the pictures
I developed of Paddy being himself. Mostly I shoot trees, rocks,
and railway ties, but secretly I'm building up a portfolio in
tribute to Paddy. I want to put them all together into a book
someday so people won't look away when they see people on
the street like my brother. Often, I'll take pictures of myself at
arm's length. Sometimes I take pictures of waterfalls.

I know Paddy won't wander when he's busy like that. I find myself moving back and forth along the fence line, trying to get a chance to shoot a rare spring flower I can see in the next farm.

She moved away a year ago, just as I was getting to know her. My parents were all hush hush about why she had to move back to Saskatchewan and live with her grandparents for a year. Since her return, I can't help noticing how she has grown up.

CLICK. *Sonja holding hands with two galvanized pails.*

I climb gingerly over the electric fence and check back to where Paddy stands, his head bowed, mesmerized in his glory. He knows how to climb under the electric wire but I know if he does wander over here he'll play dare with the invisible current that pulses through the wire. I tried showing him once, how to rest his hand on the wire between surges of shock, but he hasn't matched the click of the generator with the pinch it gives him. Somehow, he laughs when this happens. He giggles like a greedy gambler.

Sometimes, like now, Paddy's mind gets stuck on things, so I leave him and slide from tree to tree to get a closer look. She is heading to a distant shed, looking back toward her house now and then, as if she's being watched. She doesn't suspect she's being framed by my trusty Brownie from behind a Douglas fir.

Graceful, the way she walks. The pails can't be heavy. I'd like to dart out from behind my cover and offer to help her if only to find out what she's carrying from the barn to the abandoned shed at the south end of their property. Milk would make sense, except I can't see them keeping any kind of animals out in the old shed. It sits up on two large log skids, window frames open to the sky, and roof with holes big enough for swallows to swoop through.

CLICK: *Sonja walking with pails.* CLICK: *Sonja hoisting herself up to the doorway.* CLICK: *Abandoned shed with abandoned girl inside.* I like to think up names for my photos as I take them. I like the way artists do that. *Blue Boy. The Gleaners. Madonna and Child.*

I am going to leave my camera behind the tree and saunter over to the shed like I was taking a leisurely stroll, pretend I don't know she's in there. I'm thinking this, getting up the nerve and all, when her old man comes marching over the knoll of the hill. He's walking like he knows where he's going, a plaid Thermos tucked under his arm. Behind the tree, I curl up like a spring pine cone. Behind me I can hear Paddy chuckling to himself at the fence line. Her dad stops and listens in the wind like a wary deer. I can see the sun glinting off the copper fasteners on his denim overalls, hear his breath moan inside his sinus passages. He rubs his hands over a face he hasn't shaved for two or three days and continues down to the shed. One picture left on the roll. CLICK. *Father meets daughter in abandoned shed.*

I hide the roll of film in the back of my underwear drawer when I get home. There aren't enough rocks and trees on this roll to develop right away. I'll do it later when I have enough nature pictures to show Mama and Papa that I'm busy pursuing the New York Institute of Photography correspondence course I paid two hundred and fifty dollars for. I finished filling in the multiple choice questions for the whole course ages ago, but I only send a booklet off in the mail every month or two. Since I paid for the course with my own money, my parents have agreed to buy me two rolls of film every month until I'm finished. When I've completed my portfolio on Paddy, I think I might take up investigative photojournalism. Right now, I get paid for selling eggs down at the end of the driveway.

"CLICK." That's what Paddy says at the supper table most nights after the two of us go for a walk. That's how he tells Mama and Papa what we've been up to. "CLICK, CLICK, CLICK," he says over and over again, laughing to himself like he knows something we don't. Mama makes sure we're always fed the same. Tonight we both have three meatballs, but Paddy doesn't seem to notice my plate has more gravy. Most nights he gets so excited with his clicking he hardly even touches his food. Listening to my brother's antics at the table, Mama and Papa think we've had an uproarious time, while my mind keeps wandering back to how I'm going to solve the mystery of why Sonja carries those pails back and forth every day.

It is a night I'm busy developing pictures in the bathroom I have converted to a makeshift darkroom, that I find out more of what I need to know about Sonja. I find out a lot of things in there; my parents seem to think I can't listen too well in the dark. I let the water trickle into the bathtub and I lean against the door. That's how I find out important stuff, like my grandmother wanting to come to our house to die because she wants to die in the rain. After a couple of hot rums, their voices leak in from the kitchen through places even light can't enter. Sonja, it turns out, was adopted when she was five.

That much doesn't explain why she had to go away for a year but already I feel sorry for Sonja. Paddy and I don't always get things our own way, but at least we feel we belong here. It was bad enough the year my grandmother came to live with us. She kept hinting to Mama and Papa that it was their fault Paddy fell out of our upstairs window when he was little. Sometimes, when no one was around to listen, she'd tell me they must have dropped me out the window when I was young. If I had to go away and live with her for a year, I think I'd have to consider resigning from our family. I don't think Paddy could survive a prairie winter dressed in cub scout shorts anyway.

Sonja must be smart. Either that or the teachers in Saskatchewan are a lot smarter because when she left here a year ago she was in the same grade as 1 was, but since she returned they put her ahead in another school. We used to travel to school in the same van for a while. Paddy would tag along too. Now, the only time I get to work on my girl with two pails project is on weekends or after school. I worry about how I'm going to progress with Paddy around all the time. He was no bother before because he could never chase away the rocks or trees or railway ties.

Saturdays are my favourite days. Mama and Papa are both off to town most of the day and I get to stay home and have the run of the place while I look after my brother. Sometimes we wrestle in the hayloft or make a batch of red sugar icing to share. Paddy doesn't ever notice that I eat a tablespoon while he uses a teaspoon. "Two peas in a pod," Grandma used to tell us with a thin smirk on her face.

I'm teaching Paddy to do some useful things, like collect the eggs without breaking them. Mama and Papa say I've grown up a lot myself lately. My teacher says I'm doing pretty good, considering the family I come from, which makes me think nobody really understands Paddy like I do. I like our school because we get to go on field trips nearly every day.

I've been waiting for this Saturday more than most. My assistant Paddy and I plan on solving this thing once and for all. Of course, I know Paddy doesn't understand the details of our operation, but he's got to start somewhere. He can't spend the rest of his life collecting eggs.

As soon as my parents leave, we both head out, camera loaded, round the back of the Fritz property. The railway tracks slice a path quite close to the shed Sonja keeps visiting and I figure Paddy and I can sneak in there and plant ourselves under the shed between the skids. All week I've been practicing a game with Paddy called shush. I just hold my finger beside my nose and whisper shush and he shushes. An hour at a time. Someday I might include him in a partnership. CLICK: *Paddy shushing on duty.*

72

I have no way of knowing when Sonja will make her way down to the shed with her pails or if she'll even come. I've packed a snack for the two of us and figure if she hasn't shown up after lunch, Paddy and I will have to head home and get the chores done. I've got an old photography magazine in case Paddy gets bored. He likes to look at the pictures of cameras and make clicking sounds. I've also got some blank paper and crayons: Paddy can colour rainbows for hours at a time although he still needs help when it comes to colouring close to the edge.

It seems funny how Paddy and I can pass most Saturdays doing practically nothing, but we hadn't taken refuge under that old shed for more than a half hour when I found I was starting to get restless. From between the skids I could see up toward the hill where I was hoping Sonja would saunter with her pails, so I knew we were safe. I climbed up on one of the skids and peeked in through one of the window frames. The old shed looked like it might have been lived in at one time, years ago. It was dirty and shabby, but most of the floor had grey floral linoleum, spread in waves, with oily patches as if it had been used to store motors or something. One corner of the old building had the usual mess that nesting swallows leave. Nowhere inside were there any signs of farm animals. Just looking around the emptiness of the room gave me a late night feeling. I felt a tugging at my pant leg. It was Paddy. Since he's taken to wearing shorts, he seems fascinated with long pants. *Shush.* The room was bright enough with the morning light bathing the walls through the holes in the roof and the spaces that once held windows and doors. CLICK: *Empty shed without pails.* Soft warm light in a cold cold room.

Paddy heard her coming before I did. He's very perceptive about things like sound. Maybe that's why he enjoys playing the shush game so much. His head perked up, but it was my eyes that looked out between the skids and there she was, walking along in a white dress down to her sandals, the two pails at her sides. I couldn't see her doing chores with a dress on. She certainly was taller than I remembered.

Paddy didn't take much notice of the creaking timbers as she lifted herself up and into the shed, pushing the pails ahead of her. Maybe he thought someone was living upstairs from us. He turned to a full page spread of 35mm cameras and I knew he was about to start his click routine. *Shush*, I whispered. *Shush*, he whispered back. There was a frail stillness in the air. I thought perhaps she had heard us and was trying to figure out what it was. I could hear the flap of swallow wings near the nest. The two pails clinked together right above our heads.

What was she doing up there in her quiet world? Was she looking out of the hollow room, into the spring sunshine? Was she praying, down on her hands and knees, to some God she had brought back from Saskatchewan?

She began dancing on the linoleum, back and forth across the room, making her own music — a melody filled with la-de-das instead of words. I can usually imagine things pretty clearly. I imagine things that Paddy can see and hear, but right then he was busy playing shush and didn't seem to figure anything was odd. Paddy finally lifted his head from our photography magazine when her old man came walking briskly down the path.

I heard a clanking of pails. It sounded like one of them had tipped over. I couldn't hear anything spill and I could see Paddy was about to do something other than shush, so I brought out the blank paper and crayons and turned him loose.

"I want to see some real movement today." It was her father who spoke, but she never answered him. For a while there wasn't a sound, not even from a swallow's wing. She began dancing again, only this time the sounds of her feet were whispers on the floor above me and I knew she had taken her sandals off. She began to hum as she danced. I felt completely trapped. I wanted to be a part of the dance, but the cracks in the floor didn't allow me to see what she was doing. Paddy was lost in solitude so I slipped out from under the shed and crept as slowly as I could over to the open doorway. I knew that a good photojournalist would sneak along the side and peek through one of the cracks in the shed, maybe pray for a knothole to shoot through. I kept thinking this was what I should be doing as I raised my head into the doorway to watch. Sonja was floating across the room; her feet didn't seem to be touching the floor at all as she slid gracefully about, carving shapes into the air. Without warning, Sonja stopped.

"Come in and sit down. Sit right down here and watch if you want to watch." His voice didn't sound threatening like I thought it would. He sounded like he pitied me for never having witnessed such a dance, like maybe he didn't believe I could take in something like that. Without looking at Sonja, I did as I was told: he turned the second pail over and I sat obediently beside him.

Sonja never regarded me at all. She looked over at her father and when he nodded she began again to dance, as if I was of no consequence. Her movements were exhilarating, her white wide dress pushed breezes into our faces, her arms drew pictures in the air, sliced shapes through the pillars of sunlight that poured through the rough plank walls. The dance went on and on, seeming to cause her no discomfort or strain. She was a wonderful dancer. It was like she had cast a spell over the entire world and we were lucky enough to be caught in her magic. I considered excusing myself and fetching Paddy — I knew he would enjoy Sonja immensely — but I knew I was fortunate to be where I was and I was afraid that any movement on my part would shatter her dance. I was concentrating on not moving a muscle, on playing shush like Paddy did, when her father stood up from the pail, his hands thrust in his wide overall pockets.

"Now the second part."

Sonja looked at me then. It was the first time she had acknowledged my presence. She turned and stared at her father, who nodded again and assumed his position on the pail. A swallow fluttered in through the hole and, seeing that the dance was not over, darted back into the sunshine. Sonja floated over to the corner of the room and slid easily out of the white dress she wore as her only garment. Like a feather in a pirouette of wind, she whirled back to the centre of the room and continued her dance, the cream colour of her skin painting her movements now, her exposed limbs busy with angles her dress had previously hidden. Her dancing caught me like a fist in the stomach. I couldn't breathe. I realized I was clutching my Brownie camera tightly in my hands and I knew I had to do what any responsible photojournalist would do. CLICK. His eyes, his whole expression never changed, never flinched from his daughter. His hand slowly pushed my camera back into my lap. My eyes watched the marvelous dance but my mind wanted to run, to escape before he took my camera and stomped on it with his muddy boots. Sonja was in her own world now. She had passed beyond us both. The pails we were sitting on and my Brownie camera were the only real things left in the room. For a brief moment it seemed like Paddy was nowhere around, that I had come alone. I was frozen in time to the pail; I thought I would spend the rest of my life with not a worry or care, free to watch the beautiful Sonja dance.

"That was very good. You're getting much stronger."

He only took his hands out of his pockets to get down from the doorway. He walked back toward the house with the same strident pace that had brought him. Sonja was staring shyly down at her long dress. I sensed she felt awkward, my being

76

there, and yet I didn't want to get up and walk right by her to get my brother. I turned my eyes away while she pulled the dress over her head. She hesitated before she came over and sat down on the pail beside me.

"That was a beautiful dance," I said.

"Thank you."

"I'll never see a dance more beautiful."

Her eyes ran in swirls along the patterned linoleum until they found my camera, dangling innocently from its nylon strap.

"I don't understand," I said. I wanted to say I understood it all but there was no way I could. She never answered me and I felt ashamed suddenly, like I was prying beneath her skin with something sharper than my camera lens. "What is it you carry in the pails?" I asked.

"These pails are almost empty now," she answered flatly. As she spoke I looked closely at one of the pails. It was badly rusted and the bottom was full of holes.

"Is there something I can do?" My head felt numb as I spoke. I was overcome by a strong urge for Paddy to be near me.

"No," she said. "Nothing."

We both sat facing the opposite wall, snapping sideways glances now and again. The swallows seemed impatient with our staying and began to pass freely in and out between the rafters.

"I took your picture," I said. "I've taken many pictures of you. I develop my own pictures. I'll let you have some if you like." Sonja sat so still I turned toward her to make sure she was still breathing.

"You can have all of them, I don't mind. I only did it to find out what was in the pails."

She whispered thank you before she stood up. I realized she needed me to get up too so she could return with her pails. I stood in the doorway watching her until her balanced stride disappeared over the knoll of the hill. Arms swinging freely at her sides.

❖❖❖

I laid off taking pictures for a while. I stuck to my developing which gives me time to be alone and think things out. Her picture was electric, enlarged to eight by ten. It gave me a chill, watching her silhouette form against the background of the shed, defining itself slowly in the pungent liquid. I caught her moving sideways, flying, with only the ends of her fingers a blur. Paddy doesn't have the patience to work the darkroom, but I understand.

It was on one of those rare, rainy May days, a Sunday, and I was busy passing the afternoon in my darkroom. I heard her voice out in the kitchen talking to Mama. She had never visited our house before, so I hugged the door for all I was worth.

"Yes," I heard Mama saying, "he does love to take pictures. It keeps him busy."

The next thing I heard was the muffled sound of crying. Sonja's crying. It was all right, Mama told her. I didn't mean any harm by any pictures I took. She would see to it that any pictures I had taken of her would be returned. After school was out, Mama said, I would be going to Saskatchewan for the summer. At least the summer. She hated to take the camera away from me, she said, because my teachers said it was important for my development.

After Sonja left that day I destroyed all the prints I had made of her except for one. I never showed it to my parents. I promised to hand over any pictures I had of Sonja and I sort of promised to never take my camera over to her farm again. My mama never mentioned going to Saskatchewan to me although I'm sure I will be going. Since my grandmother got her wish about dying in the rain, I wonder if maybe I'll be going to the smart school that Sonja did. Mama somehow thinks it's important for me to be away from Paddy for a while.

❖❖❖

Sonja said thank you shyly when I gave her the picture and she held it fast to her side. I was disappointed because I wanted to explain the fine technical details to her. The way I had cropped the picture in the final enlargement gave it perfect balance. I think, by the expression on her face, she probably felt a little defeated and I must admit it was a picture that looked better from a distance. She never brought up the fact that she knew I was going to go away for the summer which was kind of her. I never asked why I hadn't seen her carrying the pails down to the shed lately. She did seem older, now that I think of it. I'm looking forward to coming back from my trip. I find Sonja a pretty interesting subject. I'm considering putting my Paddy project on the back burner for a while. Nobody will notice. Certainly not Paddy.

She held the picture in her hands very gently while we talked, which made me feel good. An artist needs people to believe in his work. When we finally said goodbye, I wasn't sure at all if I would see her again or when. She finally turned her back and started for home. I let her take a few strides. CLICK. *Girl walking home with the only surviving print from a negative carefully filed away.*

I know the title is too long but I'll have all summer to work on it. I looked around for Paddy, but he was nowhere to be seen. He must have grown impatient and gone home ahead of me.

Simple

THERE'S MORE THAN ONE WAY TO FIND A HUSBAND and when I look back on it I can recall exactly how I found mine. The first time I saw Harry Tulip, he jumped on my lap between my 36-D and the steering wheel, which didn't leave much room. I was wearing pants that day, instead of a skirt with no underwear like I do on hot days, and when he asked if he could try sitting behind the wheel I said yes, thinking to move over and let him feel the vibration. He flew up and sat on my lap. There was room for him because he only weighs in at one fifteen.

I was on my way to Sidney to drop a trailer off at the truck ferry and Harry Tulip asked if he could come along. I said no for no good reason. The look on his face went from sunshine to ground fog and I felt terrible. I hate to be the one to spread misery. He's a cute wisp of a kid and there's a lot of romance to driving a big rig. I could have hidden him in the glove box and nobody would have been the wiser.

The next day I stopped at the same place, The Dog House, for a burger and shake, and there's Harry Tulip walking me back to the truck asking again if he can go for a ride. I asked him if he didn't work for a living and he said he did, the late shift washing dishes, but today was his day off and could he go, could he, could he? I'm driving to Campbell River, I told him, with a load of vegetables and it would be late before I got back. He wouldn't give up so with Harry Tulip beside me, I headed north. That's how it all started. It was that simple.

When I was nineteen I walked into the offices of Island Freightways and said I wanted to drive truck. Alan Fruit was the dispatcher and he looked up from his desk, never even bothered to come up to the counter, and said there was a U-Haul just down the road, why didn't I go and rent myself a pickup. Alan and I are good friends now, but he pissed me off that day, and I kept coming back, sometimes twice a day until he realized I wasn't going anywhere soon and he hired me on as a swamper for the town jobs. I know when he did that he figured I wouldn't last till lunch time, but I'm 6' 1" and two hundred and five pounds, and I can haul freight with the best of them. When I was twenty-two I was driving the two-ton around town, and I've been driving tractor and trailer for nearly three years. So when someone like Harry Tulip begs me for the opportunity to ride up front I know where he's coming from.

The first few miles out of town, Harry watched me change gears, kind of mimicking me from the passenger seat. Not saying a word. Before long I had to pull into the weigh station so I grabbed Harry Tulip by his scrawny neck and told him to lie down on the seat. I was checking in with Bert at the scales — he's the kind of guy who likes to B.S. when it's not busy — and Harry Tulip was lying down all right, with his head on my lap and stroking my thighs with his feathery hands while I was trying to listen to Bert's explanation of why Canada had fallen behind in the series with the Russians. Try a wad of this chewing tobacco, Bert said, and while I was at it did I want to put my name down on the hockey pool he had going for a buck a pop. I was kind of listening and half smiling, and by the time Bert went back inside to fetch the chart I wasn't minding what Harry Tulip was up to. With his roaming around he'd discovered I wasn't wearing underwear. He seemed to be enjoying himself. We'd gone eight or ten miles down the hot highway before I finally organized myself to say something.

"Harry Tulip, what is it you think you're doing?"

"It's slippery down here. Like wet rubber."

"We're safely past the scales," I said. "You can sit up now."

"Harry Tulip's busy and he ain't stopping till you say he has to."

Slowing down near Ladysmith is one thing I remembered, but the rest of the trip to Campbell River was a blur. He may be a wisp of a man, but pound for pound you can't beat Harry Tulip.

Harry's shifts at The Dog House were all over the map, but when things worked out he started keeping me company on the road. Once in a while he'd come by my apartment after work and we'd watch a movie. We never ended up at his place because Harry still lived with his mother, and he said she was kind of funny. What do you mean funny? I said, and he said she kept hoping he would become a priest and his mother wasn't even Catholic. For years she'd wanted him to become a postman, but when the price of stamps went up she got mad at the post office and decided the priesthood was where he belonged. His mom definitely needed looking after he said, and there was no one left to look after her but him. I asked Harry if he wanted to be a priest and he said Hell no, he was a man looking for adventure and was he ever glad he ran into me.

I hadn't had a lot of experience with men, if you don't count foster parents, and it's safe to say I wasn't one of those loose women the devil never takes his eye off. Whenever I was around Harry Tulip I discovered a part of him that took me by surprise. His fascination with my thighs and all they had to offer was confined to our road trips. When he'd come over for dinner (toad in the hole, my specialty) or when we passed an evening in front of the TV, he would snuggle up to me and we'd kiss like distant cousins. I'd get sore some nights from driving the rig and Harry was a master at giving a back rub. He would kneed his knuckled fists up and down my spine tirelessly, and on Canada Day he bought me a bottle of vanilla-scented massage oil. We got on like two well-balanced wheels but there was something holding him back.

"Harry Tulip," I said to him one Sunday afternoon, "I need to know why it is you can explore my nether regions like some sixteenth century explorer on his way to China, yet when I try to reciprocate . . . well, you know."

I should point out I'd discovered from his driver's license that his middle name was Red and he didn't like it. "Harry" or "Harry Tulip" was fine with him, but try "Harry Red Tulip" on for size and you could see steam coming out of his ears. He was named after his Uncle Red, he said, but that was no excuse. Whenever I referred to him as Harry Tulip and left out the Red, you could feel deep appreciation floating in the air.

"I'm saving myself," he said. "For the day I get married."

The next week I was off to Calgary for a trucker's convention. I have it in good with the company and why not? I've never had an accident, I drive on schedule, and they as much as wave a shift in the air and I jump behind the wheel. I can change a tire on the road if I have to, not like that weasel Frank Foot they hired two years ago. He used to work for Canadian Freightways and since he's arrived on Vancouver Island he thinks such tasks are behind him. The candy ass drives with an orthopedic cushion, and when some of us go for a drink after work he calls us degenerates. It's easy to look good beside the likes of Frank Foot. It also doesn't hurt that the owner, Howard Menneke, thinks I'm the second coming of Christ. His wife, Marge, brags to all her friends that one of her husband's best employees is a woman, like my choice of vocation has assured women will never lose the vote. Some of the guys got their nose out of joint when they picked me to go to convention and it could be they're grooming me for something down the road.

I spent four nights in Calgary, and Harry phoned me every night at 11:30 Pacific, right after the *Bob Newhart Show* we both like to watch. It was like he was with me even when he wasn't. I would have flown back on Thursday but the company bought a used double unit and asked if I'd drive it back. Harry was at work all day Saturday, so I bought a couple of steaks after work and invited him over.

"Harry Tulip, sit down on the couch and close your eyes. Don't you dare peek, I've got a surprise for you."

Harry sat there with his hands on his lap like a grade three-er waiting to be dismissed. God, but he looked cute. I plunked a Stetson hat on his head and as soon as I did I could see I'd made a mistake. When he opened his eyes he still couldn't see a thing because the hat was resting on the bridge of his nose.

"A bit big," I said. "Sorry about that."

"It's beautiful," Harry said. "I've always wanted a real cowboy hat. It'll fit perfectly if I wear my toque underneath. Wait until my mom sees this." He rocked back and forth on the couch like he was riding bareback. You barely scratch the surface of a man and you find a boy.

"Actually, I was hoping we could discuss a few things. Including your mother."

"She thinks she's a rabbit," he said. "She's eaten nothing but carrots all week."

"Harry Tulip, I want the straight goods. You told me last week you weren't ready to get married. I need to know why not. I need to know where I stand."

He took his hat off and put it on the coffee table. He sat there thinking about something I figured he'd have a pat answer to.

"I can't marry anyone," he said. "Like you for instance. You're my kind of gal, that's for sure, but I can't commit to anything. I'm all she has left and if it weren't for her I wouldn't be here. She couldn't survive on her own, I know it. This week it's carrots, last week it was fried up garlic sausage. If I don't go along with her she won't eat a thing."

It wasn't easy for Harry Tulip to discuss his mother's condition, and although he wouldn't admit it, he needed the hug I gave him. I let it go for a while and we each tied into sixteen ounces of genuine Alberta beef. Harry couldn't finish his so I helped him out. After dinner I suggested he at least let me meet his mother — she just might take a liking to me and we could figure things out from there. He started stroking my thighs like he tends to when he feels edgy, and I knew it was just a matter of time before he agreed to Sunday afternoon.

It's funny how you carry the last song you heard around with you for a whole day. Sometimes into the next day. Last summer I was walking down Beach Avenue and this guy had a garage sale with more than a hundred eight track tapes for ten bucks. I looked them over and they were the kind of music I like, blues and country. I told him I didn't own an eight track tape player but if I did I'd buy them in a freeway minute. It was a long weekend, and everyone had gone to their favourite lake, so we chatted for a while. He begged me to take them away for nothing. I found a tape player in the pawn shop for seven dollars and I installed it in my truck at my own expense. I had a rare Saturday run to Sidney made necessary because Frank Foot had taken the day off to go in for acupuncture, and the last song on my way back was "King Of the Road" by Roger Miller. Damned if I wasn't still singing that tune as I walked up the steps to the Tulips.

I brought Harry's mom some carnations because they last two weeks if you keep them wet. I also brought a bag of carrots just in case.

"Hello, Mrs. Tulip. I'm Frieda. Happy to meet you.'

"Harry says he knows you," she said.

"Harry and I are good friends," I said. "He likes to ride in my truck."

"He should have been a truck mechanic. I've been telling Harry for years he should learn to fix them. You see hundreds of them on the road. Somebody's got to keep them running."

Harry's mom was so frail it made speech seem like a miracle. She couldn't have been more than eighty pounds. She thanked me for the flowers, put them in a vase, and Harry put the carrots in the fridge. He said she was eating potatoes this week because she felt tied to the earth.

We sat out on the front porch with our tea, and Harry suggested his mom show me her knitting. She brightened at the suggestion and hauled her knitting out of a wicker trunk that sat out on the porch.

"That looks great," I said. The truth is I know nothing about knitting. I have trouble sewing a button on.

"It's a sweater," she said. Harry winked at me. She pulled her knitting out and I saw at least ten feet of it. It was blue for a few feet, then green, then brown. "I'm knitting a sweater for Harry. He feels the winter cold."

"That's fine work, Mrs. Tulip," I said. "It must keep you busy."

"Keeps me off the street. I've tried to teach Harry but he's slow to catch on. I could teach you some day."

I heard Mrs. Tulip's version of the snowfall of 1912 and when she was finished she was exhausted and headed in for her afternoon nap. Harry and I went for a walk down by the river.

"Harry, you like to go on trips in my truck, don't you?" I asked.

"I do."

"You like my company."

"I do."

"You like my toad in the hole."

"I do."

"Then I'm going to tell you something you'd better consider because it might just be the best offer you see coming your way for a long time. I think your mother is a harmless little old woman who likes someone to talk to, and sometimes you're not much of a talker. I think you and I have a lot in common, even though it might take two of you to make one of me. There's no point in building a fence around your property unless you have something to keep safe inside, and I think on the Labour Day weekend coming up we ought to find us a justice of the peace to join us together officially and when he asks the question about you taking me to be your lawful wedded wife I think you need to be prepared to say one thing and one thing only. Do you catch my drift?"

"I do," he said, and wrapped himself around my right leg. I've got to keep an eye on him because if he gets a hankering, nothing will stop him from latching on. The first time he did it in public was in front of the deli counter at Safeway and I had to pull him by the ear to get him off.

We got back from our walk and Mrs. Tulip was back out on the porch, knitting. Harry told her we were going to get married and all live in the same house so she would have me to keep her company in the evenings. She said, "That's nice, dear. Are there any more potatoes in the fridge?" and at that precise moment in time it felt like the beginning of a happy and beautiful life.

❖❖❖

September third was the day of the wedding and it was clear and crisp, the kind of day when you realize you need the sun. Harry's mom was there and so was Eddy, Harry's lifelong friend who fixes bicycles for a living. I don't have parents to speak of, three sets of foster parents—a sorrowful lot they are, so I asked Alan Fruit to give me away, which he did. Twenty-two days later, Harry Tulip was dead.

Just before our wedding day I got Harry a job at Island Freightways doing odd jobs, swamping, cleaning trucks. Frank Foot swears he never saw him in the mirror and it's a thin man like Harry you're likely to miss. Pinned him against the dock, and it was over instantly. I tried telling his mother. Tried several times, but it just wouldn't come out. Some days she notices Harry's not around, but most of the time she carries on like I've been living with her for years. She always seems to remember I drive trucks for a living and on the days she remembers Harry, I tell her he's fixing my truck. That's wonderful, she'll say. I always knew Harry would find the right job.

There isn't a day goes by that I don't look over, astounded Harry Tulip isn't sitting beside me. Maybe it's because he was so small to begin with, but it doesn't seem like he really left this world. Every turn, every stop light, holds a memory I can't let go of. The first two weeks were particularly hard, and I could tell the office felt badly on my account. They gave me routes that got me back into town early because they knew I had to tend to my mother-in-law. It was like I was living my life in a dream, and half way through the dream I realized I was pregnant.

Island Freightways was good about it. Not long after I started to show they let me work in the office as a dispatcher. They offered me pregnancy leave with the right to come back when I was ready. That's where I've been for a long time — getting ready.

Julie Louise was born first and Harry Junior second. It just didn't seem right to leave them with someone else, and Mother Tulip certainly wasn't up to it. I went without a mother all my life and I'm not about to repeat that sad story. The thing I cherish most about my kids is between feeding and cleaning, the wide expectancy they have for the world. Mother Tulip can feel it too, and I let her take turns holding them when she's finished her knitting. I've heard hundreds of stories on the front porch about growing up on the prairies, and even though the kids are too young to understand a word of it, I can't help feeling the sentiment is right. Julie and Harry have both taken a liking to sucking on the cheeses Mother Tulip has been eating for the last two weeks. I know they'll have plenty of time to realize life's miracles have as their source such uncomplicated beginnings.

Nadine Needs Time To Think

IF ANYONE IS WONDERING WHY NADINE IS STANDING beside a B.C. Hydro transformer in the middle of a cul-de-sac at nine-thirty at night on January the 22nd while the snow crystals that have been falling for over two hours continue to fall and the temperature although no longer dropping has bottomed out to a chilly minus six degrees Celsius, it is because she has her own very good reasons. One of them is Bob.

Bob stands six foot one, stands right beside her under the yellow street light that comes on looking blue but always turns yellow. One does not normally think of light as losing confidence but this light has. In the middle of the winter month it is white. Nadine can see it is white especially on the ground, not yellow at all in the snow like the letters B 0 B would be if they were peed in the snow by a boy, or yellow like the exclamation marks a girl could make if dared, or dogs could even if not. Not yellow in the least. Not yellow at all. Nadine is suspicious of Bob, well not so much Bob as what he might say and so she has brought him out here where it is private on a winter night. Any day of any other season the sun would cast a clear light, not particularly white or yellow, but clear. The lamppost they lean on would be a flagpole, a pee-pole, a pole for home free. The shrubs that pretend the transformer is not there would be battered by children and littered with Oh Henry wrappers or cigarette butts left by men who come twice each year to weed and pick up Oh Henry wrappers. They would be, but all indiscretions are forgiven under the snow, the same snow that Nadine sees falling on Bob, on his square shoulders, on his Cossack cap, on the smiles he gives her between kisses. Nadine needs time to think.

There are five houses joined by an invisible current that emanates from the transformer, which Bob places his boot on, adjusting the shoelace that is not undone but has only one loop. That's the kind of guy Bob is, she thinks, while his back is to her, the kind of guy who always dresses smartly, who likes computers, likes their binary code, likes things in twos like loops and laces. Nadine feels the power hum under her feet out to the five houses that are all different but for the black roofs. Not now because of the snow but in real life they're black, even the ones that have been re-roofed are black. Nadine doesn't expect Bob to know this just as she doesn't expect him to know much about the lives of the people that flash through her mind, the ones who live under these black roofs, now white and somehow looking all the same.

The Jensons live at the end of the first spoke that runs under Nadine's feet. They live in a wooden house and Mr. and Mrs. are wooden spouses. They have been plainly made, finely sanded, and lacquered many times. Mr. J gets up from the couch they found on page 599 and goes to the liquor cabinet on page 610 where he rejuvenates Mrs. J's gin and tonic and pours himself another rye and water. He turns off the TV on page 566 because they have decided to play scrabble in front of the fireplace, electric, page 312. The lights around them are dim. Mr. J likes the feel of his stretch polyester and so does Mrs. J because she is allergic to wool. They share a meticulous and childless marriage. They raised a budgie named Robbie for eleven years who left them both, but Mrs. J in particular, adamant that they would never own another for the heartbreak was more than they could bear. Their lives have an unusual affinity and over the years both have taken the self-deprecating attitude that each hopes to pass out of this life first, although this article of their selfless love has never been discussed openly because in the end their fear is an enemy they refuse to let slip between them. Mrs. J does not yet know that Mr. J has contacted the Hemlock Society but some day she will. They always share each other's secrets. They have taken no notice of the falling flakes and will not until the morning when Mr. J will promptly remove all vestiges of snow from his roof and restore it to black, its normal colour. Their love is polished and firm, their habits over the years so intertwined they unknowingly mimic one another. Their smile lines are almost identical and they share their devotion like two Canada geese. Neither will win at Scrabble, for they will continue to play until they have both yawned at least once and then retire to bed, snuggle briefly, and fall asleep holding hands.

Next to the J's live the Lofts. Mr. and Mrs. L know a lot about others in the neighbourhood, even beyond the cul-de-sac, and that includes their children, boy L and girl L. That's how Mr. and Mrs. look upon their offspring, as if they were part of the neighbourhood, members of the out theres, non-members of us. Not that they don't love their children, heaven forbid, but because boy L and girl L are candidates for unsolicited advice they are automatically members of the out theres. Boy L and girl L are always prepared: well buttoned, stomachs packed with wholesome lunches, and versed in all the safety rules documented by the Red Cross, Ministry of Health, fire department, and Boy Scouts of America. Boy L always pushes the lawnmower when he helps Mr. L, never leaves himself vulnerable by pulling it toward his toes. Girl L peels carrots with a down stroke only, with all the peels falling into a double layer of biodegradable newspaper for easy clean up. The two of them share equally in taking organic materials to compost. Both ride mountain bikes with patch kits and kryptonite locks and fluorescent stripes that can be seen from all angles. Mr. L and Mrs. L work very hard at developing relationships between people that might be described as responsible and they are proud of the progress demonstrated by their children. Alarm systems, Neighbourhood Watch, and pit bull terriers are obsolete because of them. Mr. L is watching Nadine and Bob at this very moment. He sees where their footprints have come from but cannot fathom their intent. The eccentricity of young love is not something he has forgotten, but something he has never known. Mr. L is the only member of his graduating class (engineering) who can truthfully declare that he has never written a single line of poetry. He will stare out of the end bedroom which is dark and shares his anonymity, for another twelve-and-a-half minutes, which, coupled with the previous two-and-a-half, will equal the time it takes Mrs. L to complete her once monthly telephone call to her mother in Bourne-mouth, England. He will then return to the kitchen, inquire about "Mother's" health, and join Mrs. L for a drink while they plan strategy for safe winter fun. They will both have their usual nightcap (eggnog) and Mrs. L will pretend not to notice that Mr. L has spiked both drinks with a dash of brandy. What she will not know is that the images of the blue movie, *Emmanuelle Infiltrates the IBM*, shown at the Lions general meeting the night before (his one night out, hers is quilting Monday), are coursing through his veins. In the en suite she will run a stripe of Estée Lauder up the inside of each thigh while he checks for lights out. He will forgo the national news on the radio at ten in order to rid himself of these ghosts that have tormented him for twenty-four hours. Children need proper care and what they have managed to accomplish with two they might just as easily do with three, and so tonight as Mrs. L accepts his lunge she will whisper in Mr. L's ear, "I am off the pill" and the whisper will seem to her quite loud enough.

The Szabos live next to the L's. They have seven grand-children and leukemia has taken an eighth. They both wear sadness on their faces, a sadness that came long before the death. They use work to ease their minds. They are country folk in the city: they use every last square inch of their yard for gardens and sheds and fruit trees, a greenhouse, a doghouse, a boat shed, a garage, and a brick barbecue pit. Mr. S does not have a lawn to mow. He likes the rain when it rains, likes the sun when it shines, hates progress whether it affects him or not. Mrs. S bakes, cans, freezes, dries, and smokes for her three sons and their families. Mr. and Mrs. S don't talk to each other much, they step over one another, lie beside one another, sit silently at opposite ends of the table every morning without so much as a newspaper between them. Their love smacks of servitude, not to one another but to the way things are supposed to be. They never discuss returning to their homeland even for a visit but they both wish they had never left. People here are too nosey or too snobby. People over here either bite each other on the ankle or fuck one another at key-swapping parties, and they wonder if they'll live to see the bomb. People think highly of the S's because they hand fresh buns over the fence and take a thank you in return. Nothing more. Mrs. S has never been inside another house in the neighbourhood but Mr. S. helped the J's when their basement flooded. Mrs. S is sitting downstairs listening to the T.V. and knitting now while Mr. S is in the garage sharpening and waxing his snow shovel for tomorrow. He worries about retiring from janitorial work next year because he is not ready to sit, stand, or lean about the house. On his way back to the house he sees two people standing under the white light in the white snow but it is not because of the snow that he does not know it is Nadine. He wouldn't recognize

Nadine if he saw her at the bus stop. He only remembers her as a little girl who loved to run naked through the sprinkler in the summertime. He stops when he sees them though. Two people like that, close together in the snow, send a flood of warmth over him and he cannot explain why it is he feels ashamed.

Mrs. Petronni lives next to the S's on the curve. She sometimes acts divorced, sometimes single, sometimes separated, sometimes even married which she still is if you want to go by the books. She doesn't seem to mind if her three young P's run barefoot around the neighbourhood, eating globby peanut butter and jelly sandwiches, thinking of ways to boost their reputation as little bastards. They enjoy being little bastards and it's no wonder because they're getting good at it. Mrs. P doesn't know the half of what they do and when people tell the half she hears about she pulls a sweater, a tea towel, whatever is handy, over her head and cries and says I don't know what to do about the little runabouts. People have told Mrs. P. what to do but she is often gone into town doing whatever it is she does when the little bastards are doing the half she doesn't hear about. The oldest little bastard liked to use the phone and he could change his voice well enough to order a load of slab wood from the East Indian Fuel Company to be delivered to the J's driveway, to order a birthday cake for Mrs. L that says Happy Birthday Mrs. L! even though it isn't her birthday for nine months, and to tell Mr. S that if he can name the two colours on the Canadian flag and get down to the local radio station within the hour he will win ten thousand dollars and a trip for two to Hungary. Mrs. P is, despite all her troubles, a happy lady. She dresses up pretty every afternoon and wiggles downtown and has learned to get by just fine now that the phone has been disconnected. She always seems to have enough money and everybody says she has an awful lot of friends. She doesn't think her life is on the skids, she just hasn't found the right man yet, she tells people when they ask and they do ask. The little P's think Mom is the greatest. They like playing hide-and-seek in the tall grass that grows up around the house every summer. The only thing their mom has them do is make their own peanut butter and jelly sandwiches and they get to watch anything on TV they want. They think boy L and girl L live in prison and they don't understand why everybody doesn't live just like them. Mrs. P. knows that not everybody thinks her family is funky but has learned to tolerate x-ray eyes. She remembers the Bible saying "He that is without sin among you, let him first cast a stone" and except for the one that the little bastards pitched through Mr. S's greenhouse, she figures things are rolling right along thank you very much. The little P's have fallen asleep around a pot of cold Kraft Dinner that sits in front of the TV. Mrs. P is off work early because of the snow. She comes down the street feeling pretty good about herself — about the world. She walks silently in the snow and comes upon Nadine and Bob, wrapped in a kiss, before they see her. "Isn't it a lovely night?" Mrs. P says and they smile. She enters the house knowing that at least with this snow the roof will not be leaking.

The Bedfords also live on the cul-de-sac, at the other end of the horseshoe-shaped street. Nadine is a Bedford. Mr. and Mrs. B have just had a tiff. They knew Bob was coming over, they saw him sitting at their table, tucking into a fine turkey dinner, though Mrs. B had her mind on other things and burned the Brussels sprouts. This knowledge didn't stop them having their tiff. These tiffs seem to be tripping over one another lately. It's an old story really. Nothing new. Mrs. B feels neglected and wants to make her point. She makes her point, even when Bob is there, and then Mr. B feels neglected. Knows he's neglected. Nadine has tried to keep Bob pinned against the wall all evening, behind the curtains, anywhere she can to minimize the damage. But a tiff leaves a funny smell in the air that doesn't go away for a while. That's partly why Nadine has gone, flown the coop, is standing in the predictable fall of crystals. The tiff will end of course. The smell will go away, but Nadine doesn't know this. She is not yet able to forecast moods with any regularity, with any degree of comfort. Bob is not just a friend — he is serious. He has been hinting at marriage. She doesn't know. This may be the night. Still might be. That's why she had to come. Had to get out to this haven in the street. Bob likes to think in twos. Nadine needs time. Time to think.

Learning To Cha Cha

RUDY FREEMASON WAS PLANTING ANNUALS for his mother with his shirt off. He liked the heat on his skin, the promise of an early start on his tan. He wouldn't be able to put it all in perspective until he was much older, but there had been huge changes in his world during the past year. Spit, a dog he'd had since he started school, had been deliberately poisoned according to their vet. His grandmother, who wintered in Sedona every year, died in her sleep on her flight back to Victoria, and a month after that his dad left on a business trip and didn't return. That was nearly a year ago, and his mom said good riddance to bad rubbish. She told Rudy his dad wouldn't be allowed to step back into the house even if he did return, and she said it in a way that made him believe her. Not all the changes had been bad. Rudy was in love with Monica Shepherd who lived right across the street. He'd heard her mention once she liked the look of a man with a deep, dark tan, and it was possible she was watching him work in the garden at this very moment.

"Rudy, put your shirt back on," his mom said. "*I* have a light coat on and *I'm* chilly."

"I'm not cold. You just have to keep moving. The sun feels great."

He asked his mom, more to change the subject than anything else, if she'd considered alternating the pink polyanthus with the purple ones.

It was exactly one year ago his grandmother died, but Rudy hadn't found out about it until the day after because he'd been camping in Brian Smolenski's back yard. Nicholas and Theodore were also there, and the four of them crammed into a pup tent. The tent belonged to Theodore but everyone liked the idea of camping over at Brian's house because Mr. Smolenski drove a potato chip truck and there were always plenty of potato chips and cheesies around, and Mrs. Smolenski had a new electric frying pan. It wasn't new exactly, it was six-months-old, but she was still amazed at the ease with which she could fry pancakes and have them come out golden brown every time, and she would use any excuse to invite Brian's friends over for breakfast.

Late that night, after Mr. Smolenski had made two trips out to the tent to tell them to pipe down, something happened that changed Rudy's life forever. They had been reading *Superman* comics and trading baseball cards with the aid of a lantern flashlight, when Theodore pulled a *Playboy* magazine out of his sleeping bag. The flashlight had given off a strong light when the night began, but was quickly fading to a dull yellow. Nicholas, who was the best student in school and got invited to camping trips at Brian's because he lived right next door, always had something to say, but he was speechless while the four of them huddled over a wide selection of pink flesh.

That's when Theodore said, "Any of you guys ever whacked off before?"

Nobody said anything. Rudy was certain he knew what it meant, but he wasn't willing to risk looking stupid. Earlier, they'd taken a package of Marlboro Lights Theodore had stolen from his brother, Alfie, out to the sawdust shed, and Rudy had taken a coughing fit and felt so dizzy he had to sit down on a sawdust bucket.

"It's easy when you know how. My brother showed me. Once you learn how you'll want to do it all the time. But you have to be old enough."

Theodore opened the magazine to the centerfold, then changed his mind and found a cheerleader from Pennsylvania he liked better.

"First you got to get an image like this in your mind. Think about what it would be like to be right up beside her. Then you grab your cock and pump it up and down until it gets hard. Then you keep going."

The flashlight was so weak Rudy could see the outline of the bulb inside, but there was still enough light to see Theodore was working on something they'd all heard about but never seen, something that had emerged like a miracle out of his Peter Pan pajamas. He pumped harder and harder until a spurt of white dribble oozed over the Pennsylvania pony tail.

"Alfie says if it happens when you're sleeping it's called a wet dream. I haven't had one of those yet, but I keep hoping. So . . . who's next?"

Everyone tried without results. The flashlight finally gave up and everyone found a pillow. Nicholas borrowed Theodore's lighter and started reading about a guy who met Marilyn Monroe in a park before she became famous and the adventure she took him on before the sun came up. Rudy fell into a regretful sleep, thinking it was only a lousy flashlight that stood between his childhood and what was yet to come.

In one year, Rudy *had* come a long way. He discovered his mind was an imaginative instrument with the ability to engineer the same feat Theodore had demonstrated that night in the pup tent. Theodore continued to get old *Playboy* magazines from his brother, and even though they were more than a year old, they were well worth the twenty-five cents a week rental fee Theodore charged. Rudy noticed most of the girls his own age didn't have the same effect as the ones in the magazines. Alfie was seventeen, and he explained to the four of them one night why this was. He said that women have to learn how to be sexy, it doesn't come naturally. A beautiful woman, he said, wears makeup like it's part of her beauty, which it is, but only if you don't notice it. They have to learn how to carry themselves, how to cross their legs just so and answer questions like they don't care about the answer they give. Receiving a first kiss from a girl is like kissing an ice cube, he said: it's either sealed lips or a gnashing of teeth. The good news, Alfie said, is that all girls get there eventually. The bad news is most of them don't get there until they are at least sixteen, sometimes much older. Your best bet, he said, is to enjoy yourself until you're old enough to attract a woman who knows how to be sexy. You'll know when you find one, because you can smell it on them a block away.

Rudy thought about what Alfie had said, and found at least part of it to be true. Even a girl like Lois Barahowsky would invite you into her tree fort for cookies and Kool-Aid, then pick away at a scab on her leg while you were eating, and she'd do it as if it was as much fun for the person watching the scab bleed as it was for the person who got to pick it. In the summer, it was Theodore's suggestion they go down to the beach where there were all kinds of girls. The four of them would sit on their towels and rate the girls they saw on a scale of one to ten. Maybe because of the magazines they all had wedged between their mattresses, there were rarely any tens. When they came across one they agreed was an eight or a nine, she wouldn't give them the time of day and they would all return home and invest their energy in their personal pursuits. Another gem of wisdom Alfie told them was: use it or lose it, but their attempts to tap into the world Alfie had intricately charted out were sporadic. After two or three days of serious deliberation, they would return to hunting squirrels or playing baseball. But Rudy was persistent, and everything fell into place when he discovered Monica Shepherd.

❖❖❖

"I went out to the front garden this afternoon to water and I noticed someone had already done it. Thank you, Rudy. You've been a real help around here lately and you're not even finished grade six.. Where have you been?"

"Just the library."

"What did you take out?"

"Just a book and a record. Nothing special."

"Let's see. Well now, don't we have eclectic tastes. A book on Marilyn Monroe and a cha cha album."

"I've decided to pick something once a week I know nothing about and learn it. It's a trick Nicholas taught me."

Rudy closed his bedroom door before his mom could ask any more questions. It seemed to him she asked more questions now than when his dad was around. He put the record on and started leafing through the book. The cover had a spectacular picture of Marilyn Monroe standing over a vent and half-heartedly holding her skirt down against the rush of air that was sharing her thighs with the world. If Monica dyed her hair blonde and wore bright red lipstick, she could be mistaken for Marilyn Monroe. It seemed to Rudy, Marilyn Monroe embodied all the qualities Alfie insisted a woman should have: she was confident — the way she carried herself, her make up was flawless, she talked in a way that invited you in, and if her movies were any indication, she knew exactly how to kiss. The more he stared at the pictures the more he realized that Monica Shepherd could easily be Marilyn Monroe reincarnated. Nicholas said everyone was reincarnated from a past life and the reason we come back to earth again is because we still have lessons to learn. Maybe Monica Shepherd was sent back to learn how to be a sexy woman who wouldn't kill herself. Maybe it was Rudy's job to help her learn how to be that kind of person.

One, two, cha cha cha.

The record stopped, so Rudy turned it over. He was lying on his back, searching through his book, trying to discover the secret Marilyn Monroe clearly had going for her. He wondered if Monica had any aspirations to be an actress. Maybe she would become a famous dancer instead.

"Rudy? Can I come in."

"Yeah."

"There's another babysitting job for you if you're interested."

"Monica phoned?"

"Mrs. Shepherd phoned. I've told you before it's not polite to refer to her by her first name."

"She doesn't mind. I asked her. She said Monica's fine with her."

"She wants you over there at quarter to seven. She has her dancing lessons so it will just be a couple of hours. Both of the boys have colds so you're not to keep them up late. Rudy? Did you hear what I said?"

"Yeah, I'm interested. I'll be there at quarter to seven."

After supper the clouds moved in and it started pouring rain. The weather hadn't been very good for tanning lately, and Rudy felt like he was falling behind schedule. He took his mother's umbrella to Monica's because he didn't want to risk damaging the album cover.

"Hi, Monica. I brought you a record I got out of the library. It's cha cha."

"Rudy, how thoughtful. I keep saying to myself you're the sweetest young man I know. We got rid of our turntable years ago and I'm in a bit of a rush right now, but you can tell me all about it when I get back. I have two CD's that you might want to listen to. I had no idea you were interested in cha cha."

Rudy got the usual run down on Trevor and Jamie and instructions on how much cough syrup they were allowed before bedtime. Monica was in a real hurry to get to her dance class. He stood at the living room window with the two boys, but Monica didn't even look up to wave.

Mr. Shepherd was in the navy and out to sea again. Only for a month this time. It seemed to Rudy he was away more than he was home and that the neighbourhood was more peaceful when he was gone because he was the kind of man who yelled. Monica never seemed to mind his going away; she carried on as usual. Rudy imagined her being very lonely and brave.

The boys wanted to play Connect Four, a game he despised because he really had to concentrate in order for them to win. He let them watch TV for half an hour, substituted their usual cocoa with orange juice, gave them their cough medicine and tucked them into bed. He read them a Robert Munch book and left the light on so they would sleep.

They finally fell asleep. He had the house to himself and he liked to explore: he opened the medicine cabinet in the bathroom and smelled the perfume, examined the different kinds of makeup Monica used. She never seemed to wear much makeup, but like Alfie said, that probably meant she knew how to wear it like a real woman. The CD collection was huge and it took him a while to find one of the cha cha albums. While the music was playing he did up the supper dishes because he knew it was the kind of thing that made Monica happy. He tried to imagine what dancing to cha cha music would be like. He thought he would ask Monica to teach him when she got home. It seemed like the natural thing to do.

In the cupboard he found a package of Oreo cookies, took three from the top layer and one from the layer below. He liked Oreo cookies, loved to open them up and lick the soft insides, leaving just enough icing so eating the outer layers wasn't a chore. When he was sure the boys were asleep, Rudy turned their light off and went into the master bedroom. Monica's bedroom had a large walk-in closet. He looked through her clothes and remembered seeing her in each outfit. He turned the lights off to see what it would be like to be in Monica's bedroom at night. He lay down on the bed, the side he could tell Monica didn't sleep on because the night table on the other side had magazines and a round container of pills. It felt very peaceful just to lie down by himself. The bed was big, and he thought two people could lie on it and there would still be a huge gap between them. His eyes adjusted to the darkness, and with the glow from the street light he could see the picture of Monica on the wall. Mr. Shepherd was in the picture too, but when he looked at it for a while, all he could see was Monica smiling down on him.

"Rudy. Rudy, wake up. You had me worried."

"What?"

"You weren't in the living room and I called your name. You usually sleep on the couch if you're tired."

"Oh, sorry."

"Not a problem. Did the boys fall asleep okay?"

Rudy nodded his head and yawned.

"How was dance?"

"It was fun. So much fun. I went out for a drink with some of the gang after. That's why I'm so late. That's good for you though, right? You look like you're still half asleep. Are you going to be all right getting home?"

"I could sleep here I guess."

"I don't think that's a good idea. Your mother will be wondering where you've got to."

Monica stuffed a twenty dollar bill into his shirt pocket and guided him over to his shoes by the door.

"Will you teach me to do the cha cha?"

"You want to learn the cha cha? I can't believe it. Sure I'll teach you. Maybe some Saturday."

"There's no school tomorrow. Teacher's day off."

"That's perfect. Why don't you come over tomorrow after lunch. The boys usually have a nap and even if they don't it won't matter. Consider it a date."

Monica ran her fingers through his hair while he fumbled with the door. People were always trying to part his hair the opposite from where it wanted to go.

❖❖❖

In the morning, Rudy faced a list of chores. Since his dad had disappeared it was what his mom resorted to. He was always a free man once the list had been crossed off.

He was on his way down to the strip mall to pick up the dry cleaning and drop off a video. His mother said he could rent one for himself and gave him a note to explain. Rudy spent a long time in the section dedicated to Marilyn Monroe. One thing she was obviously good at was titles. *Clash by Night, Gentlemen Prefer Blondes, Some Like It Hot.* He was drawn to *Let's Make Love,* but ruled it out because he knew what his mother would say. Alfie sometimes rented movies from the Adults Only section. Maybe he would take it out some day and they could watch it at Theodore's. He finally decided on *River of No Return.* The title wouldn't offend his mother and the pictures on the back of the video looked good. He went through them all one more time before he made his way up to the counter.

"I was wondering. You don't have any Marilyn Monroe posters you were going to throw out, do you?"

The man behind the counter was shaped like an Easter egg, and what hair he had was thin and unsure about which way to go. He was wearing a short sleeved T-shirt. Both arms had identical tattoos of a woman with a snake coiled around her. He stared at Rudy for a while, as if he wished he hadn't heard what was said.

"I loved Marilyn Monroe. Loved her since I was about your age. All I ever wanted to do was talk to her. When I got my driver's license I started saving money to drive down to Hollywood and talk to her. That's all I really wanted, you know? Just a chance to talk to her and listen to her side of the story. When you're a beautiful star like that you're surrounded by people who don't know how to listen. I wanted to give her that chance."

Rudy watched as the man massaged his face with his hands. He wasn't crying, but it looked like he could start any time. He walked into the back of the store, and when he came out he had a poster which he carefully unrolled on the counter.

"I was watching you over in the Marilyn Monroe section. I could tell right away you knew what so many people don't. I bought this poster from a collector in 1960. It means a lot to me, but I don't want it thrown in the garbage or sold to someone who doesn't understand. If I gave it to you, you'd look after it, wouldn't you?"

"I'd look after it with my life. I wouldn't let anyone touch it. I'd get it framed in glass so nothing bad would ever happen to it."

"Non-glare glass would be best," the man said. "It costs a little extra, but it would be worth it."

"I'll get non-glare glass. I promise."

The man carefully wrapped brown paper over the rolled up poster, then covered it in a plastic bag and secured the package

with elastic bands. He checked out the video Rudy had selected
and handed the poster over the counter. The man didn't have
any other words he wanted to say, or if he did, he couldn't find
them.

❖❖❖

There was tomato soup and crackers for lunch when he got
home. His mom had started buying crackers without salt
because she said there was enough salt in the soup to grow
shrimp. Rudy lathered the unsalted crackers with butter so he
could eat them.

It was Friday and his mom agreed he could have Theodore
and Brian sleep over to watch the movie he'd picked out.

"You can invite them over this afternoon if you like."

"I'm busy this afternoon. I've got a date with Monica to learn
how to do the cha cha."

"Since when have you wanted to learn to dance?"

"I already told you. You pick something new each week you
wouldn't normally be interested in and you get interested.
That's why Nicholas is so smart."

Rudy hid his poster underneath his bed and grabbed two root
beers and a bag of chips he'd bought to share with Monica. It
occurred to him, crossing the street, that if the boys were awake
he'd have to split everything four ways. When he got to the door
he found a note explaining that she'd had to take Jamie to the
clinic, so he trudged home. He was disappointed Monica hadn't
suggested he go too. She must have had to leave in a hurry.

His mom persuaded him to phone his friends early and they
ended up watching *River of No Return* in the afternoon. Brian
and Theodore thought the movie was okay, and when it was
over he took them into his bedroom and explained to them
how important Marilyn Monroe was as a sex goddess. He told
them about the poster and laid it out on his bed. It's from the

108

movie *Seven Year Itch* he explained, and he was going to have it framed, and if Alfie wanted to see it he would have to come over to his house because it was going up on the wall forever. Women like Marilyn Monroe come around only once or twice in a century, if that.

He carefully wrapped the poster back up they and started a game of Monopoly. When Monica phoned to apologize for canceling the dance lesson and rescheduled for Saturday night, Rudy knew everything was going to work out.

❖❖❖

"This is a great movie and I thought you'd like to see it. I've got it for seven days so it's good till next Friday. I brought us some pop and chips too. In case you get hungry."

It was Saturday night and Trevor and Jamie were in bed. Rudy had told Monica he couldn't come until eight o'clock and she said that would be fine.

"How thoughtful. Rudy, tell me, what do you think of this dress? Our dance class winds up this week and we're having a party at the end of the month to celebrate. I can't make up my mind what to wear."

Rudy sat on the couch and watched as Monica swiveled her hips and turned around. It was a long red dress that had sparkles around the collar and down the sides.

"It's all right. I kind of like it. What else have you got?"

Monica ran to the bedroom and came out in a tight, blue dress. It had a zipper down the back and she had to bend over and have him zip it up. That's when he knew for sure Nicholas was right about reincarnation. She had moles, just like Marilyn Monroe. She pranced around the room while Rudy sat on the couch with his mouth open.

"Well? What do you think?"

"I like the dress. But you should dye your hair blonde if you're going to wear it. And wear bright red lipstick."

"I think you're right. The dress doesn't really go with my hair. It doesn't clash exactly, but it doesn't do anything for me. Wait right here."

It took a while for Monica to come back out of the bedroom and when she did, Rudy was disappointed she didn't need his help with a zipper. She was wearing a cream-coloured blouse with a pattern and a black skirt that came down to just above her knees.

"You don't have a white skirt with pleats, do you? I think that would be perfect."

"No, I don't. Who knows, I may have to buy a dress. It has to be something I can move in. Some dresses make you look all right but you just can't move."

"I agree," Rudy said. "That's why I suggested a skirt with pleats."

Monica opened the pop and got two fancy glasses from the buffet in the dining room. She put the chips in a wooden bowl and helped herself.

"All right, Mr. Rudy. If you want to learn how to dance, you came to the right place. This might seem difficult at first, but it's easy once you learn the moves."

Monica put some cha cha music on and had Rudy stand beside her to mimic the steps. Then she took control and Rudy found himself flying around the living room in a blur. He wondered if his hands felt as moist to touch as hers did.

After the dance lesson they sat down on the couch, and Monica showed him pictures from her honeymoon in Acapulco. There was a picture of Monica with an iguana on her arm. She looked a lot different in a bikini.

"It looks like your mom is popping over for a visit," Monica said.

Rudy looked out the window and saw his mom walking up the sidewalk. She was carrying something covered with a towel.

"Hi, Monica. I thought two hard working dancers might like some fresh-out-of-the oven cookies."

Rudy resisted having a cookie at first, then the smell overcame his resistance. He was disappointed his mom had intruded, just when they were having such a good time. His only consolation was that Monica seemed disappointed too.

❖❖❖

When Rudy got to Theodore's house, Alfie answered the door.

"Theodore's gone fishing. He left about an hour ago."

"That's okay. I need to ask you some things."

Alfie let Rudy in and turned the music down. Alfie was smoking in the house which meant no one else was home.

"What's up, sport? Still keeping a stiff rope?"

"Yeah. It's stiff when I want it to be. I need to know what you're supposed to do when you get a girl."

"You got a girl in mind?"

"Sort of."

"I thought I told you guys to bide your time until you found a girl old enough to be sexy."

"She knows all about it, don't worry. I need to know what to do next."

"Who is it?"

"I can't tell. She made me promise to keep it secret."

"Okay. Is she younger or older?"

"Older. But she's just like Marilyn Monroe."

"So, Rudy's after older women, is he? Well, if she's old enough, chances are she'll know exactly what to do. How far have you got?"

"We danced. At her house. And we sat on the couch for a while."

111

"Well, like I said, she'll probably know the ropes. Just in case, you should have one of these with you. It's like whacking off but you can't get any inside her. You know what will happen then. You'll be cutting lawns for the rest of your life."

Alfie went to his bedroom. When he came back he handed a condom to Rudy, then told him it would cost him fifty cents or he could buy his own at the drug store. Rudy put the condom in his pocket and pulled out two quarters.

"When you open it up — "

"It's okay. We got the banana lesson at school last month. It's just that I don't know how you get started."

"Rudy, my boy, if she's in the mood all you need to do is make sure you're wearing the hardware. If she's been around the block she'll give you a tour. Are you sure you're not too young? When I was your age I was learning how to fly fish."

Alfie continued talking about his own exploits with the opposite gender. Rudy listened with some interest, but when he left he still didn't have the answer he was looking for. He decided Alfie was probably right, Monica would know exactly what to do. She would help him and he would help her.

Rudy didn't see Monica around for several days. He phoned a couple of times but there was no answer. Finally, he asked his mom where she was.

"Monica went to visit her parents with the boys for a few days. She'll be back on Saturday."

"Saturday! That's no good. She borrowed my video. I need to return it by Friday."

"Not to worry. I've got a key to her house to water the plants. I'll look for it when I go over tomorrow."

"I'll go. I'll water the plants and find my video at the same time."

His mom gave him the key and told him to be sure to water the mother-in-law's tongue that was in the upstairs bathroom and not to get any water on the leaves of the African violets. "When you lock up, make sure you try the door," she said.

The video was sitting on the VCR. He wondered if she'd had a chance to see it. He took the plastic watering can and tended to all the plants, even though they looked watered already. Then he went into Monica's bedroom. He lay on Monica's side of the bed and imagined what they would talk about. Even in the movies, there was always talking first. Then he saw it — draped over a chair in the corner of the room. A cream-coloured skirt, pleated, just like the one he'd imagined Monica wearing. That was a sign she respected his opinion. A very good sign.

In the kitchen he found some note paper and he wrote: *This dress is perfect. It will make you look even more beautiful.* Then he crossed out dress and wrote skirt and signed his name at the bottom. He left the note on the chair in the bedroom. He was sure Monica would call him as soon as she got home and offer to model her new outfit. Maybe she'd even dyed her hair blonde.

A whole week went by and Monica didn't phone once. He saw her driving off in the car on Wednesday. She waved but didn't roll down the window. When he got home from school on Friday, his mother told him Monica needed him to babysit on Saturday at five o'clock. She was going to a wind-up dinner and dance put on by the dance academy and wouldn't be home until late.

Rudy tried to sleep in on Saturday but he couldn't, he was so excited. He wanted to make sure he was wide awake when Monica arrived home from the party, so he attempted a nap in the afternoon, but to no avail. She would be tired out from the dance party, he figured, and would be ready to go to bed as soon as she got home. His mom didn't expect him home until late. Everything was working out just as he'd hoped it would.

His mom said, "There's some coke left over in the fridge. You can take it over for the boys if you want."

"I don't think that would be a good idea. If they drink a lot of coke they don't fall asleep right away and then they wake up and have to pee. I think I'll stick to my routine."

"My boy is maturing right before my eyes," his mom said. Rudy volunteered a hug before he headed across the street.

When Rudy walked up the driveway he noticed a huge Harley-Davidson motorcycle parked right by the front door. It was the shiniest motorcycle he'd ever seen.

"Come on in, Rudy. I'm almost ready. How do you like my outfit? I took your suggestion and borrowed a skirt. What do you think?" She didn't even mention his note.

Before Rudy had a chance to answer, a tall, lanky man walked out from the kitchen with a beer in his hand.

"Rudy, this is Brett. He's in the dance class too. He's going to give me a ride there and back on his motorcycle. Isn't that exciting?"

"Motorcycles are dangerous," Rudy said.

"You're right, Rudy. They can be. But Brett's a safe driver and sometimes you just have to throw caution to the wind. I might be late tonight, so you can sleep once you're sure the two hooligans are down for the night. Okay?"

"Sure."

Brett finished off his beer and put it on the kitchen counter. Then he helped Monica into a motorcycle helmet. "Don't worry," he said, "this will do more to keep your hair in place than if you weren't wearing one."

Jamie and Trevor were watching a *Batman* movie and took no interest in their mother's departure. Rudy watched them roar off down the street and noticed Monica seemed to be sitting closer to Brett on the seat than was necessary. It wouldn't take much speed on a machine like that for the wind to play tricks with her pleated skirt.

There were instructions to microwave three TV dinners. When they finished eating, Trevor and Jamie wanted to watch *Batman* again. Rudy let them and kept his mind occupied by browsing through the photo albums Monica had in the living room. A second set of instructions was to allow them to share a bath before bedtime, which he did. Then he read them three stories until they finally fell asleep. He cleaned up the kitchen and it was still only eight-thirty.

Alfie was planning a push up competition on Sunday so Rudy did twenty-four in a row to practise. He could have done more, but he didn't want to use up all his energy. Brian Smolinski would win anyway, just like he won the arm wrestling championship the week before. Monica said she would likely be late which could mean ten thirty or eleven, or even twelve. By ten o'clock he was starting to fade in front of the television. He wished now that he'd brought a Marilyn Monroe movie to help him stay awake. It was time to come up with a plan.

Monica had said if he got tired he could sleep. She didn't specify where. He considered taking his pants off before he got under the sheets, then changed his mind. He turned the covers down slightly on Monica's side of the bed. She'd appreciate that. He left the lamp by her side on so she wouldn't be startled. His plan was to pretend he was sleeping when she arrived, but to really be awake. He would say if it was all right with her, he'd stay the night and then see where things went. Alfie said she would know what to do and he was counting on it. Then he remembered the condom he had in his pants pocket. However, if his pants came off, he figured it would be awkward to keep track of the condom, so he slid it under the pillow on his side of the bed. Alfie said some girls, even if they were on birth control, wouldn't let you do it if you didn't have one, so if it came down to that he had it within easy reach. The curtains were open and he could see stars. He tried to imagine the constellation of moles Monica had on her back. He thought she might have some on her legs too, but it was the heavenly stars on her back he was drawn to. It sounded like a car had pulled up at the curb and it scared him. He could feel his breathing tighten and he almost jumped out of bed and abandoned his plan, but soon the car drove off and he relaxed. He started to dream about how surprised Monica would be to find him in bed, under the covers. What a thoughtful boy he was to understand how important it is to have someone to come home to.

❖❖❖

In his dream a voice was calling "Monica, Monica." Monica was kissing him and someone was calling her away. He started calling her back. "Monica, Monica, Monica." When a light came on he woke up and turned to see Mr. Shepherd standing at the door in his sailor garb.

"Rudy? What are you doing sleeping here? Where's Monica?"

Rudy couldn't remember what day it was. He jumped out of bed and ran for the door. Mr. Shepherd backed down the hall like was afraid he was going to be tackled, so Rudy turned into the bathroom, closed and locked the door. Then there was silence.

"Rudy, are you okay? You're not sick are you?"

Rudy didn't say anything. He looked in the mirror and then he remembered why he had come and what he'd planned to cap off the evening. Monica was supposed to come home, not Mr. Shepherd.

"You're babysitting, right? Where did Monica go? Rudy?"

He could hear him walking around the house. Checking on the boys, most likely.

"Rudy, come on out. I'll pay you and you can be on your way. Come out now, Rudy. I'm losing my patience."

Rudy could hear the Harley-Davidson pull into the driveway. He heard the door open and close.

"Johnny. I thought you were coming home tomorrow afternoon. What happened?"

"They cancelled Nanoose Bay. That's what happened."

"This is Brett. He was my partner in the cha cha and guess what? We won. Isn't that amazing? Brett's been taking dance for years but I'm so new to it all. I just can't believe it. Did you pay Rudy?"

"Rudy's locked himself in the bathroom and he won't come out. He was sleeping in our bed."

"He does that sometimes. I told him we'd be late because it was our wind-up party. It's okay, really. Rudy? Come out now. It's time to go home. I don't need you anymore."

"Oh, for Christ sake, Monica. If he doesn't get out of there I'll break the bloody door down."

"I guess I'll get going," Brett said. "Nice to meet you, Johnny. Your wife's an amazing dancer. My next wife will be a dancer, you can count on that."

Rudy could hear whispering then, but he couldn't make out what was being said. He heard Mr. Shepherd mumbling and the TV on in the living room.

"It's okay, Rudy. You can come out. Everyone's gone. It's just me. Rudy, you have to say something so I know you're not sick or anything. You're not sick are you?"

"No."

"Good. You had us worried. Did it scare you when Mr. Shepherd showed up? I can imagine it might have. I didn't expect him home until tomorrow or I would have warned you. Are you ready to come out now?"

"No."

"I had a really fine time tonight, Rudy. I won the cha cha and I think I know why I won. It's because you helped me practice. Tell you what, you don't need to come out, just let me in and I'll show you the trophy they gave me, okay?"

Rudy thought about it. "You don't need me anymore."

"Of course I need you. You're very important to me. You know what, I'm planning on taking salsa lessons in the fall and who will I practice with if you're not around? Johnny can't dance, or at least he says he can't. Please open the door, Rudy. Please."

Rudy unlocked the door but he didn't open it. Monica opened the door quietly and stepped into the bathroom. As soon as Monica hugged him he started crying.

"It's okay. You were confused, that's all. I was looking forward to coming home to tell you the news about the dancing contest. I thought you and I could make a cup of cocoa and share the trophy together. Brett said he wanted to come in and have another beer, but I told him he'd have to head home because I was coming home to Rudy. That's the honest truth. So you see, I do need you. You're very important to me."

"I don't see any trophy," Rudy said.

"It's in the living room. I'm going to pay you for babysitting and you can see it on your way out, but only under one condition. You have to promise to come back tomorrow when it's light out, and I'll get Mr. Shepherd to take a picture of the two of us with the trophy. Promise?"

Rudy could see the back of Mr. Shepherd's head in the living room. He was watching *Batman*, but he didn't turn around to say good night. Monica showed Rudy the golden trophy of two dancers in each other's arms, sitting on a wood base. She put her own shoes on and walked him across the street to his house, and it was then that Rudy remembered what he'd left under the pillow.

"I think I left something of mine in your bedroom," he said.

"That's okay. We won't worry about it tonight. You're coming back tomorrow, remember. You promised."

"Monica, do you think I could kiss you good night?"

"When you ask like such a gentleman, how could I refuse?"

Monica held his head between her hands and took control of the situation, just like Alfie had suggested she would. She kissed him once on the lips, softly.

The Only Sign Of Fire

LIFE LOOKS A LOT DIFFERENT FROM UP IN A TREE. You see things you don't normally see. Of course I didn't know that when I climbed up. There are a lot of things about climbing up in a tree you don't know before you actually climb up. It's funny how life works that way.

Anyway, it was a Friday night I took the notion to climb up. It was my "night out with the boys" as Peggy liked to put it. Some nights I just don't feel like being with the boys and it's kind of informal down at the local pool hall — whoever shows up, plays. My game has been off lately and the cue just hasn't felt at home in my hands.

It's actually quite a comfortable tree — a huge maple like the others that line the one side of our street. When I say the tree is comfortable, it's not in a comparative way. I don't do this sort of thing as a rule, but the one in front of our house has a particularly large sloping branch that I found quite cozy. Instead of walking all the way into town, I stopped at the 7-11, bought a special thermal cup I'd always wanted, a ham and cheese sandwich, and headed back toward our house. The truth is I was planning on puttering around in the garage for the night, maybe stacking the cord of wood I'd split. The blade on my band saw was dull and it's one of those things you never get around to, and the next thing I know I'm sitting up in the tree right in front of our house with quite a nice snack and a warm cup of coffee in my new 7-11 mug. I'm thinking it would have been a good idea to have grabbed a danish or a Sweet Marie, but realistically you can never come completely prepared for wherever it is you go.

It's amazing to me how life never seems to go like you've planned it. That's the way it is with me, anyway. If I had my life to live over I wouldn't plan a thing. Just go with the flow like a kite in the wind. A kite never knows when it will be dragged out of the attic and set free and I'm sure it doesn't care. A kite never plans anything. I certainly never made plans to climb up in a tree on a Friday night and I think that would have been okay if I hadn't planned so many things in the past.

The view was great from where I was sitting. I could see all the way to the end of the street and it felt like I could look right in on my own house. Peggy was moving around a lot. First one light would go on, then another. She finally settled down to talking on the phone. She's always on the phone and she's mastered the art of switching from ear to ear. Me, I get sore just ordering pizza. Talking on the phone doesn't so much apply to Peggy, now that I think of it: she mostly listens and ah-hahs. My wife has a lot of friends.

I thought maybe she'd be watching a movie. She's seen *Gone With the Wind* hundreds of times. I told her she should keep track on the calendar and send it in to the Guinness people. She told me it was the stupidest idea she'd ever heard and this made me think that some of the other ideas I'd come up with over the last seventeen years weren't so bad.

It was comfy with my hunting vest and my hot coffee. It was hot, too. I'd recommend one of those 7-11 cups to anyone in my situation. It really did the trick.

She was on the phone for a long time so I knew she wasn't talking to Jessie. Jessie's our fifteen year old who has a car-driving boyfriend. That's what they do a lot — drive around. Up and down our main street, mufflers rumbling, holding up two finger salutes to their friends who drive down main street going the other way. Jessie snuggled right up beside him, holding on for dear life, which can be hard to take for some dads. I figure Jessie has a head on her shoulders that knows what to do with the rest of her body. Peggy doesn't see it that way which is why I knew it wasn't Jessie on the other end of the line. Their conversations lately have been short and brittle.

Then the bathroom light went on, which doesn't exclude her from still being on the screamer. We got a real deal on the cell, evenings and weekends. I can see why women like a fancy bathroom. I really can. Presentation means a lot.

I could swear there's a special kind of mayonnaise they throw on the ham and cheese. It's the kids working in there late at night that make them — I've seen them do it. Some genius deserves a pat on the back, I can tell you. It's either the mayonnaise or a secret spice.

From where I was sitting I could hear the pathetic bark of the McGinty's dog across the street. I feel kind of sorry for the mangy mutt, now that he's seventeen years and nearly blind with cataracts. Poor thing wouldn't walk out of the yard if you left the gate open. It wasn't always so. Jason was afraid to deliver the newspaper after the dog took a bite out of his ankle. I don't get mad very often, but when your kid loses flesh it's time to stand up. That's why I know how old the McGinty's dog is because he and Jason have been the same age since the McGintys moved in.

The vanity in the master bedroom is where the final touches are applied. The last layer, so to speak. When Peggy approached the three-panel mirror without a phone in her hand, it was clear that arrangements had been made.

When the garage door finally opened, Peggy started up the '56 Caddy. It doesn't sound like much but it's been completely redone, inside and out. They call it a vintage car, a genuine antique. I've got a couple of guys in town who've offered me an embarrassing amount of money for it but I couldn't sell the old beast. Some things in life become part of you after a while. Tony, who works down at a small independent on the edge of town, says if I use this special additive in the gas, the car will outlast me. I know Tony would love to buy my car — he's done most of the work on it over the years. I can't stop by for a tank of gas without him seeing me off by taking a rag out of his back pocket to massage the fenders. Tony never asks if I want to sell. Some people know better.

She wasn't heading over to visit her sister, that much was clear. Beulah only sees Peggy drive up in the old Toyota pickup that's wedged in beside my workbench. It's got a bit of rust and the clutch is slipping but it runs. The Japanese make it hard to sell. Grey, overcast skies sum up how Buelah sees the world. If you want to catch Peggy's sister in a good mood, wait until it's rained for three days in a row and invite her over to watch news coverage of flood victims in China. Put cream in her coffee that's off two or three days. There's nothing in the world Beulah hasn't come across that doesn't need improving. She's been legally separated from her husband, Fred, for five years now with no sign of divorce. When she and Peggy get together it's time to review life's misery. Having to drive our old pickup truck can only stand in the shadow of Beulah's having put up with Fred, but at least it's something.

Driving away in the Caddy meant she was in the mood to taunt the brighter side of life. She drove right underneath me on the way out and stopped for a last minute inspection in the rear view mirror before heading into town. The left backup light was out. It had to be new or Tony would have noticed it.

I didn't have to wait long. I just finished the second half of my ham and cheese and she was back again. I wish she'd learn to take the curb gently and it's not that I haven't asked. The front shocks are on the edge and they're expensive. I can see she's not alone. Naturally, any man slouched in a maple tree outside his yard who sees his wife drive up with a man in the car would be curious and that was me to a tee. I could tell right off it was Fred she had with her. Fred always walks with a cane and limps wherever he goes. I've see him cross the kitchen floor, when he was still with his wife, and help himself to a beer with no cane and no limp. He said his father brought the cane back from the Boer War but I don't know how much of that to believe.

My first thought was Peggy had a plan. She was good at leading other people's lives. Maybe she'd had enough of her sister's stories of missing Fred one minute and despising him the next. Any minute Beulah would pull up for a game of crib that would turn out to be three-handed. These things are always touchy and after the weather you can always talk about fifteen twos. The kitchen was out of the question from where I was sitting. Fred liked his beer and I was sure there were two or three in the fridge. Otherwise, he'd take scotch straight up.

Fred eventually limped into the living room and Peggy followed. He took a seat in my leather wingbacked recliner I got second hand after a house fire. Peggy put on some music. Music is always nice. It kind of soothes the nerves, makes you relax even if you're not in the mood. That's how I met Peggy in an off way. Everyone deserves to feel angry and I was bar hopping after I'd been fired as a car salesman. Let go, Harry Stoke the manager said. Looking back, it was as it should have been. I hadn't sold a car in two months and cars were selling. I'd gone out, drinking up the nerve to slug someone in the face and I distinctly remember thinking that was what I needed to do to find peace. It didn't have to be Harry Stoke, anyone would have done. I ended up having a drink with Peggy Malone who wore a white pearl necklace around her neck. It was a fine neck and I could see why she wore a necklace there. We ended up back at her place and she put on some music. Albums in those days. I'd never heard such music before and I couldn't tell you the name of it to this day, but there I was, as comfortable as anyone could get on a smelly old couch with a dozen cats crawling up your leg, but relaxed. Music can do wonders.

The leaves weren't full out on the maple, but just the same I had to stand up to get a good view of the guest bedroom. Peggy got there first and I imagined Fred making a big production of hobbling up those stairs. He never went anywhere without his ancient pocket watch and long gold chain. I could envision the chain swaying side to side as he tilted his way up the stairs. I'm not even sure the watch worked. Any time you asked Fred what time it was, he always took a guess.

A dark night brings with it a fragile security. It can make the best of us unreasonably brave and a dark night on the second floor never asks for curtains. It didn't take them long to finish. Fred always struck me as an efficient man and to be fair, he may have felt time was against him. He used to peel an orange the same way.

It was the perfect venue for Beulah but she was no where to be found. Timing is everything. After Peggy drove off to return Fred to the bachelor apartment he'd taken, I decided to go for a walk. I was dangerously low on coffee and for some reason I felt the need for dessert. Sometimes the selection of sweets is so low, choosing is easy. There was a new clerk on and he was kind enough to point out which row of chocolate eclairs was fresh. I guess it didn't make any difference to him. I felt like telling him not to worry, that the pimples that had blossomed around his nose would disappear in time. I thought better of it and wished him a good night.

It would have been more comfortable with a pillow, but I did manage to catch some sleep up in the maple. Before I did,

Jessie pulled up and her boyfriend had his boom box turned way down, which was nice. He walked her to the porch and all the lights were out except one in the kitchen. The two of them sat for a while, snuggling on the porch steps, sharing a discman. It was obvious they hadn't mastered the art of fondling but were both open to exploration. Everything comes in stages.

Time flies by faster when you're up in a tree. I don't claim to have any scientific evidence for this, but I believe it just the same. Jessie came out on Sunday afternoon to look around the yard. It's not often a fifteen-year-old will take the time to look around the yard. I liked to think she was looking for me. Monday rolled around and the kids were off to school. Jason was late as usual. He's not a morning person and he takes showers that stop when the hot water runs out. Peggy left shortly after for work. She works down at the local health clinic where she counsels people on birth control and such. I hopped down and went in for a shower and a change of clothes. I'd decided to pop into the office and tell them I'd be out of town for the rest of the week. Most of my accounts were closed so it wouldn't be a problem.

It didn't take me long to make the tree more comfortable. I had some old wood around that was supposed to be made into shelves in the rec room. I made it over into two levels. There's nothing worse than living somewhere thinking there's nowhere else to go. I found the old down sleeping bag I used to use when I was into duck hunting, and a few pillows. I ran a hose down the fence line and had running water available not more than ten feet away. Fresh air has a taste all its own in the unfolding leaves of a maple tree. It's the kind of thing I'd recommend to anyone.

By Wednesday, Peggy got into the habit of meeting Fred for lunch at the house. If she skips her coffee break, she can take an extended lunch. The neighbours knew I was up in the maple

126

tree, but Peggy didn't. Information can have big gaps when you least expect it. One day, old Mr. McGinty shuffled over when I was fashioning a make-shift closet.

"What are you up to, Hester?" he said. I've told him on more than one occasion that my name is Lester but it's the kind of thing you let go.

"Building a tree house," I said.

"I thought so. I said to Eleanor last night when we were eating supper that it looks like Hester is building a tree house. You should have done it years ago when the kids were little."

He watched me for a while, steadied the ladder once or twice to make himself feel like he was a part of it all. His dog made a feeble attempt at lifting his leg to pee against the trunk of the tree.

Late one Saturday afternoon, Jessie came out and sat at the base of the tree and started painting her toenails. She loves gummy bears, particularly the black ones, so I dropped one down that I swear made a hollow sound when it hit her head.

"How's my little muffin?" I said.

"Dad. It's you. Where have you been?"

"You know me. Never far from home."

"We've been worried about you. Mom's beside herself."

It was hard for me not to tell her that this was not the case twenty-four hours a day. My reserve startled me. I explained as metaphorically as I could that I needed some time to myself for a while. It's not always easy to determine how much a fifteen year old can comprehend. I threw her down a few more black gummy bears and soon we could hear her boyfriend's muffler coming down our street. She asked if she could come and visit and I told her that would defeat the purpose of my being alone.

I had to straighten up a few affairs at the office and make a some phone calls to out of town customers. I worked late into the night, I guess, because when I woke up slumped over my desk, the birds were starting to sing even though it wasn't yet light out. I helped Charlie at the 7-11 haul in the newspapers that had just arrived. He said I must be pretty anxious to find out what's going on in the world to be up at such an hour. He's a well-meaning kid, really.

When I got back to my maple tree, I was in for a shock. The electric cord I use for my weed whacker was strung from the house and up the tree and connected to the TV set from Jason's room. It's only fourteen inch, but still. It's times like that when you realize why you bothered to have kids.

Kids will teach you stuff about yourself you don't want to know. Peggy didn't want any children at first. May have been the line of work she was preparing for. Life can be complicated enough without kids, she used to say, which inferred that life would be too complex with them.

It didn't take long for Fred to move in. I could see it coming, I really could. I figured it had been at least a week since Peggy realized I was living in the maple tree right outside her front door, so what she was trying to pull, having Fred park his Impala down at the end of the street in the middle of the night and pack two large suitcases up the street and into the house, was beyond me. I was growing quite fond of my maple tree by that time, but a man living in a tree only sleeps in fits and starts. Some people don't need to practice being naive.

With rabbit ears I was able to pull in one station only, but it was better than nothing. The thing I liked about it was the loyalty you develop. The talk show host becomes your minister. Newscasters read you a bedtime story every night. I'd never given daytime TV a thought before but I can see now how people get hooked. It's easy to become immersed in the lives of people you know, and before you realize it you care what happens to them. Imagine having a twin brother dying of cancer and you've never lost a game of chess to him before and you know you should lose for his sake but you're afraid he'll know you're doing it out of pity which is worse than winning and so you feel trapped. Every day you play him in the hospice recreational room and every day you try to find a way to lose, but as close as you get you keep winning and the net result is you feel like such a loser. God, life is so unfair. This was where I was one day, watching a man tell his twin brother that he felt terrible being such a good chess player, bawling his eyes out, when I was interrupted.

"Lester, get the hell out of that tree. Right now. It's no place for a grown man."

Beulah had her hands on her hips which was the first stage of a tantrum. I wasn't so much surprised by her appearance as disappointed. I thought she'd have shown up weeks ago.

"Can't you see I'm busy, Beulah? You've picked a bad time," I said.

"How can you make a spectacle of yourself? Here you are sitting up in a tree while your wife is shacked up in your own house with my husband. Don't you feel any shame?"

She did her little stutter step then, back and forth beside the tree. Whenever she got herself worked up, she found it necessary to fidget with her feet.

"I have nothing to be ashamed about, Beulah. This is my tree house and I built it all by myself and I happen to like it. I'm catching one of my favourite shows, if you didn't notice, and I'd rather not be disturbed."

"You're frittering your time away watching *Days of Our Lives*. For your information, you're watching a rerun."

"You're kidding?"

"No, I'm not kidding. Sammy finally lets him win a game and his cancer goes into remission. Now I want you out of that tree this instant and I want you to throw my husband out of your house."

"Can't do it, Beulah. It's not my place to do such a thing. His cancer just disappears? I've heard of that happening before."

Beulah took off her shoes then, and started throwing them up at me. She has pudgy little feet with the middle toe longer than her big toe, just like Peggy. "Well if it's not your place, whose is it? You haven't turned religious or something, have you, Lester?"

"Would you like a hot cup of coffee?" I asked. "I don't have much room up here for visitors, but I could send a cup down if you don't mind it black."

She walked barefoot to the house and tried the garage door first. Of course all the doors were locked so she picked up one of the folding chairs from the porch and smashed the living room window. Had I been able to predict what she was going to do with that chair I would have told her we kept an emergency key under the garden gnome. The sound of broken glass tends to draw neighbours out of their houses. Just curiosity I suppose. Some of the neighbours who weren't privileged with a satisfactory view began to gather at the sidewalk. There was definitely a ruckus going on inside and as Beulah made her way from room to room we were all able to follow her progress by listening to the sounds of smashing china, mirrors, the toppling of bookcases. By the time she made her way upstairs there was smoke making a straight line out of the chimney. She didn't break any upstairs windows, but instead opened them up and threw out a wide variety of clothing that belonged to Peggy and to Fred. I hadn't realized until that moment that Fred favoured boxer shorts.

The only sign of fire was smoke coming out of the chimney but someone called the fire department anyway. They pulled up with sirens blaring and ran the hose from the McGinty's side of the street and smashed the front door down. What they found when they got in there I don't know but Rachmaninov was pouring out of the house. We always kept a fair selection of liqueurs on hand and Beulah may have been going through them by this time. While it's one thing I'll never know for certain, my guess is she never found one that suited her.

Things settled down soon after they discovered there was no real fire and Beulah came out, finally, and walked shoeless down the street, leaving her car as her signature. I knew it was just a matter of time before someone came home. Reruns aren't so bad if you've never seen them in the first place.

The Short Life Of Carmelita

SOME DAY CARMELITA WILL KNOW EVERYTHING.

Her first days in this world will be yellow, jaundiced, and wrinkled. This will not be a problem. They will put her under the lights for a few days and the wrinkles will disappear once she adjusts to her arrival and, like all babies, realizes she has to make the best of her predicament. During this period, her mother will worry needlessly and her father will solicit the opinion of a specialist from out of town.

She will toilet train easily. Girls seem to be better at this. She will spend too much time in her walker which will not only inhibit her progress from ape-like crawling but will turn her right foot in, requiring special orthopedic shoes at age six. It will be a hassle fitting them on every night before she goes to bed, but the doctor will insist that her problem can be solved in her sleep. If only all problems could be solved this way.

School will be a breeze for Carmelita. She will be in the ravens, the top reading group, right from the start and she will add numbers just by staring into space instead of counting on her fingers like everyone else. Her teacher will call her amazing. She will require glasses, however, something that will puzzle her parents as both of them have flawless vision. The optometrist, who wears glasses himself, will smile and say you can't be good at everything. Everyone in school will say the name Carmelita is a colourful and pretty name.

Athletics she will take or leave. In grade four she will represent her school in the district track meet and come third in the relay race. Her father will question whether or not they should have placed her second. Her mother will be happy she did not drop the baton.

When she enters junior high, Carmelita will become Carma. Again, everyone thinks this is a fine name. She will wear her clothes too tight and too short according to some. Her CD collection will be average but her posters will be the envy of her friends. Her marks will continue to suffice, except for cooking class because she will make a disparaging remark toward Miss Wilks about having to prepare an omelet. She will be hit by a severe case of acne at fourteen, but it will be brief. Everything will clear up nicely thanks to a prescription for adapalene, which will have the blessing of her mother. Her father will be none the wiser.

Flirting at the wrong time will cause her to fall awkwardly down the thirty-six steps at the pool hall and she will end up with a broken arm and a black eye. Her parents will both question the wisdom of her frequenting such a dive in the wrong part of town, especially on her own. Carma will not share with them the fact that she was not alone and that was why she fell.

When she is sixteen, Carma will lose her virginity. She will plan for this to happen exactly the day she turns sweet sixteen, but nature creates her own monthly calendar. The mission will be accomplished, not with Butt Fozanni who she will be dating on her birthday, but with Vince Madden whose parents will be on a four day weekend in Reno the week after her birthday. Her mother will have faith in their frequent talks, hoping the school system will have filled in the gaps. Carma will know you can't be too careful these days.

By grade twelve, Carma will become sly. She will work part time at the Tastey Freeze Drive-In and feel confused about her future. Her close friends will refer to her as Car and the name will stick. She will survive the confusion and strive to be independent. There will be no steady boyfriend in the cards for her. The boys in her graduating class, mostly out of wishful thinking, will say things like it must be fun to drive around in a Car. Because she understands confusion, Car will forgive them.

College is not for everyone. That is the conclusion Car will come to. At her first full time job as an apprentice travel consultant with The Bay, she will meet a man six years older who has been waiting for her all his life. The marriage will be a hurried affair, not because she is pregnant, but because he is a businessman who has business to tend to. They will move to Toronto where Car will enroll in a decoupage class at the Ontario College of Art and Design. She will phone her parents every weekend on a special long distance plan her father will pay for. One Sunday she will cry so desperately into the phone, her mother will feel the tears right through the handset. She will tell her mother how one night after her class she went for coffee with her friends and found her husband groping another woman's legs in the window booth. Her mother will tell her to hang tough, try to work things out, but Car will know this is the beginning of the end. Thank God, she will think, she has continued on the pill.

Car will ask for nothing in the divorce. She will later regret this. It will not be until she is twenty-five that she will meet Hammy Atkinson. Hammy will appeal to her in a way she won't be able to describe to her mother, but this too will pass. Hammy will be stable. And fertile. Hammy and Car will have three children but will only be left with two. Hammy will tell everyone they only have two children because the second was only alive a matter of hours. To Car, this will still be a child to remember. Within a month of their losing the second of three children, Car's father will die of cancer. This will begin the second phase of Car's confusion. Why me? she will ask. The gods of fate will answer, why not?

The two children that do survive will be boys and she will name them Butch and Vinney. Hammy will think the names are strange but will not stand in her way. Hammy will prove to be more than stable, he will be an astute investor. They will move into the Shaunnesey district of Vancouver and there will be two basketball hoops and a Jaguar in the driveway. The basketball hoops will be off to the side. Car will dye her hair seven different shades before she will let the gray have its way and her friends will begin to call her by her first initial. C's mother will grow very old in what seems like a very short time and an offer will be made to move her to Vancouver to live in the self-contained suite in the basement where C can keep an eye on her. Her mother will say thank you, dear, for the offer, but I just couldn't. You have your own life now. C will think about her mother's response a lot. There is so much, she will realize, she still has to learn. So much to learn before she knows everything.

Hope

I ONLY IRON WHEN I'M NERVOUS and Tuesday I ironed all afternoon. It was the way the planets were lined up. Mercury was retrograde, but I didn't tell anyone, not even my wife. I'm a lot of things, but I'm not an alarmist.

I was brought up to respect the number three. Three meals a day, three baths a week, that sort of thing. It was my mother's fault. I don't blame her for much, but with the number three there's nowhere else to turn. In our house if you woke up and stubbed your toe first thing in the morning, you acknowledged it as number one. You were wary. After school you might get into a fight with Dom, the butcher's son, who never let up till he saw the sight of blood. That was two. And then you'd wait. You'd try for something mellow, suggest a game of crib with your dad after supper, the loser to wash and dry the dishes, clean the counter and make the lunches. But inevitably you'd win. Some nights you'd wait for number three and if nothing came down the pike before bedtime you'd wake up in the middle of the night with the flu. There was no way of escaping the number three.

I've been driving bus for twenty-seven years (that's nine groups of three). That's what I tell people, but there were three years I missed after the accident (making it really only eight groups of three), but I was driving bus in my mind the whole time. It gets in the blood; it's hard to explain. It was icy and the school buses shouldn't have been on the road in the first

136

place. I wasn't the only one to slide off the road but my bus hit a pole. A freckle-faced kid named Nathan broke his expensive braces and even though that was the extent of it, I was suspended. They offered me a job cleaning the buses, but I couldn't take it. Driving is my life.

When you turn fifty-two your reactions aren't what they used to be, but experience makes up for lost time. That's a fact. My eyesight is impeccable, and I've never needed glasses. After my suspension from the school district it was tough to get a leg up. I've been driving for West Coast Transport for a few years now, and I like it. Variety. After thirteen years of driving the same school route I yearned for change anyway — road construction, anything — because kids are ornery on their way to school and who can blame them. I don't have to listen to a bunch of rug rats singing "The wheels on the bus go round and round" and if you think I miss it, you've got a few lug nuts loose. West Coast does promotional tours, the Adams River run, holidays for the elderly, and so on. Every five years they put you through a battery of tests, and now they say my reactions are borderline. Bernie is twenty-eight and he started the same time I did. His reactions test out A+ and lately Bernie has been getting most of the trips passed his way. Bernie can drive a straight line, but doesn't know how to cozy up to people. That's my strength, being able to swing a line and keep their interest. There are only so many trees you can stare at out the window of a bus.

I was nervous as hell and it wasn't just the planets. Fifteen days ago I took a group on the Canadian Winds Rambo Tour which has been big around here since they filmed *First Blood*. It was a good trip but a short one, and I haven't been called back since. There was no sense phoning the office again because Ruby can bite a chunk out of your ear if you're not a paying customer. I like Ruby, though. In fact she's the only woman who doesn't shave her armpits I've taken a shine to.

Beryl, that's my chubby bundle of love, reminded me we've only got two and a half years of mortgage left. She's been through the wringer with her first husband, Beryl has, and she knows I'm the kind of man to give her what she deserves. It's a powerful thing when another human being has that kind of faith in you. They can lay me to rest after that, but until then I need to drive twice a week to keep my end up.

I ironed my burgundy blazer like I did every day and hung it up by the door just in case. We're the only company with burgundy blazers and personally I think they look sharp. What they say about a man in a uniform still holds true for ladies with a cane in each hand. I ironed every shirt I own and most of Beryl's. Because she was out of the house I started in on the sheets. It kept me busy and I was curious to see if she'd notice.

I was about to put the ironing board away when I got a call from Ruby. She can be soft spoken when she needs someone and I was a someone again. Ruby never calls with straight forward information. Everything comes wrapped up like a fancy *hors d'oeuvre*.

"Francis, you haven't broken any limbs lately have you?" she said.

"No, Ruby," I said. "I'm still standing."

"Good for you. I like a man who can stand on his own two feet. Frank has a trip for you. You'll be gone four days. He specifically asked for you."

Frank is the office manager who inherited the job when his old man passed away, and he's the kind of guy who makes me nervous. The last time he lined me up with a "specifically asked for you" job I had to drive the Marchment twins along with their dead mother laid out in a casket from Hope to Penticton and back to watch the Peach Festival parade. It was in the old lady's will, according to Frank, and there wasn't a thing he could do about it.

"This doesn't involve any dead people, does it?" I asked.

"As far as I know, you'll be dealing with live cargo," Ruby continued. "Frank said to be in by eight in the morning. Four days means bring your pajamas. You do wear pajamas don't you?" Then she laughed the way only a hairy person can.

Beryl was pleased as hell when I told her. She works two days a week in front of Canadian Tire selling Mr. Tube Steaks and I can tell she's not fussy about taking on any more than that.

The next morning I went into work with an extra pair of pants and three extra shirts packed in an old Mr. Seam laundry bag and found out I had a real doozy. My job was to drive from Hope, north to a place called Elkness Camp just out of Prince George. I was to spend the night in a cabin already paid for. It was a summer camp for the mentally challenged and I was to bring four of them to Hope, but not before I took them and some of their camp mates to Clearwater Camp for two days, one hundred and twenty-five miles out of Kamloops. The four I was bringing back didn't have all their marbles but their families had lots of coin and wanted them on the West Coast, closer to home.

Frank wasn't there when I signed the bus out. He probably thought I'd have something to say about his relatives.

I filled out the paper work and checked the bus over. I was about to leave when Beryl drove up in one big hurry. She always drives that way and I now include a brake job as one of our yearly expenses. You forgot your pills, she said. You need them in case you get those dizzy spells again. I sometimes look back with regret that it was Beryl who landed me the job. She sold a tube steak to one of the drivers who told her they were hiring and ever since it's been like she's the only one with a reputation to protect. I hadn't had a dizzy spell for at least six weeks, but she was right. I knew she was right.

The trip up the Fraser Canyon was uneventful. One stretch of re-paving, but that was it. I stopped for a burger at The Burger House and got into camp with plenty of light.

A tall red-headed man came out of the office and offered me his hand. "My name's Andrew Beaverpelt," he said. "I see you found the place all right." I was mulling over what he'd said. It was obvious I'd found the place or I wouldn't be there. I was wondering to myself why people say such things, and at the same time thinking that if I had a name like Beaverpelt, I'd change it quicker than underwear. I grew up with a guy called Gordie Draper whose family name had been Raper, and I always thought that was a smart thing to do. While I was running these thoughts around in my head I was intrigued by a woman who kept walking around the bus and wiping the lights using her dress as a chamois. She never touched the rest of the bus, which was plenty dusty, but when she finished the lights were like new.

"The directions were pretty straight forward," I said.

"Well, you wouldn't have been the first driver to get lost up here." Andrew Beaverpelt wore a long, droopy mustache, and after every statement he'd guide an end of it into his mouth to suck on.

I followed him over to the cabin where I was to sleep. The mosquitoes were everywhere and you had to keep moving, but they didn't go near Andrew Beaverpelt. He said I could join them for breakfast at seven-thirty, and after that I was to take his son, Charlie Beaverpelt, a level one camp counselor, and fourteen campers down to Clearwater. They all went for a one mile run before breakfast, he said, and after they'd eaten, most of the campers would sleep on the bus.

"Make yourself at home," he said. "After we get everyone into bed, Charlie and I always play a couple of games of Parcheesi. You're welcome to join us."

I thanked him but figured if I could get through the first half of a Jeffrey Archer novel I could get through the second. I had a cabin to myself which was fortunate. Someone was having a bout of cabin fever not too far away, and I didn't sleep much.

After breakfast, I was told it would take half an hour to get the fourteen people moving on to the next camp ready to go. This turned out to be optimistic. Three of them got on the bus immediately and sat in the front seat together. I explained the best I could that it might be more comfortable two to a seat, but their close proximity to one another seemed more important to them than creature comforts. All three sat looking straight ahead like we would be arriving at a carnival any minute. It took almost an hour for Bernie to round up the rest of the recruits, and I couldn't help feeling odd as they made their way aboard. I'm used to giving customers a line when they get on my bus, but I didn't know what to say to these people. One man kept saying "Bussy, bussy, bussy" with no indication he planned on stopping any time soon, and the lady who'd taken such care cleaning the headlights got on and ran her hand over my burgundy blazer.

I drove through a hot stretch to get to Kamloops. We have two air conditioned buses, but of course I wasn't driving one of those. Once we got out on the highway, most of them nodded off. The three men in the front seat would have none of that. Their eyes never left the road the whole trip. Charlie said to stop at McDonalds, which I did. He came out with a box full of food, and we headed down to a park by the river. By the time everyone ate and found the washrooms it was the middle of the afternoon, and I was on page 597 of my novel.

We got into Clearwater Camp late. Charlie said he knew the way which turned out to be the wrong way. Everyone had finished supper and they had to work up an extra spread for us. I could tell the cook wasn't pleased, which didn't surprise me, but what did surprise me was his red hair. Charlie called him Uncle Gus and I left it at that.

For the next two days I stayed out of the way of their Bible meetings and their field trips into the bush to make wooden crosses. Their ages ranged from twenty-five to fifty and they were serious about everything they did. I couldn't help wondering how much, if any of it, they understood.

Sunday morning, right after an outdoor church service, I was ready to head out on the final leg of my trip when Charlie came up to me and said one of the camp counselors had been re-visited with something associated with polio and, seeing as they were short-staffed, would I mind taking the four passengers destined for Hope down on my own. I told him I thought polio was under control these days, but he said once you get it there's always a chance, and they were praying for him in any case. The four in question, according to Charlie, were well-adjusted and they were going to a group home in the country where they would help out with odd jobs and be part of the community. They'll just sit there, he said. They might even sleep.

So Martha, John, Harold and Muneesh collected their things and away we went. I thought the four or five hour trip should get us in by five o'clock and there would be plenty of time to ready the bus for the next morning. It was hot as Hades, but Martha refused to take her coat off.

Harold had a portable radio with him and while I usually don't encourage such things on my bus, I didn't think it was worth making a fuss about. One thing stood out in the heat — the frequency of beer ads on the radio. *This Bud's for you.* *Kokanee — the beer around here.* I hadn't counted on stopping, partly because it was safer if we just kept moving, and I didn't want to supervise a bathroom break. Harold kept repeating the beer ads as we made our way through the canyon and by the time we got to Lytton, I thought my mouth was going to crack. Then, just like a miracle had been willed by my friend Harold, I spotted a bar and grill sign on the horizon with a banner for Kokanee beer hanging limp in the heat. I pulled in and shut off the bus. All four of them were looking at me like the trip was over.

"You wait here," I said. "I'll just be a minute. Stay on the bus."

No one responded, although Martha smiled. I went in to see if I could get a cold beer to hit the road but beer sales, I was told, were closed on Sundays.

"You're welcome to drink one inside," the waitress said, "but you'll have to order food to go with it." She smacked her chewing gum loudly and looked around impatiently as if there was a lineup behind me.

"Sure," I said. "Order me up two Kokanees and some nacho chips. But first I'll take four Cokes." The waitress, whose name tag read Marlene even though she looked more like a Barb, stared at me for a minute before she moved into action. Some people take longer than others to process even basic information.

I took the four Cokes to the bus and handed them out. John had trouble opening his so I gave him a hand. It was getting hot inside the bus so I opened a couple of windows to let a cross draft through.

The first beer slid down my throat and would have tasted better if I hadn't kept thinking of how hot it was in the bus. When the nacho chips arrived I played with them a bit, but the beer was a saving grace. I've never been one to hit the bottle hard, especially after what my Beryl's been through. But when you're as thirsty as I was, even Kokanee tastes good.

I wasn't more than fifteen minutes, I swear to God, and when I came back out they were gone. At first I thought they were hiding further back in the bus, but they were gone all right and so were the three backpacks and the shopping bag Martha had brought with her. I checked back inside the restaurant in case they'd slipped in when I was in the washroom. I asked the guy who was pumping gas next door, but he said the only thing he could recall were some hitchhikers heading toward Vancouver.

"How many were there?" I asked.

"I'm paid to pump gas not count hitchhikers."

My only chance was they would get a ride south but not too far south, and I'd be able to retrieve them. It was my slim hope of salvation.

I pulled over in Boston Bar and asked a few people if they'd seen my payload. I got *the look* from a few of them, I can tell you. I guess it's not everyday a bus loses its passengers. I wasn't speeding, that's for damn sure, my eyes roaming the countryside like I was a predator and not a bus driver who'd stopped to quench his thirst. Finally, I spotted a man with a back pack hitchhiking, but he was on the other side of the road. I pulled over, and he came up to the open door.

"You haven't by any chance seen four people hitchhiking south in the last half hour, have you?"

"Nobody hitchhike," the man said, in an accent that was a deliberate mouthing of vowels. "You give me ride?" he asked.

"I thought you were heading the other way?"

"I don't mind," he said, and got on.

I didn't say anything because I didn't have time to argue. I'd let him off down the road a ways and that would be that.

There are two kinds of hitchhikers. Some are out there because they have a destination but no car. I can see it on their face. Then there are the ones who scurry across the earth, hoping to find a place to survive. I see it all the time driving bus and understand how thin the line is between them. I could see him in the mirror, all hunched over, like he'd just been scolded. We carried on down the Fraser Canyon, and just north of Spuzzum I spotted a lady at the side of the road, so I pulled over.

"Hi," I said. "Have you seen any hitchhikers on the road on your way down?"

She stood there, a blue and white bandana around her forehead, her hair in pigtails and a big smile that indicated a tooth was missing.

"Tom," she yelled into the bushes and two men came sauntering out. They were either drunk or sleepy but they sure weren't moving fast. "These two is hitchhikers," she said. "They're both called Tom."

I looked at them and didn't know what to say. I was feeling a little woozy, maybe from the heat, maybe from the beer. Then inspiration slapped me in the face. "Hop in," I said. "I'll take you as far as Hope."

They got in, but not before retrieving a large duffel bag from the side of the road. I was only an hour out of Hope, so I took out the directions to the group home.

"We's looking for a cheap place to stay," the lady said. She'd moved up two seats from the two Toms so she could talk to me. "Got to be pretty cheap cause we got no money. We got music. Tom can play harmonica and Tom can sing."

She turned around to point at the Toms and they both smiled like what she'd said was gospel.

"Do you play something?" I asked.

"I wail and play drums. That's what's in the bag," she said, then started beating out a rhythm on the back of the seat with her hands, but hard as I listened, I couldn't catch the tune. The man who wasn't Tom was nodding his head to the music and wore a look of recognition. I knew exactly how he felt — music doesn't have to be great as long as it's familiar.

Everybody needs somewhere to go and these four looked like they could use a good meal. When you get older you realize there's an art to survival.

By the time I found the place it was already five-thirty. I shut the bus off and turned to my passengers. "I know the people who live here," I said. "They'll let you stay as long as you help out once and a while and read the Bible."

"What if you can't read, Mister?" the woman said. I was about to explain that listening to the Bible would be just as good, when a man came out on the front porch. He stood there with his thumbs hitched in his suspenders, and I wasn't really surprised to see he had red hair. I knew there had to be a third one out there somewhere.

"So, you made it, I see." He said it like he was genuinely surprised, and it occurred to me that astonishment might be hereditary. We took turns down the steps. "Hello, " he said. "My name is Wil. And you must be Martha."

"Name's Cornelia."

"A rose by any other name," I said, and the man laughed. I helped them up to the porch with the duffel bag. "They've had a hard week of camping. They'll be very grateful for a shower and a home-cooked meal," I said, and that part, at least, was true.

I headed back to the office, but being late on a Sunday there was no one in. I turned in my log sheet and phoned Beryl to come and pick me up. "How did it go?" she asked over the phone.

"Fine," I said, "not a dizzy spell the whole trip." That's all I told Beryl and with any luck that's all she'll ever know. She worries enough about my job as it is.

When we got home, I sat out on the verandah and had one of my home brews. Beryl brought out a left over tube steak, warmed up and smothered with onions just the way I like them, and I realized it's the little things we'll remember when it's all over.

Hot Wheels

"VROOOOM, VROOOOM. UUUUURK!"

The housekeeper was scheduled to clean the house from top to bottom on Mondays, but by Monday everything would be over. The kitchen had to be spotless. The kitchen was the heart and soul of a house, a room where people made judgments. Her excuse for not coming to help sooner was Asian flu, but Mel had her doubts. Why wouldn't she have doubts when a housekeeper who'd been with them for nearly eight years added "Asian" to an already powerful word like flu.

"Speed bump. Vroooom, vroooom!"

"Michael, stop that. Get out of the kitchen. I've had enough."

Michael remembered it wasn't long ago when running his hot wheels cars up his mother's leg was entertainment for everyone. He cowered under the kitchen table and pretended to change a tire.

Richard had relented and offered to clean the bathrooms but not without a battle. Richard didn't appreciate being called a lazy slob. There was a time when it wouldn't have bothered him in the least, when he would have called the description dead on. Mel would go in after him and do both bathrooms over. When people made judgments about bathrooms they were never anything but scandalous.

Michael was motoring with his whispering voice. "Vroooom, vroooom," loud enough for his mother to hear if she were

148

focused, background noise if something else had taken over. Thirteen hot wheels cars were stored on the frame of the table and many more were kept in his room and in Tag's room. Tag was older and only played hot wheels when he had nothing better to do.

The phone rang and Mel stared at it. Richard didn't believe in answering machines, and some people, like her friend Marjorie, would phone until it rang twenty or thirty times if she didn't pick up.

"Hello."

"Mel, Marj here. How *are* you holding up?"

No matter what the circumstances, Marjorie was the one person Mel could talk to. She had been Mel's best friend for three decades and Mel regarded her as a saint. Marj had agreed to field the out of town calls from relatives, most of whom Marjorie had broken the news to.

"As good as could be expected, thanks. It's going to take time for Richard. After all that's been said around here these last few months, he's got a lot of sorting out to do. Despite what he thinks, it hasn't hit home yet."

"Twenty-three confirmed," Marjorie said, "and that may be what we're looking at. The Uncle John from Weyburn is still waiting on a date for his bypass and can't make it, but Uncle John and Aunt Edwina from Vancouver are coming. They've all been told you're taking your mother in and that's all you can cope with. I've given everyone prices for Super 8 and Best Western. It's up to them. Now I know you mentioned catering, but I'm bringing a double batch of date squares. I'll cut them small. Is there anything else I can do?"

"Marjorie, you are an absolute saint."

"Oh, Mel. You don't have to say things like that."

Marjorie paused, waiting for Mel to repeat it one more time.

❖❖❖

Richard finished the bathrooms and made his way to the garage that was separate and set back on the double lot. It was the first time he'd gone to the garage in the last four days and he knew it was something he would have to face eventually. He opened the door and his '69 Ranchero sat innocently enough, the windows still rolled down. It was a car that had defined who he was. He insured it only from May to October each year and had turned down offers to sell, most of them wishful thinking, but some from serious collectors south of the border. For a brief stint, Richard had raced stock cars, and just being around his pride and joy took him back to his glory days. The sponsorship he'd finally arranged had been pulled out from under him, and gone forever were his dreams of becoming a professional driver. Keeping the vintage car was his pacifier. Now, the deep maroon and glistening chrome that had been his inspiration for so many years, stared back as if to say it knew what it had done and didn't care one way or another. A sawhorse was turned over on its side, but otherwise everything in the garage was as it had always been.

"Vroooom, vroooom. Vroooom, vroooom."

Richard heard Michael coming across the yard. It occurred to him he had no idea how long he'd been standing in the garage staring at the car.

"Get back in the house, Michael."

"Tag play hot wheels. Hot wheels, hot wheels."

"I said get back in the house. What are you doing out here in your bare feet? Get out of here before I smack you one."

Michael took the two cars he had with him and slowly made his way toward the house. He liked it when only he and Tag were home and they could play in the garage without any yelling. Tag would pretend the big car was a hot wheels car and he would start it up and let Michael beep the horn. When Tag sat inside the big car, Michael had to play hot wheels by himself because Tag liked big hot wheels better than toy ones. Tag would sneak out of the house and hide in the big car and Michael would have to come and find him. Sometimes Tag would hide in it with his friend, Philipe, and then he couldn't come in. It was okay to play hot wheels inside the car but not outside because the paint might get scratched and Tag would get mad at him.

❖❖❖

Kraft Dinner was Michael's favourite and they'd had it two nights in a row. After dinner, Mel went to the bus depot to pick up her mother and Richard sat in the Lazy-boy and stared into space. Michael had his small hot wheels circuit out on the carpet and was imagining how fast his cars would go if they could go faster than they did. The big circuit was in Tag's room, but he'd been told not to go in there. If his dad got up to fetch a beer, Michael would get up into the Lazy-boy and run his cars off the foot rest, but his dad didn't move. Instead he turned on the hockey game then turned it off right away.

"Tag play hot wheels with me tomorrow," Michael said.

"Bring Daddy a beer from the fridge. Okay, Michael? Go and get Daddy a beer."

Michael gave his dad the beer and climbed up to sit in the Lazy-boy with him. He ran his hot wheels up and down his dad's leg and he didn't seem to mind.

When Mel's mom arrived there was no cheery hello. Richard put his beer down on the rug and went to the door. He hugged his mother-in-law for a long time and it was difficult to tell who started crying first.

"Only God knows why these things happen," Dorothy Grovier said, reaching up and rubbing Richard's back.

"One day at a time," Richard said.

"Michael, how did I know before I got in here you'd have a car in each hand? Give Granny a big hug." Michael liked when his granny came to visit because she always gave him something before she got back on the bus. That's why he didn't mind that she smelled of lavender.

When they were finished, Richard went back to sitting in his chair and Mel helped her mother up the stairs with her suitcase. Michael grabbed his favourite car and followed, taking the necessary time to maneuver his car up each stair. By the time he drove down the hall they were in the den and putting sheets on the pullout couch. This was another room Michael was not allowed to enter except when he was home alone with Tag because his hot wheels would skid and mess up his dad's papers, and one day the mouse ball mysteriously went missing. Half way down the hall it was time to fuel up.

"Tomorrow will be an emotional day for all of us," Dorothy said. "I can't imagine the pain you've been through these last few days. You're a strong woman and I'm proud of you."

"Thanks, Mom. A celebration of life. That's how I've been told to think of it all, and I'm trying to do just that. It's the regrets that get to you. We all have regrets."

Adult hugs could last forever. Michael went into the bathroom.

"Michael, what are you doing in there?"

"Car wash."

Michael drove slowly down the hall and still caught up to his mom and granny. They paused outside Tag's room.

"Michael, go and tell your dad to make Granny some tea. Way you go."

Michael slipped on wet tires just as they opened the door to Tag's room. If Tag was in there he wasn't on his bed — it was covered with stuffed animals. He could be under the bed. Sometimes they'd both hide under there and listen while the search was on. That's where Tag kept the big hot wheels circuit hidden.

❖❖❖

In the morning, Dorothy was up well before anyone else. By the time Michael came downstairs, she had a tower of pancakes ready to go. Mel and Richard were a long time coming for breakfast, and their yelling voices could be heard from the kitchen. When they finally came to the table, the frayed ends of their conversation trailed after them.

"You can't change someone's nature," Mel said. "If that's one thing you didn't know, you sure as hell do now. And don't you dare start in with that 'No son of mine' bit. Don't even think about it."

They found Michael running one of his cars through the syrup on his plate, but before he got in trouble, Granny grabbed the car and washed it in the sink.

"How many more pancakes can my race car driver eat?" Granny asked. Michael held up five fingers and she put three golden pancakes in the syrup puddle on his plate. She had attempted to make them into the shape of racing cars, but no one, including Michael, had noticed. He grabbed for the syrup but Richard put it out of reach. Richard put his usual two sugars in his coffee and stirred it for a long time before taking a sip.

"I want to be there a half hour early," Mel said. "I want to be seated before everyone arrives."

"I don't see what difference that will make," Richard said.

"It will make a lot of difference to me. That's why we'll do it."

Richard took a third spoonful of sugar and continued stirring his coffee. Yes, he'd gained ten or fifteen pounds, but he knew he could head right upstairs and put his charcoal suit on and it would fit. Fifteen pounds wasn't much these days, despite what his wife thought. And when they got there he would say something if and only if he had something to say. The newspaper on the table remained beside yesterday's, both in their plastic sleeves, untouched.

After breakfast, Granny offered to help Michael into his good clothes. Michael's yellow hot wheels car made it to his bedroom long before his granny arrived. It was never a good idea to leave a car idling too long.

"Come into the bathroom first," she said. "We've got to clean behind those ears."

That was one thing Michael hated about granny visits. Behind the ears meant in the ears and down his neck and she always rubbed his face with the washcloth until his nose felt hot.

"This is a cute outfit, isn't it? I believe it's the one I bought you for Christmas."

Michael had never seen the grey pants, white shirt and grey vest. Good clothes meant clothes he'd never worn before.

"When we get there you're not to talk. And no cars. I suspect your mother has already told you that. Some people will talk, but you and I don't talk. We're going to listen to what people want to say about your brother. You got that?"

Michael was waiting for his granny to spit on her fingers and tame his cow lick and was only half listening.

"Michael can't talk and Tag can't talk."

"That's right. Tag will be listening to all the stories too."

❖❖❖

When they arrived, Mel could see her sister's Cadillac parked by the front entrance. She'd chosen to leave her partner in life, Amelia, at home. Richard found it easy to be mean to Amelia. When Mel approached the car, her sister rolled down the window.

"I figured you'd be here early and want to get settled. I'll wait before I come in."

Mel nodded, Granny retrieved a car from Michael's back pocket, and they made their way into the chapel. It was decorated with daisies, the flowers Tag liked to pick as a child, despite Mel's aversion to their skunky smell. On a table at the front were pictures of Tag, one for each of his sixteen years. Mel and Richard went into a back room to meet with their host, Mr. Melanby. Granny took a seat in the front row and Michael went up to explore the pictures.

"Is this one Tag?"

"Yes, that's Tag when he was a baby."

"Is this one Tag?"

"Yes, that's Tag all right."

"Is this — "

"They're *all* pictures of Tag. Come and sit down. We're here to listen, remember. Not talk."

It didn't take long for the place to fill up. By the time the service began, there was a crowd of teenagers standing at the back.

Mr. Melanby began the service with a few motherhood statements about the mystery of life and our need to accept the unexpected. The tone of his voice and the intention of his words were to soothe those in mourning, but the speech was so universal it came out sounding like an astrology chart in the newspaper. An invitation was made for others to make a dedication to Tag and many accepted. The school principal talked about what a spirit Tag had been around the school. What an impact he'd had on his fellow students, and how the tragedy would leave them all with an emptiness for years to come. Several of Tag's friends spoke emotionally of their loss, and eight students sang a song of peace and everlasting love they'd written specifically for Tag, followed by his closest friend,

Philipe, who repeated the chorus in French. When he was done, Philipe stared up at the ceiling and cried, "Tag, I will love you forever," then overtaken by grief, had to be helped back to his seat.

With each tribute, Richard could feel his wife's eyes drawing an arrow to the front of the room.

"I thought you would have something to say," Richard said. "After all, you are his mother."

The timing may have been wrong, but Richard was relieved he had spoken. He began to relax, as if his comment had somehow absolved him from any responsibility to make a speech. Mr. Melanby made a few closing remarks. Some left immediately while others mingled around the relatives and the pictures, the artifacts that remained. Marjorie said she would stay behind to retrieve the pictures. An important juncture in their lives was over.

"I want to drive the long way home," Mel said. "The route along the ocean."

"I think it would make more sense to get back and help the caterers set up," Richard said, but obediently drove the car along the ocean. Slowly, personal recollections were made: Clover Point where Tag had successfully flown his first kite, the bike route he liked to take during his brief stint as a competitive cyclist, the ball diamond where he'd struck out three times in one game.

"I like my Tag," Michael said. "He plays with me . . . hot wheels."

❖❖❖

Michael got more than his share of attention once they returned to the house and people began to arrive. Aunts he'd never seen before would pick him up and hug him or straighten his bow tie and pinch his cheeks. He took his favourite car out on the front porch and ran it along the railing. He liked being around the uncles with their pipes and cigars and rye. He alternated between the living room and the egg salad sandwiches, and the porch and the smell of his uncles, driving his car back and forth through heavy traffic, careful not to run anyone over. People kept talking about Tag, but Tag was not in the kitchen or on the front porch. Michael headed upstairs, but Tag wasn't in his bedroom or in the den. He opened the door to Tag's room. He checked the closet. He looked under the bed. The big hot wheels circuit was still there, but Tag was not. The shiny trumpet Tag hadn't played for years and the purple hot wheels car he claimed was the fastest of them all, were sitting on the dresser under the shadow of a Michael Jackson poster. He shoved the car in his pocket. Tag probably thought he'd lost it again.

Tag could hide better than anyone. Michael went out into the yard and checked the tree fort. He heard voices in the garage and he crouched down behind the wheelbarrow. Tag sometimes gave him rides in it, and when he did, Michael had to hang on tight. His dad was not alone in the garage.

"They said he'd been gone for hours before we got home," he heard his dad say. "There was only a quarter tank left so it must have been on all morning. You couldn't get near him it was so thick. And the car was hot as hell."

"Have you decided what you're going to do with the car?"

"I'll get rid of it. I couldn't find any enjoyment in it now. I hate the damn thing."

"Richard," Mel yelled from the back door. "Have you seen Michael? I can't find him anywhere."

"He was on the front porch."

"Well he's not now. Keep an eye out for him."

When his dad and Uncle John went back inside the house, Michael went to explore the garage. "Tag?" he called, but got no answer. He couldn't find his brother in any of the three stave barrels at the back. He wasn't hiding on the shelves littered with scraps of lumber.

The first thing Michael noticed when he opened the car door was the smell. The pine tree air fresher was shriveled up, and the car didn't smell the same. He rolled the window up and down and back up again with both hands like Tag had taught him, and from inside the car he could faintly hear people drinking and talking up at the house. He took out his favourite hot wheels and left the purple one Tag liked sitting on the dash. Tag was not here now, but when he came home and saw all these people standing around he wouldn't know about the egg salad sandwiches, and there was one place Michael knew for sure he would want to come.

Tag didn't come and Tag didn't come again. At the bottom of the glove box he found the key Tag had hidden as a spare. You needed the key to listen to the radio and Tag had taught him how to do it. It was way more fun with Tag around because he knew which stations played the good music. After a while listening to the music wasn't much fun all alone, so he reached up and turned the key some more, like he'd seen Tag do many times. He turned the radio down and realized he had been able to start the car all by himself. He could still hear the aunts and uncles up at the house so he turned the music up loud.

Michael grabbed the steering wheel. He felt powerful inside. "Vroooom, vroooom!" This was way more fun than hot wheels, and more than anything, he couldn't wait to see the look on Tag's face.

Lonnie And The Man With An Even Keel

"JEEZ, BUT THAT'S A PAIN IN THE BEHIND when one of your lashes turns in on you," Lonnie yelled in the general direction of Jason P. Riley who was concentrating on the oil light of his Ford truck which had started flaring up on the idle ever since the first stop light out of Duncan. He wondered what she'd been doing with her head out the window and staring into the cracked oval mirror. "Excuse my language," she added, "but that was a common phrase around our house."

"What's that?"

"Pain in the BE-hind. Mother wouldn't stand for any swearing even if you pounded your thumb with a hammer or burned yourself frying bacon. If us kids got in her hair that's what she'd tell us — that we were a pain in the behind."

"You don't say," he said lazily, the syllables measured.

"Yep. That and Milko. Milko was kind of our family's universal, all purpose swear word. It could take the place of . . . well, you know, all the regular swear words. I'll never forget what our dad said the night Floyd Patterson got knocked out on channel four."

"Uh-huh."

"Milko is what he said. Said it like he meant it too."

Riley was in the middle of a first date with Lonnie that had started out at the Odeon watching *The Good, the Bad, and the Ugly* until he didn't think he could handle her colour commentary filtering in through his right ear. *Which one's*

*supposed to be the ugly one? It must be hard for a cowboy to keep
so clean shaven I bet. Are horses ever twins, J. P.?* She had, he
noticed, the habit of pushing her voice high up at the end of
every sentence. Lonnie agreed to leave as soon as she finished
her popcorn. It was hard to get acquainted at a show, she said.

Jason P. Riley would come back though and catch the show
another night. He liked Clint Eastwood. He liked the strong,
silent type.

"I reckon you'll see this movie sometime."

"I will."

"You like westerns a lot."

'1 do."

Every so often Lonnie stuck her head back out into the 50
mph wind to see if her eyelash had mysteriously retained its
former shape. Jason P. Riley sat with his shoulders hunched over
the steering wheel, trying to remember if he had a spare quart
in the back shed. Out of her purse, Lonnie dug an emery board
and sat meticulously smoothing the edges of her long, pointed
nails. Watching her, he'd swear she was chewing gum. As they
moved out into the country, she kicked off her shoes and sat
back, her feet resting on the glove box. She liked being without
shoes. It was an old Ford truck.

"Has anyone died in your family?" she asked.

"Not lately."

"Just curious is all. You seem the serious type then. I had a
sister die once two years back. The big C. makes a person think,
don't it? You never know when your lease'll run out. Of course,
coming from a family of six girls teaches you to go after things
if nothing else. Everybody at the funeral cried except me. It
wasn't that I loved her any less, but she told me once she didn't
want anyone bawling their eyes out when she died. She knew
where she was going she said and it wouldn't be half bad. I don't
think she told that to my sisters, or if so, they didn't listen."

"Got to stop and get some oil," he said, slowing down and swinging into a double-pump Texaco.

"More time than money," she said.

Lonnie could hear him muttering to the mechanic under the hood.

"Hey, J. P.? Buy me a chocolate bar, will you? You pick."

"Took nearly two quarts," he said when they were back out on the road. "Must be leaking 'cause it sure as hell ain't burning oil."

"You work at the government weigh scales south of town, don't you?"

"Uh-huh."

'That must really be something, I bet. Weighing people's things for a living."

"Steady."

Jason P. Riley pushed the cigarette lighter in but then remembered all his cigarettes were at home.

"You're not married I hope."

He shook his head.

"Life has enough problems without getting mixed up in domestics. I been through the wringer, believe me. Actually Marla told me all about you. Said you were a man with an even keel. You ever dated Marla at all?"

"No, no. Marla and I just talk a bit over the counter."

"Oh yeah? I like Marla. She still makes the milkshakes too thick, but I figure if no one complains. Marla sure does want to marry bad. Real bad. Worries too much about her shallow bust if you ask me. Marla, I told her, think positive. You got a nice smile. Slim waist. You'll outgrow those pimples."

Jason P. Riley gave his oil light a sharp flick with his finger as if not convinced the light was out for good.

"All my sisters are married now except Eloise. Eloise is the one who's gone to heaven. Yep, married every single one. But can you believe it? No kids! It doesn't seem right to me, I'd like to have a whole raft of kids but all we've got to show so far is one miscarriage."

A hollow twang sounded as the lighter popped out.

"Your lighter still works," she said, and threw her Mars bar wrapper into the ditch.

When they got to his house, Lonnie slid out the driver's side under the steering wheel. She gave him a bear hug and then kissed him three times on the cheek.

"I appreciate you bringing me all the way out here for a visit. I don't much care for cowboy shows."

He wasn't sure how she'd take to the place and it showed in his walk. He hadn't done a thing to the place except dust since his mother had moved into a rest home a year ago. He was waiting for a leak before he put on a new roof.

He stood and watched her mosey around like she was interested in buying.

"J. P., this is re-e-e-eal cozy. If you weren't so even keeled, I'd swear you were already married."

"Sits on ten acres," he said. "Damn good well."

"You don't have a dog, do you? I don't see how a man could live way out here in all this peace and quiet and not own a dog. Listen!" They both listened. "You can hear fir-tree crickets out here. J. P., you've got to get yourself a dog."

"You want black coffee and Triple Sec on the side or light beer? It's all I've got."

"I'll try your coffee. I never get tired of coffee."

They sat out on the back porch with their first drink, watched the sun lie down, and between conversations, listened to the crickets and the slow drip that leaked out of the eaves and onto the railing. When they finally moved inside, Jason P. Riley turned on the corner lamps, low, so a soft yellow light melted over the furniture.

"It won't bother you if I smoke," he said in a tone that only hinted at compromise.

"Heavens no. Winston Churchill smoked cigars his whole life and he didn't catch the big C. I'm used to kissing men who smoke anyway."

He poured them both another coffee and liqueur and left the bottle on the table. He sat down at the end of the couch and she snuggled in beside him.

'This is real nice."

"Uh-huh."

"Nice and cozy."

"Uh-huh."

"It's a nice name, J. P. I knew a D.J. once but never a J. P. You'll never guess how I got my name."

"Probably not."

"I knew you couldn't. We could sit here till the roof falls in and the real source of my name would be a mystery. My name's Lonnie, right? Well it's not really Lonnie. You see I was number six and each time one of us came along they had us figured to be a boy. Well the first five times they had a girl's name ready, kind of like stand by? But when it was my turn they were sure the odds were in favour of a boy so they didn't have a clue. I was alive three days and my mother says to the nurse, my but that's nice lipstick you have on what kind is it. It was what shade she meant, but the nurse said Revlon thinking she meant the maker and it sounded kind of musical to mother. R-E-V-LON, sort of like that, but of course as you know most people call me Lonnie. You could call me Revlon if you like. My parents still do. Which do you like better, J. P.?"

"Lonnie."

"I figured. It's okay, though. I'm not much of a romantic myself."

Jason P. Riley crossed his legs and allowed her to light his cigarette.

"We could turn the lights right off, J. P. I like being in the dark."

"Then we couldn't play cards," he said, standing up to fetch a deck from the bureau. "You like a game of cards?"

"Depends which game. I don't know a lot about cards but I'm willing to learn."

"What do you know?"

"Let's see. I used to play fish with my grandpa. That was before he died. And my sisters used to play snap."

"Is that all?"

"That's it."

He threw the deck onto the table and several cards slid off onto the floor.

"You're not cross at me because I don't know much about cards are you, J. P.?"

"No, it doesn't matter."

"I know another one. Fifty-two pickup. You want to play fifty-two pickup, J. P.?"

Jason P. Riley started laughing then. She certainly had spunk, he thought, and they started play-wrestling on the couch.

Lonnie pulled her shoes off one at a time. Slowly, deliberately. She tucked her feet under her legs and wrapped her skirt over her knees but not before she was sure he'd helped himself to a little peek.

"The Triple Sec sure throws some heat into you though, doesn't it?" she said, sounding amazed.

"You want to see my rock collection?"

"You got one?"

"All kinds, come on I'll show you."

He pulled her off the couch. She kept nudging him from behind on the way to the basement like she wanted to ride him piggyback down the stairs.

The basement was low and dark and full of posts and beams and smelled earthy. All along one wall stood oak cabinets with glass tops and inside were neatly mounted samples of rocks, each assigned a typewritten label.

"The case over there has all the minerals, but I'm mostly interested in rocks. Latin name's in brackets."

"You sure got a lot of rocks, J. P. I didn't know there were so many."

"There's some I don't have. You can buy samples from the government, but I like to go out and get my own. The truck's handy that way."

Lonnie saw a spider slide across the cement floor, so they went back upstairs.

"My goal is to someday discover a rock nobody else has. Some kind of special gem."

"You want me to make us a grilled cheese?" she asked.

"Sure."

"I like mine burnt. That the way you like yours?"

"Sure."

"Some people down at Whimpie's think I burn them by accident, but they always eat up what I serve them."

Lonnie served the grilled cheese laid out with green pickles in the shape of a flower, over the charcoal coating. "Pretty food tastes better," she said. "I see you have a record player."

He got up and put on Gordon Lightfoot's *Greatest Hits* without asking.

"I'll make us another pot," he offered and wandered into the kitchen.

"Use a filter this time, will ya," she yelled after him. "I hate the grinds in my teeth."

When he returned with the coffee, there was only one lamp on and a solitary candle burning on the table.

"You just sit down and put your feet up," she said and kissed him on the lips like she knew a secret. "I'm just going to step into the bathroom and freshen up.

The bathroom was the colour of earth. Muted browns and quartz swirled beiges complemented the chocolate brown tub. In the mirror her hair looked like a tossed salad but it suited her, she thought. She touched up her tangerine lipstick before taking a look inside his vanity. Aftershave, razor, toothpaste, a jar of Vaseline. Band-Aids, dental floss. The usual, except that on the bottom shelf a blue bottle fly lay on its back with its legs poking out, dry and stiff. It looked noble in the fluorescent light. She wondered how long he'd been there. She was drawn to the bathtub. She'd never seen water sitting in a brown tub before. The water didn't smell bleachy like city water did, she noticed. She adjusted the hot and cold to a comfortable, equalizing temperature. She resisted looking inside the white wicker clothes hamper that she neatly folded her clothes on, and waited until the water was nearly to the top before sliding into the clear warm liquid. There was a faint essence of rose in the soap he kept at the side of the tub. The rose water seemed softer the way it caressed her skin, and she took her time, massaging each toe individually. She couldn't help herself singing "Some Day Soon". Sad songs always made her feel happy. After a while she drained some of the water and added more until she felt so relaxed she caught herself nodding off.

Hanging on the back of the door was a bathrobe, two-tone brown. Her clothes didn't appeal to her after she'd dried off. Under the cupboard she found a pair of mugwump slippers.

When she came out of the bathroom she was startled to find she was completely alone. She checked the back porch and the basement before she noticed his truck was gone. Lonnie stood at the front door for a long time staring into the country black, trying to make everything real. The darkness made the house seem all the more cozy. It was as if she had lived there since she was a little girl.

She went into the kitchen and began to tidy up. There wasn't much to tidy really. Things had their own place. She ran the dishrag behind each individual canister and shined up the stainless steel trim on the gas range. A bachelor didn't know how to spell the word dust. Inside the fridge the eggs were lined up on the shelf with a strip of masking tape: older — newer measuring the length of their stay. His bedroom was plain and tidy. The closet held an assortment of plaid shirts, khaki trousers, blue jeans. In the corner she could see a hunting rifle wedged behind a single grey suit that was neatly fitted with a dust jacket. A picture of a man and woman, middle-aged, his parents she guessed, and a pocket watch sat on a starched doily on the one dresser in the room.

She felt helpless all of a sudden. There wasn't much she could find that needed doing. The longer she remained alone the less likely it seemed he'd gone off for cigarettes or beer. Pouring herself another glass of liqueur, she curled up on the couch. She felt warm and not at all alone, listening to the owls asking questions in the woods outside.

When she woke up in the morning she opened her eyes to find him sitting at his place on the couch. The cup of coffee in front of him was steaming. It took her a minute to run the sequence of events through her mind before she realized where she was.

"J. P., you're back." She sauntered over to the couch and leaned against him. "You had me so worried," she said, "well, not really worried but wondering, you know? I thought you'd be here when I came out of the bathroom — I had a bath, I hope you don't mind, and when I came out you weren't here.

I looked everywhere and when I saw your truck was missing I thought you'd gone to the store. You didn't go to the store though, did you? I didn't think so. Then I wondered if maybe you were working night shift or something, and because I'd taken so long you just had to go, but I thought that would be crazy, I mean you would have knocked or left a note or something. I waited and waited and I didn't know what to do I mean I didn't know how long you'd be and for all I knew you might have been in an accident or maybe you were out of oil. I remembered how you were having oil problems. So I just lay down here on the couch and listened for your truck and listened and listened and oh, J. P., I'm so glad you're back. I should be at work by now, but it's okay, I'll phone in. Arty won't mind. I'm not mad at you, J. P., honest I'm not. You're not mad either, J. P., are you?"

Lonnie stopped and listened. Listened to something she heard in the absence of her own voice.

"I bought a dog," Jason P. Riley said. "He's sleeping in the kitchen."

"A dog! Oh, J. P., you little devil you."

Lonnie went and retrieved the German shepherd pup who came bouncing into the living room and plopped himself down on the couch between them.

"Cute, cute, cute. Oh, J. P., this is just the place for a dog. Is it . . . let's take a look. Yep it's a boy dog. That's smart, J. P. Boy dogs don't go into heat. Hey there, little fella. Isn't he friendly, J. P.? Don't you just love him? We'll have to think up a good name, something original. Some people call dogs like him Rover but I think it's a bit overdone, don't you? . . . J.P.?"

Jason P. Riley sat slumped on the sofa. It wasn't that he didn't want to speak up. He just didn't know what to say.

"Where you going, J. P.?"

"Check the shed for oil. Might need it for the trip back to town."

Lonnie let the dog chew on her knuckles. She couldn't wait till J. P. got back. If it was okay with him she'd let the dog have the window seat wherever it was they decided to go.

A *Place You've Never Been*

"DONNY, YOU OLD SIDEWINDER YOU. Name the one place in the world you'd like to go right now?"

Asia was lying on her back on the floor of my apartment when she asked the question. She was looking up at the ceiling fan that wasn't turning. Maybe wishing it was.

"How could you think up a question like that?" I said. "There are a thousand things that must be crossing your mind right now and you want to know where I want to travel?"

"Fiji . . . London . . . Greece. Walla Walla, Washington. The book's wide open, Donny. Shift that imagination of yours into gear. Where do you *really* want to go?"

The apartment was messy, I'll admit that right now. It always gets that way when Delores is out of town. The first day or two I make an effort, and then everything starts to crumble. I can always find things. I know where everything is. I don't get visitors much and I certainly didn't plan on Asia Mooney sprawled out between the magazines and beer cans.

"Do you want a pillow for your head?" I asked, and it made me think of Delores again. I think of her often, even when she's not here. If Delores doesn't position her head just so, it's off to the bone crusher the next day.

"No, I'm fine," she said, "but you know what I'd like to do? I'd like to get out an atlas, blindfold myself and stick a push pin in, and just go there. Go there for say a month just to get away from it all. Chances are you'd end up in a place you've never been."

"Chances are," I said.

Asia grabbed the little makeup bag she had slung over her shoulder and got out a tube of orange lipstick. Without getting up from her prone position, she ran it methodically over her lips and rubbed them together like she was tasting wine. "So, you got an atlas or not?"

"Asia, I hardly think this is the time."

It wasn't the time. Any fool could see that. Almost anything was possible if the time was right. I hadn't had much of anything to do with Asia for fifteen years, and then out of the blue she phones. Would you come down to the cop shop? she says. I'm in a jam and the first person I thought of was Donny Hamilton. I said hi to her at the rodeo three years ago and that was the last time I'd talked to her. What are the chances? I'm always trying to do the right thing, so I go down to see what she needs and she's in over her head. It's no big deal since the Raptors are behind by more than twenty points. Turns out she's in for hit and run. Hit an old lady in a crosswalk. She refused to take a breathalyzer and got into a big argument with the cops. A thousand bucks later and some goodwill on my part and you'd never guess anything had happened.

"What's the matter, Donny? Imagination all run out? That happened to me once. I felt like dying. Life never stops, that's what I learned. Once I realized that I was back in the saddle."

"But I don't understand how you — "

"I can see that. I can see your lack of understanding, Donny, I really can. But you'll get over it. Something in your life will trigger it, and wham, you'll realize you're never without a future."

"Don."

"What's that?"

"People call me Don, now," I said.

"Whatever."

I met Asia years ago when I first moved to Duncan. People new to town usually meet other new people first. Most people can only keep as many friends as you can fit into a phone booth, and unless someone jumps out, there's no room for anyone new. Asia and I were part of a new phone booth for a while. We met at parties and she kissed me once on New Years. She was different from most of the people we hung out with. For one thing, she was shapely. Shapely, outgoing, but a little scary. We planned a weeklong hiking trip up into Strathcona Park and I was looking forward to it, but I cancelled after Delores got serious. Funny thing is, after you get married there's never room for you *and* your spouse in an existing phone booth unless it's evacuated for unforeseen circumstances, and who would want to go there anyway?

"You should get yourself a good lawyer, Asia. This is serious."

"Good old Donny Hamilton. We had some good times, didn't we? Remember the time a bunch of us went skinny dipping down at the river? You were the last one in and the first one out. I'll never forget that."

"What do you plan to do, Asia? For example, tonight?"

"I'll do something. I always do. That was sweet of you to come down and bail me out. I'll probably head home later. Maybe I'll crash here. Say, where's that Delores of yours?"

"She's away a lot. Marketing seminars. Sometimes she's gone for two or three weeks. I never know when she'll be home."

"And you still work at . . . "

"Copps Shoe Store. Yeah, I'm still there. Sixteen years now. You came in and a bought a pair of shoes off me a few years ago. I remember, they were red pumps you needed for a wedding."

I remembered more than that. Asia had the most delicate feet. Narrow and easy to fit.

"My wedding, actually. I probably never mentioned that because I knew I shouldn't have been getting married. It's a long story. Life moves on. With us or without us."

"You feel all right?" I said. "Your head hurt or anything? I've got some aspirin."

"I feel great. I didn't have much to drink. Two or three. And it wasn't hit and run, really. I was going around the block is all. Someone told the cops I drove off, which I did, but it's a one way street because of the detour, and I was coming back."

I tried to imagine myself hitting an old woman in a crosswalk. Even with two or three drinks your reactions are usually pretty good.

"God, I'm hungry," Asia said, and rolled around on the carpet until she found some old pizza boxes. "Never mind, found some day old pizza."

"That might be more than a day old," I said.

"Not to worry. Cheese keeps longer than beauty."

Even if they don't have kids, most women relax and spread out over time. If anything, Asia seemed the same, possibly tighter than when we used to hang around. She looked like someone who worked out on a regular basis with no intention of letting the jelly doughnuts hang over her belt like mine do.

"My God," she said, "do you collect CDs or what?" She crawled over to my stereo on all fours. "I've got a great idea. You pick something out and put it on and we'll dance."

"I don't think so," I said.

"Oh come on, Donny-wonny. Just like the good old days."

"I'm not much for dancing. You can ask Delores."

"Delores-bores isn't here, Donny-wonny and I want to dance. I'll lead."

I remembered then, dancing with Asia. She was a great dancer in a frenetic kind of way. When the music slowed, she could hold you in her arms and take you places you'd never imagined.

"I found it, Donny. 'Stairway to Heaven'. That must have been a hit for a decade."

The next thing I knew I was being paraded around the living room with Asia Mooney in charge. After two or three turns she had most of the pizza boxes and beer cans kicked out of our way. God the woman has rhythm.

"I like the way you've got this place decorated. It looks lived in or something. Jeez, Donny. I'm peakin'. I'm just peakin'."

When the song ended she spread her blue skirt out wide and curtsied, then pulled me onto the couch. With Asia, you never know what's next.

"You did me a big favour tonight, Donny. I'm never going to forget that."

"Don't mention it. What are friends for?"

"See, there you go again. A man who aims to please. I'm going to ask one more favour, Donny Hamilton. I'd like your help."

"What's that?"

"I'd like you to rub me right here." Asia grabbed my hand and guided it between her legs. It was like I was watching someone else's hand moving up her thigh. It was my hand. It had to be — there was no one else in the room.

"Asia," I said. "That wasn't called for."

"Oh yes it was," she said. "What's the matter? Donny doesn't want to climb the stairway to heaven?"

"Asia, we're friends and that's all. Well sort of. We really haven't been friends for years."

She stood up then, loosened her panties and did a little two step until they fell to her ankles. When she stepped out of them, she stuffed them in her makeup bag.

"God, I hate wearing those things. They make you feel so encumbered. I think that's the word. Anyway, I feel un-encumbered now."

I crossed the room and sat on the sofa chair. I didn't really know what to say. Asia sprawled out on the couch and slid her own hand between her legs.

"I'm just going to lie here. You'll have to excuse me, Donny. It won't take long. You keep talking. Please."

I couldn't think of anything to say, so I got up and put on some Dave Brubeck. Something discordant to drown out her moaning. She might be in shock, I thought. Or maybe wired on something. Even if I hadn't averted my eyes, I couldn't see anything.

"That was a great choice," she said, when she'd finished. "You're the kind of guy who's helpful even when you don't mean to be. And patient as a fence post."

"Asia, for Christ sake, what about her?"

"Who?"

"The woman you hit. Aren't you going to phone the hospital to find out if she's okay?"

"Oh, she's dead. Dead the second I hit her they said. I guess I kind of knew that. That's why I wasn't in any hurry to drive around the block. There was nothing I could have done at that point."

Asia found a *Car and Driver* and started mindlessly leafing through it. I watched her not read and thought about what I'd be doing in her situation. Religion, booze, a best friend all crossed my mind. Maybe meditation if I knew how.

"You know what kills me?" she said, without looking up from her magazine. "They design these great cars of the future, tell you what cars will look like in five years, and I'm thinking if it's such a good idea for five years down the road, why not make them right away? Doesn't that strike you as funny?"

"In a way," I said.

"I don't think I'd be caught dead in a car like this one anyway. Too low to the ground. Hey, you know what? We should go bowling. I love ten pin bowling. Love to stick my fingers deep into that sixteen ounce ball."

"I've only bowled five pin."

"See? That's your problem, Donny. Everybody has a block of some kind. You're a man with no ten pin bowling experience."

❖❖❖

By the time I convinced Asia it was time to head home, the bowling alley was closed, so I told her it was a great idea, maybe some other time. On the way back from her place, I drove slowly down the street where the accident had happened. There were no cars, no people, only some chalk lines from the police investigation. I'd driven down Canada Avenue hundreds of times before and never come close to hitting anyone. What had happened to Asia seemed bizarre. Like a lot of things you look back on.

When I finally got home I was surprised to see Delores there. She was supposed to be home either this Friday or next Friday, but when there's a choice it's usually the latter.

"Delores, I didn't expect you till next Friday."

"Sorry to disappoint," she said, wrapping my stupid statement around my neck. She was wearing the snub-nosed Van Eli's she'd purchased in Ontario. To her they were sensible travelling shoes, but her back won't stand more than a five-eighths heel, and she's a woman who demands a strong arch support.

"Of course I'm not disappointed. It's just that I would have cleaned the place up a bit. How was your trip?"

I wasn't sure if Delores had caught my question. She was sniffing the air. I looked around but there didn't appear to be any traces of Asia Mooney to be found. Thank God, I thought, she was the kind of hit and run driver with enough common sense to put her panties in her makeup bag.

"If I go through one more seminar on this whole Y2K thing I'm going to slit my wrists. Even some of the people I work with are buying generators and storing oatmeal. I'll bet you've never met anyone who's stowed away a thirty day supply of socks and underwear."

"Not a one," I said.

"Well, I've met two of them."

I could see Delores was upset. It did concern me she'd mentioned the slitting of wrists because she tried that after we found out it wasn't going to be possible for her to have children. That's when her career took over.

"Where were you just now?" she asked.

"Bowling." I said it without thinking, but it could have been the truth.

"Bowling? Well, I'd like to think you're making progress but bowling doesn't qualify."

"Well, it was ten pin bowling. It's not easy you know."

Delores wheeled her suitcase into the bedroom and started unpacking. Her clothes were clean and neatly folded, thanks to room service. She put them back in her closet or into her dresser. Next, she would lounge in a bubble bath, the tub surrounded by scented candles, and by the time she came to bed and lay her head on her orthopedic pillow, I would be in the dead of sleep. Sex would be out of the question. Today was now the twenty-third, actually, the early hours of the twenty-fourth. Ever since conception had been ruled out, Delores saw sex as her one obligation in marriage. Kind of like an allowance for my paying half the rent. These conjugal visits took place once a month, always in the first week.

❖❖❖

Most people think of selling shoes as one step up from working at McDonalds, but I actually enjoy it. I pretty much run the place since Mr. Copps passed away. Myrna Copps still owns the store and she trusts my judgement. That's definitely what you need to be a good shoe salesman. Some people come in at the end of a working day, all sweaty, and I swear sometimes you can actually see the odor emanating from their feet. They don't mean anything by it. They're on their way home to their wife and kids and dog and two cats and they've got to mow the lawn before the neighbours complain. A visit to the shoe store is hard to fit in on a Saturday, what with baseball, soccer and swim team, and the promise to walk Granny in the park is hard to break. So you smile, breathe through your mouth, try to narrow down their choices first so the whole process doesn't take too long. I always have my customers walk the whole length of the store, even take a jaunt down the street. They've got to look me in the eye and tell me these are the shoes they've been waiting for all their life or I won't let them out of the store. They seem to appreciate my care and attention and I have hundreds of repeat customers.

When things are slow, I nip into the back for my coffee. I can always hear the door chime if someone comes in. Delores had been home for a whole week, but tonight was her last night. We hadn't yet got it all together, so I was thinking maybe I'd take her out for dinner or a movie, her choice. If we do both she ends up being too tired.

"Hey, Donny-wonny. You in there?" I popped my head around the corner and there was Asia, dressed to kill in something short and red.

"How did you get in here?"

"The door, silly. Don't think I didn't give the chimney some consideration but I didn't want to scare you."

"I usually hear the door chime."

"Donny old boy, you're mind must be wandering. You were probably thinking of taking me bowling tonight, am I right?"

"Well no — "

"League goes until nine, nine-thirty. Say, you don't sell bowling shoes do you?"

"No we don't. I can't bowl tonight, Asia. I'm tied up. I've been worried about you. Have you got a court date yet?"

"I couldn't tell you, Donny. My lawyer is looking after it all. He told me I'd better stay put for three or four weeks. But then guess what?"

"What?"

"I'm off to Italy. Want to come?"

"Italy? Why Italy? No I can't go. You know that."

"The push pin landed on Italy. What can I say? Italy is the shape of a foot you know. You could do research on Italian leather shoes. I think it's your destiny, Donny."

"I'm taking Delores to a movie tonight. That's what I mean by tied up."

"You mean tied down. What movie you going to see?"

"*Life is Beautiful*, probably."

"Seen it. Otherwise I'd join you. No I wouldn't either. I have flamenco lessons at six. Well, I got to fly. Say howdy-do to Delores for me and tell that boss of yours to consider bowling shoes. Serious bowlers own their own you know."

There was no one in the store after Asia left but it seemed more than empty. I'd seen Roberto Benigni give his acceptance speech at the Academy Awards and that's who she reminded me of. Always water flowing over the dam when Asia's around.

Life is Beautiful was a great movie. I can't say I'd care to see it again, but it was moving. Delores ordered a jumbo popcorn and was too full when we got home to consider anything adventurous. She apologized and lay her head down on her thin pillow and in the morning she was gone. Mississauga is where the company might want to send her if she gets the promotion she has her eye on. Would I want to go there? she wanted to know. She told me there had to be at least a dozen shoe stores in Mississauga, but that wasn't the kind of detail I found particularly reassuring.

❖❖❖

I never heard a word from Asia for two weeks, then one night I was sitting in front of the TV with Kraft Dinner and wiener chunks and she started banging on the door.

"Don't eat too much of that," Asia said. "I've got something much better in mind. Is Delores in?"

"No."

"Good. Show me your best suit."

"What do you mean show you my best suit?"

"Donny, we've only got an hour, so don't fool with me. Come on." Asia led me to the bedroom and started rifling through my clothes. "This blue one is gorgeous. God, I'll bet you're a handsome devil in this. Here, put it on."

Sometimes people say things to you and you don't know what to say back. An hour later, the perfect response comes filtering through, but at the time.

"Okay, okay," she said. "I'll go into the living room. You never used to be this bashful. Hope you don't mind if I change the channel."

When I came out in my suit, Asia was momentarily breathless. With Asia, being breathless is always momentary. She ran over and gave me a big hug and led me back into the bedroom where we both stood in front of Delores's three way mirror.

"Are we both dressed to the nines or what?" she said, then went through my shoe collection which is colossal. Myrna Copps lets me buy my shoes at cost. Asia rubbed her hands along the souls of several pairs, turning occasionally to match colours with my suit. "Here, these spunky brogues will do the trick. Not bad considering they're not Italian."

"I don't know what you have in mind, Asia, but if you think I'm wearing this to go out tonight, you've got another thing coming."

"I always have another thing coming, Donny. You know, I think you're beginning to catch on. When was the last time you wore this suit?"

"Probably two years."

"I rest my case. Would you keep your can opener around if you never used it for two years? Of course not. Clothes are fun things and we've got to learn to enjoy them. We'd better get a move on. I want to run through the car wash before we get too far."

"I'm not keen on fancy restaurants," I said. "I'd better warn you."

"Relax, Donny. This evening won't cost you a penny."

We took my car because Asia's was still being held and she insisted she drive. It wasn't until the car wash that I had a legality moment. "I thought they took your license away?" I said.

"They did. What they don't know won't hurt them. Hey, Ron," she yelled out the window. "Do a number on those hubcaps will you? We're on a mystery date and we want everything to be perfect."

Between layers of lipstick, Asia muttered that I didn't need to worry, Ron owed her one. "You must remember Ron the pole vaulter, don't you?"

"No I don't. What do you mean a mystery date?"

"You don't know where you're going. Can you think of a better name for it?"

Sometimes the more you talk to Asia the less the world makes sense. I realized that was probably the buffer that kept us apart years ago. I'm the kind of guy who likes to know the weather forecast every night before I go to bed.

After Ron had finished washing and rinsing, we pulled over to the side and got out to watch him run the chamois over everything. The old Buick looked fine, all spruced up. "You ever watched *Moonstruck*?" Asia asked.

"I think I saw it years go."

"I watch it once a month. It's my favourite movie of all time. I don't know why I didn't think of Italy on my own, but next week, Donny, I'm out of here. It's not too late for you to come. It's never too late to live until you're dead. Remember that, Donny."

Before we got back into the car, Asia got out a shopping bag she'd brought and started taping tissue paper flowers of every imaginable colour up both sides of the car. Each flower was meticulously placed one hand width from the previous one, done as if to suggest this small act of perfection balanced out the rest of her life.

"Where are we going?" I asked.

"To our destination. It's only ten minutes away, so just sit back and relax. You're in good hands, you just don't know it yet."

Asia drove slower than usual, probably to protect the flowers. Soon we were at The Moose Lodge and there were at least a hundred cars already parked there. It's a picturesque spot right on the lake and we had to park a hundred yards from the hall, but even from where we were you could hear the din of voices filling the air with two-foot conversations.

"Asia, this looks like a wedding reception or something."

"Bingo! Donny Hamilton to the front of the class."

"But who's getting married? Do I know them?"

"I doubt it. I know I don't but it's an Italian affair and they're rich. The meal should be marvelous."

"We can't go in there and not know a soul. That's absurd."

"Life's absurd, Donny. That's what I've been trying to tell you. Wrap your arms around it and you'll feel a lot better. The groom will assume we know the bride and the bride will assume we know the groom. This is how I met my former husband. Besides, what do they care? The more people that show up the bigger the celebration. Come on, I'll show you how it's done."

Asia grabbed my hand and led me to an empty table, then left to get us a drink from the bar. The bride and groom hadn't arrived yet and people were milling around, discussing how stunning the bride was. What a perfect ceremony it had been. I nervously kept retying my shoes.

"Okay," Asia said. "Here's a beer to loosen you up. The groom's name is Cosmo, nick name, The King. His bride is Roxanne. She's not Italian and that's a bit of an irritant. Got it?"

Before I could answer, two couples descended upon our table. Asia smiled and made them feel at home.

"That was some wedding, now wasn't it?" The elderly man who asked the question had white hair and a white moustache and yet his skin was smooth as porcelain.

"Grand," Asia said. "The most grand wedding I've ever been to."

"Are you friends of the bride or the groom?" he asked.

"The groom," Asia said. "Donny's a good friend of The King."

Everyone at the table stared at me, as if friendship needed an explanation.

"I sold Cosmo a pair of shoes years ago. They made him very happy," I said.

"Cosmo buys all his shoes at his uncle's store in Vancouver," the man said. "Why would he buy shoes behind his uncle's back?"

"They were bowling shoes," I said. "Special order. They had air in the heel."

"I didn't know Cosmo was a bowler," the man's wife said.

"You'd be surprised how many closet bowlers there are out there," I said. "I sold a pair to a man just last week who bowls on Wednesdays at midnight. His wife knows nothing about it."

Everybody at the table nodded, suggesting my explanation was more than reasonable. Asia wore a look of genuine admiration. I glanced under the table and saw a pair of Florsheim Lexington Wing Tips. Undoubtedly bought from Cosmo's uncle.

Italian wine is very good and Italian weddings don't stop until all the wine is gone. By the time it was over I'd made my contribution. *You're a hell of a flamenco dancer, Donny. A hell of a flamenco dancer.* That's the only thing Asia said on the way home, repeating it over and over until she threw up into her purse. After that, she never said a word.

❖❖❖

When I went back to work on Monday, my head felt thick. A lady came in and bought a pair of sandals and she had the same kind of purse Asia had had the night of the wedding reception—soft Tuscany leather. It made me cringe when she opened the purse to fetch her credit card. I was afraid she'd stick her hand in there and get sick to her stomach. It was a ridiculous thought and I knew it even while I was thinking it. Funny how the mind works.

I'd been having recurring dreams about lying on my back in Italy with Asia Mooney standing between me the blue sky, dropping grapes into my mouth. In the dream, the grapes tasted delicious, and normally I never eat grapes.

On Wednesday Asia phoned me at home. Had I given any more thought to Italy? She had a Friday morning flight out of Vancouver and the last time she checked there was still room. I told her I couldn't go but that she was right, we did have a really good time on our mystery date. I couldn't go, I said, because I was moving to Mississauga at the end of the month. Some things just pop up out of nowhere, I said, if you know what I mean. Asia said she understood completely. Her bail had been lifted, the case was closed and I could get my thousand bucks back. It was a real shame the lady was wearing black that night. Her lawyer did a bang up job and the weather was on her side.

Saying goodbye to Asia on the phone like that was a real emotional stew. It was like getting over the flu and appreciating your good health once again. But there's a part of Asia Mooney in all of us. If you're ever in Mississauga drop by, I told her. Maybe we can go bowling. She said she would, but I know for that to happen it would take something completely out of the blue.

Wise Men Don't Have Speaking Parts

WHEN YOU FALL FROM GRACE only God knows where you'll land. If you believe in God, he knows. If you don't, not a damn soul knows until you hit the ground.

War and lust are a bad combination, and they teamed up to send my parents on different paths to salvation. My father stayed put in the house he built and rose to the position of churchwarden, sang in the choir, licked his wounds. He was the kind of man who was easy to feel sorry for. He never said much about his situation in life, but you got the feeling he knew the war wasn't his fault. He ate seven different herbs a day and sang into his eighties. Even after his voice was gone, he'd mouth the words and smile toward heaven.

My habit of running away came from my mother. We left Nelson on a bus early in the morning, and I was allowed to pack my hatchet in my suitcase. I was only five at the time and considered myself privileged for owning my own hatchet. I don't remember much about the journey, just the leaving and arriving. Mom billed herself as a "homemaker" and was looking for a job. The irony of her resume is something that doesn't occur to a five-year-old, though it may have occurred to her. The bus took the ferry to Vancouver Island, and we landed in Nanaimo, on our way to Victoria. There was a stopover in Duncan for an hour, and Mom suggested we go for a walk. It was early spring, and I was hot in the sports coat she insisted I wear. She stopped at a taxi stand near the bus depot and told the dispatcher she was looking for work as a homemaker. She may have used the term housekeeper, but whatever it was she said, she said it at the right place and the right time. "Hey, George," the man yelled, running out onto the sidewalk. "George, there's a lady here who'll clean your house."

Two days earlier I'd chopped down my first tree with my own hatchet, and now I found myself in the back seat of a taxi with a mother frantically applying lipstick and a Hungarian I could barely understand.

One of the benefits of being a kid is you never think of yourself as a liability. Running away by yourself is one thing, but with a five-year-old in tow we must have presented ourselves as something on the sidewalk to step over. It was a small house, but once Mom saw that we'd have our own room to sleep in, some kind of arrangement for wages in return for cooking and cleaning was made, and we brought our luggage in from the cab. The house was right in town and the lot was huge, in the shape of a shoebox. Out in the back, there was a pond overgrown with willow bushes and skunk cabbage. I spent the first few days hacking away at an old log that floated in the pond, waiting to see where we would go next, but after waking up in the same bed for a few days in a row, I realized I was staying put. We were going to be all right here, Mom said. It would take her a few months of salary to save up, but eventually she would see that accordion lessons and religion were part of my life.

George Szabolcsi was the name of my mother's employer. It didn't take me long to learn how to spell his last name, because being such a mouthful it was always being spelled over the phone. George couldn't read or write in English, and sentences were often repeated before we could understand what he was saying. He was a logger and got up early in the morning, much earlier than I did, and went to work in the yellow crummy that picked him up on the corner. He came home eleven hours later and my mom had dinner ready. George loved cabbage rolls. My mother soon learned to make them and we learned to eat them. He also loved pickled onions, but I couldn't say if I liked them or not because I never dared try. He made homemade wine which he kept under the house in a crawl space, always in half gallon jugs, and one night my mother and I were woken up by a huge explosion. She turned on the light, put on her housecoat and went to see what had gone wrong. George sometimes fastened the caps on the half gallon jugs sooner than he should have and two or three months after he'd started the process, the bottles would explode right under our bedroom. We found all of this out the next day. The explosions must have been routine for George because he never woke up.

Next to our small house was an even smaller house where the Widow Jantz lived. She was friendly and George helped out by splitting firewood for her. She had a small wood-burning stove and an oven to keep warm but no fridge. She kept her vegetables in the back yard in plastic bags under a tap that dripped water twenty-four hours a day, and once a week she would make fresh buns, glazed with butter and sugar on top, and she would always bring six over in a pan, fresh out of the oven. I was getting pretty good with my hatchet, and I would take some of the small pieces from her woodpile and make kindling for her. I thought she was the best of neighbours until my mother started talking religion with her. She said getting me to Sunday School would not be a problem because the Reverend Morley came by every Sunday, and he would be glad to pick me up.

You don't know how to pronounce a word like hypocritical when you're on the verge of going into grade one, but that doesn't mean you don't know the definition. My mother hadn't been to church since she was a kid, had no interest in it whatsoever, but there she was making arrangements for me to learn a life of purity. I complained. Oh how I complained, but to no avail.

There I stood out on the street the next Sunday morning beside Mrs. Jantz, who I was re-evaluating since the whole Sunday School arrangement had been made, dressed up again in my sports coat and a bolo tie with a horse's head, waiting for Reverend Morley to drive around the block in his black Studebaker. The front seat was reserved for Mrs. Ella Morley, and I sat in the back with Mrs. Jantz and the first boy my own age I'd met in my new town, Obadiah Morley. When I got in he said, "Hi, my name's Obadiah and my name comes from the Bible." I guess with a name like Obadiah, it's the kind of question that gets asked.

I felt more dressed up than the preacher's son, who wore black pants and a white shirt. We got there early, and Obadiah took it upon himself to show me the room at the back of the church where they stored the extra chairs and the Christmas manger. It looked like a dusty storage room to me, but he said we weren't supposed to go in there, and he didn't show it to just anybody. Sunday School was run by Mrs. Ella Morley, and we sat around and coloured a picture of Jesus walking on the water between two fishing boats. There was a rainbow we got to colour too, but the crayons were in short supply and mine turned out purple and brown. Twelve of us in all and everyone except me was supposed to recite the verse they had been given the week before. Obadiah, and a fat, freckled girl named Naomi were the only ones who knew their verse. Mrs. Ella Morley said that was okay so long as they had it *and* a new one memorized for the following Sunday, then she put a gold star on our pictures and set us free.

After Sunday School finished up, most of the kids got to go home. Obadiah and I had to wait for a ride home, so we had to sit through the church service. He showed me one of the hymn books that had the word *fuk* printed in it, and he told me not to tell anyone.

"So, how was your first day of Sunday School?" Mom asked when I got home.

"Boring. I hated it."

"Well, I'm sure you'll enjoy it if you give it a chance. You'll meet some kids your own age and it won't hurt you to listen to what they have to say."

"Why don't you come? I could ask Mrs. Jantz if you could. There's room for one more in the back seat. You get to shout Hallelujah."

"I learned a lot from the Bible when I was your age. I went to Sunday School for three years and I haven't forgotten what I learned. That's why I don't need to go anymore. Now change out of your Sunday clothes if you plan on going outside." My mother was ironing the sheets while she was talking. That gave her an excuse not to look me in the eye.

"Where's George?"

"George has gone to town. He's checking into a surprise for you."

"What is it?"

"It wouldn't be a surprise if I told you, now would it? Go on and get changed. If he comes back with his surprise you won't want to be dressed in your good clothes."

I was out at the pond when they called me in for lunch. I was trying to figure out a way to get out of going to Sunday School ever again but still qualify for Mrs. Jantz's fresh buns once a week. When I got inside there was a shorthaired puppy curled up in a basket by the stove. It was white with tiny black and brown spots all over. When I came into the kitchen, it jumped out of the basket, little tail wagging back and forth. First it licked my hand, then it peed on the floor.

"She's a girl," my mother said, while gathering some old newspaper. "Any idea what you want to call her?"

"Naomi," I said. It was the first thing that popped into my mind and I'd already forgotten about my Sunday School experience which was to turn into a weekly ritual I couldn't avoid. By the end of the summer I had the three-quarter bed all to myself and my mother acted like she'd finally found the job she'd been looking for.

George not only couldn't read or write English, he couldn't drive either. Neither could my mother and I didn't know how to ride a bicycle, so consequently we walked wherever we needed to go. Naomi went with me everywhere I went, mostly out to the pond to chop away at the big floating log. About three weeks after George got the puppy from the S.P.C.A., he had another surprise for me which he presented on a Saturday afternoon. It was my very own bicycle. The problem was it was a woman's bicycle, maroon with big balloon tires. Even with the seat set as low as it could go, I couldn't come close to reaching the pedals. Still, owning your own bike is something and the following day when the Morleys came by to pick me up, I told Obadiah I had my very own bike. After Sunday School was out, I took it over to his house to show him, but I had to push it around the block because there was no way I was ever going to ride that bike. George wired two chunks of two-by-four onto each pedal the following Saturday, but I still couldn't reach. Obadiah said I was lucky to have my own bike and we made up a circuit in his back yard and timed ourselves pushing the bike through the raspberry canes.

"That looks like a nifty bike. Mind if I ride it?" It was Obadiah's older sister, Beulah, who'd come out on the back porch with her boyfriend, Tommy.

I shrugged my shoulders and didn't say anything. Beulah took this as a yes and lunged for my bike and was gone for a long time. I didn't know Obadiah had a sister because she never went to church when we did, which was hard to figure seeing as her father was the preacher. While she was gone, Tommy showed us how to flip someone with judo moves he'd learned. He didn't have any trouble flipping me and Obadiah on our backs, but he said it didn't matter how big the enemy was, even someone our size could flip him if we knew how, then he sat back on the porch and watched us practice while he smoked cigarettes.

"That's a great bike," Beulah said. "With those big tires you don't feel the bumps at all." She tousled my hair and handed me my bike. "What's your name?"

"Jessie. But it's not out of the Bible."

"Do you know how to ride yet, Jessie?"

I shook my head. I hadn't really concerned myself with riding it until now, just owning it had been enough. But when Beulah asked me then, I wanted more than anything in the world to tell her yes, I could ride like a champion.

"Don't worry," she said. "You'll learn in your own time. Come on, Tommy. Let's go upstairs."

"Your parents aren't going out, are they?" Tommy asked.

"It doesn't look like it."

"Then I think I'll head home. I'll see you around."

Obadiah was ready for another round of circuit-bike-pushing, but I wasn't. It was a stupid thing to do with a bike anyway.

"I didn't know you had a sister."

"Got a brother too. His name's Frank, but he's in jail for two years."

"Jail? How come he's in jail?"

192

Beulah appeared at the upstairs window and waved. I waved back.

"He stole some money from a Chinese store. He hit the Chinaman over the head with a bottle of Dr. Pepper. My mother and father pray for him every day and Frank reads the Bible all the time now. He might be out before next Christmas if he's good."

I was thinking about what Obadiah had said. I wondered what it would be like to be in jail, away from everyone you knew. I had an older brother who had joined the navy when he turned seventeen and he got to live a grand life. Every post card he sent us had pictures of beautiful women and sandy beaches. What was it that made some people join the navy and others go to jail? I looked up to the bedroom window again, but Beulah was gone.

When school starts what you don't realize is that you've just begun a routine that will continue until you retire or die and that weekends are of the utmost importance. My Sunday mornings were taken up with Pentecostal Sunday School, and as if that wasn't bad enough, Mom rented an accordion by the month and signed me up for lessons on Saturdays at three o'clock. That September I felt like all my free time had come to an end and I was sure I knew what Frank Morley faced on a daily basis. I had to stop building forts or fishing on Saturdays at two o'clock, and pack my accordion down to Carter's Music Store. All of the Carters were huge people and they all taught music to forlorn souls such as me. I had Mrs. Carter, who was the roundest woman I'd ever seen and she was covered in talcum powder: her arms, her legs, her face. She taught me "Every Good Boy Deserves Favors" and said I was a natural talent. I'm sure she told everyone that so their parents would keep sending them back. In Nelson we'd had our own piano and I guess my mother figured this was the closest thing she could arrange, since we didn't have a lot of money. It meant a lot to her that I was able to take music lessons, even accordion lessons, and I didn't have the heart to push too hard to have them cancelled. I think I even went to my first lesson eagerly, but after that it was all down hill. George got me a dog that I loved and a bike I would grow into eventually; later he bought me a slingshot and a bee-bee gun. My mother, meanwhile, signed me up for grade one when I already knew how to read and filled my weekends with accordion lessons.

I decided to work on freeing up my Sundays. They were already planning on a Christmas pageant and I'd decided I didn't want to have anything to do with it.

"Did you ever have to go to church when you lived in Hungary?"

George and I had chopped enough wood for Mrs. Jantz to survive the winter and we were now working on our own pile. I thought getting him on my side wouldn't hurt my cause. He told me when he was older than I was he'd been caught with his hand up a girl's skirt and had to crawl on his hands and knees up forty stairs to the church and ask for absolution. He said there was dried corn sprinkled on the granite stairs and he had to plow his way through it, and by the time he made it into the church, his knees were bleeding through his pants. When he got there, he asked God for forgiveness, but it didn't stop him from chasing girls. What it taught him, he said, was to be more careful.

I thought about the small church I went to every Sunday. There weren't more than two steps to get in and I hadn't seen any sign of corn. Obadiah said in the pageant it's best to be one of the three wise men who come bearing gifts because you get to walk around with a big staff and wise men don't have any speaking parts. He said unless someone showed up soon, Naomi would be the Virgin Mary for the third year in a row. The one good thing about Sundays was I usually went to the Morley's for lunch and Beulah was good to me. She'd pretend to steal my nose and get me to pronounce long words out of the dictionary. Once, when we were in the living room alone, she read my palm and said I would grow up to be a wise old man.

Sunday School never took too long and Mrs. Ella Morley was the kindest woman you could imagine. If you started acting up or giggling during the time for thoughtful prayers, she would walk over and put her hand on your head and say a silent prayer of her own, then carry on as if something like that would never happen again. She was the kind of lady who, when she smiled at you, you had to stare at her until she decided it was time for her smile to let you go. She bought everyone in the class a book of lifesavers for Christmas and when Easter rolled around, we all made a wooden cross with a figure of Jesus we glued on and a fan of palm leaves. It was in the spring that Obadiah started making a fuss about us having to sit through church, but his father said sitting through the church service every Sunday was exactly what young men like us needed the most. He was never as kindly as Mrs. Ella Morley, and when he gave his sermon he'd yell up into the rafters as if God was hard of hearing. Eventually, Obadiah got to his mother, and if it wasn't raining we were allowed to walk home right after Sunday School.

We used the first few weeks of our newfound freedom to head to my house to play for an hour before we went back to his house for lunch. I had received an electric train set for my birthday and Obadiah loved it. He never got new toys of any kind, and he had very few used ones. When he'd come over, my mother insisted I play something for him on my accordion. I'd gotten to the point where I could play "Beautiful Brown Eyes" without the music and yet I loathed the instrument, and the time I had to spend on it, as much as ever. Following my mother's cue, Obadiah always clapped, which didn't make things any better. He grew tired of my accordion concerts, and one Sunday he suggested we go directly from Sunday School to his house instead. I think it was the first time I said hallelujah and meant it.

The weather was warm and people were out mowing their lawns. When we got close to his house, Obadiah said he was going to show me something he bet I'd never seen before. He said if he showed me I had to promise not to tell anyone because if I did we would both go straight to hell. I agreed and we went into the house.

We each grabbed a cookie, and I followed him upstairs to his room. I looked around, for something special that would make me keep a secret or face eternal damnation. He went out into the hall, and we could hear music on the radio from his sister's room. The Morleys weren't keen on Elvis Presley. They said he was a young man who once sang gospel but had been reeled in by the devil, so the only time the radio was on was when Mr. and Mrs. Morley were away.

"Beulah, Jessie and I are going out to play baseball at the park. Okay?"

She turned the radio down just long enough to say that was fine, but to be home by 12:30 for lunch. Obadiah then led me stealthily back into his room. He said we had to be quiet as church mice, then he took me over to a door that separated his room from his sister's. He bent over, peeking through the keyhole for a long time before he let me take a look. Beulah and Tommy were both naked and going at one another like dogs do in the park when we play baseball. When that happens everyone stops the game and gathers around to watch, and it was with the same fascination that I found myself staring through the keyhole. Beulah didn't move around much, but Tommy was moving to the beat of the music. I wondered if that was what Reverend Morley meant when he talked about rock-and-roll being the work of the devil. We watched them for a while, and when they finished and went downstairs, Obadiah and I went out onto the roof and shinnied down the drainpipe.

"Bet you've never seen that before," Obadiah said, once we'd made it to the back yard.

I told him no, of course I hadn't. I asked him if he thought they were going to have a baby.

"Beulah doesn't care. She doesn't care about going to hell or anything. She says hell is so full there's no room for her."

When we came in for lunch we didn't have our baseball gloves, but no one seemed to notice. I looked at Beulah once while we ate. She smiled at me. She had the same endearing smile as her mother.

The following week was eventful. Naomi bit the mailman and had to be kept in the house until after one o'clock every afternoon, whether we were home or not. Mom announced that she and George were going to be married as soon as George found a suit he liked, and out in front of the house was parked a grey, 1949 Ford that George bought for $100. It was sitting patiently, waiting for the day my mother got her learner's license. Despite the myriad of distractions, I couldn't stop picturing what I'd witnessed through Obadiah's keyhole. Unlike watching dogs, it wasn't something to joke about.

I was glad when it poured rain the following Sunday. I tried to concentrate on pure thoughts while I sat through the drawn out Sunday service. The sermon dealt with our obligation to raise children in a God-fearing manner, and I wondered how the Reverend Morley would rate his own child raising. His son

Frank was due to get out in three months, after being behind bars for more than a year, and that couldn't have been easy for him to live with. I wondered if he knew what his own daughter did to fulfill the Sabbath every week.

The next Sunday, Obadiah didn't come to Sunday School. He had a tooth that was growing in instead of out and he missed school the entire week. On Friday after school I went to his house with some of my old racing cars. I figured I'd leave them there for a while to give him something to do. We played in his room until his mother called him and said he had to have a checkup at the dentist. He asked if I could stay for supper, his mother said yes, and off he went, leaving me to play with my racing cars by myself. As soon as their car pulled out of the driveway, the radio came on in Beulah's room.

At first all I heard was the radio, then I could hear voices. Tommy was in there with Beulah and they were talking loudly at first, then yelling. The argument grew heated, and even above the radio I recognized words I'd heard between my mother and father before they parted ways. I continued playing with my cars, minding my own business, until I heard the unmistakable sound of someone being slapped. I maneuvered my cars over to the keyhole. "Bitch," Tommy yelled. "You can be such a bitch." Beulah didn't look any worse for wear and I thought it must have been Tommy who'd been slapped. He got dressed in a hurry, slammed the door and stomped down the stairs. When I turned away from the door I was heading for Obadiah's bed against the far wall. I was going to hide under the covers and pretend I was none the wiser. That's what I intended until I kicked one of my racing cars.

"Jessie? Jessie, are you in there?"

I ran and lay on the bed, staring at the door, praying it wouldn't open.

"Jessie? There you are. I didn't know you were here all by yourself."

I turned away from Beulah, who was standing in the room, a housecoat draped over her shoulders. I could feel her walking toward me. I could feel the heat of her body. She sat down on the edge of the bed and put her hand on my shoulder. It felt like my shoulder was burning, and then, for a reason I couldn't explain, I began to cry. Beulah put her hand on my head to soothe me and I realized she must have learned that from her mother.

"You're upset," she said, "and it's all my fault. There's nothing to worry about. These things happen sometimes, you know."

She said some other things, about her and Tommy. I couldn't get my mind around it all. I could only think of one thing.

"You're going to end up in hell," I finally blurted out. "You're father knows it and even Obadiah knows it. Why would you do that and end up in hell? I saw you in there and now I'm going to hell too."

Beulah lay down beside me and started making cooing noises like pigeons do. She said she didn't think either of us would be going to hell any time soon. She said she was sorry I had to be in the room when it all happened. She asked me to promise to keep this afternoon a secret between us, and even though I didn't say I would, I nodded my head and she thanked me and gave me one last hug. As soon as I heard the door to her room close, I made my way out the bedroom window, down the drain pipe and ran home the short way through the Dutchman's cabbage patch.

❖❖❖

"You didn't stay long," my mother said, when I returned. She was sitting behind the wheel of the car, studying for her driver's test. George liked it when she sat inside while he washed the outside, so I climbed in and sat beside her.

"No, not long."

"How's Obadiah's tooth?"

"Better," I said.

George kept soaping the windows so we couldn't see out, then hosing them off so we could. Mom was leery of the prospect of driving. I think it had occurred to her that if she failed her written test then the car would be sold and that would be the end of it.

"I think I've learned all I need to know about Sunday School. I've been going for quite a few months now and I'm a quick learner. I've got heaven and hell all figured out. I want to start playing baseball anyway. I can join Marty's farm league team and they practice on Sundays sometimes."

"I thought you enjoyed going to church with the Morleys and to their house for lunch once a week. Why such a sudden change of heart?"

Without being completely sure what it was I'd understood, I knew I'd made a promise to Beulah and I was going to keep that promise forever. Whatever was going to happen, I knew it would happen to both of us. When there's no good answer to a question, the wisest thing to do is say nothing at all.

As Good A Town As Any

MARSHA HAMILTON WAS RUNNING AWAY FROM HOME. She'd been gone twenty-six hours, and six of those hours had been spent in dingy bus depots in towns people would drive around on purpose, little towns just off the highway so no one took notice of them. Some were so small they shared a police force with the town down the road, and even then an emergency call in the middle of the night would pull an officer out of bed, reluctantly, like a stubborn molar. Sometimes the bus depot was an all night garage with a BUS DEPOT sign. All of them, in the middle of the night, served burnt, stale coffee so that even three creamers didn't make a dint.

Running away was the only plan Marsha Hamilton had. She could have stopped riding the bus at any one of a dozen stops along the way, and she wasn't sure why she'd chosen this one. After twenty-six hours on the bus, any town becomes a candidate. When the bus pulled in she was able to see the town was large enough to have a real bus depot with a small restaurant that served lemon meringue pie at five in the morning. This, she took as a sign.

When she told the bus driver she wanted off, the look on his face said she was crazy. He retrieved her three large suitcases from the bowels of the bus like it interfered with his own getting into the cafeteria to have lemon meringue pie. He didn't move for the longest time, as if she might change her mind.

She had her three cases stacked in the waiting room where she could sit at the counter and keep an eye on them while she ate. The whole trip she hadn't chatted with anyone. For a stretch she'd sat beside a little old lady who looked kindly and understanding, but when she began to tell her about her life, the lady fell asleep and gave off tiny, abbreviated snores. After doing some business with tickets in the office, the bus driver came into the cafeteria. He didn't sit beside her, though he could have, and he didn't order lemon meringue pie; he ordered a cherry tart.

Had he looked the least bit interested, she would have told him something like this: my name is Marsha Hamilton and I'm running away from my former life. It sounds dreadful, I know, but it all depends on the perspective. I used to live in Swift Current and that's where this running away all started. Bert, he's my husband of thirteen years, came home from work earlier than usual one day, and when I asked him what was the matter he said he didn't love me any more. I figured he was kidding or sick, but when he started crying, I knew. Why not? I asked, and he said he didn't have a clue, he just didn't. Then he cried some more. *And* he refused to go to work. This went on for a week and a half, and even when his boss dropped by the house he wouldn't budge. He started sleeping on a small cot we keep out on the front porch for when it gets hot, but that's not for another two months. He slept there at night and walked around town during the day and he looked like hell. Completely depressed and his face sagging like a bloodhound's. He would go down to Merilee's Burgers for lunch and skip breakfast and supper. Is there someone else you're in love with, Bert? I asked him, but he shook his head and said no, he just didn't love me. I could hear him crying out on the porch every single night, and I thought if he was a real man who wanted out that's what he'd do, he'd move out, but instead he wandered around town, moping, not looking anyone in the eye except Merilee when he ordered his burger. That's when I decided it was up to me to make a move because it sure wasn't going to be him. I know when I'm not wanted, so I packed my bags, one a day for three days, but there was still no sign of change. I even put them out on the porch on the third day so my intentions were clear, but he just rolled over and started crying again, so I called a cab and got on a bus. Marsha Hamilton on her own little adventure.

It was quarter to six when the bus pulled away in search of another little town, and she was left in the cafeteria with a perky man about twenty-five who was doing the dishes, polishing the tables and filling the salt and pepper shakers, a man who looked a decade too old to be wearing pimples. There was no one else, and he kept putting quarters in the jukebox and playing oldies songs, singing like you could never imagine him being sad his entire life. Marsha Hamilton watched and listened and read the classified ads in the town's weekly newspaper, because now that she was here she had to find an answer to the question, What next?

Room in private house. Separate. Small fridge, hot plate, bed and dresser. One nosy cat. 244-1758. It was too early to phone so she decided to walk around the downtown. You can't tell much about a town late at night and she hadn't made her mind up about this one. A hardware store with wheelbarrows in three different colours can be viewed in several ways.

It was only five minutes to seven when she returned from her tour. It would be almost eight back home, so she decided to give her number a ring. She let the phone ring for five minutes exactly which meant Bert was out walking, or wouldn't pick up. It was just a whim she'd decided to call, and like most whims it felt like a footstep that went on forever and never landed. Her next call was to inquire about the room for rent, and it was picked up on the first ring.

❖❖❖

The driver took his time and kept yawning. She could tell by his breath he'd just started his shift and hadn't brushed his teeth yet. She asked him to wait while she looked the place over. He'd already shut the meter off, and he shrugged his shoulders as if to say, What can you expect so early in the morning?

It wasn't the prettiest part of town from what she'd seen on the drive over, but at least it was in town. She could walk anywhere.

Marsha Hamilton rang the bell, and the door opened immediately like the owners were standing on the other side of the door, waiting for her the whole time.

"You must be the lady that phoned earlier," the man said. "I'm Howard and this is my wife, Louise. You said your name is Marsha Hamilton."

"It is Marsha Hamilton."

"Well, good. Come this way. You'd come in through this door with the same key we use, but your room is just down the hall. No stairs, which is handy for packing groceries."

The hallway was hardwood, and when they walked over the black metal grate that sat in the middle she could feel the heat climbing her legs. It felt so good she almost backed up.

They opened the door to a room exactly as described in the ad. It had a bed, a dresser, a fridge that was only four feet tall and a table under the window with a hot plate. The L-shaped window afforded a partial view of the street.

"Louise, why don't you show Marsha Hamilton around? I'll carry on with my crossword puzzle."

"It's not a large room, as you can see," Louise said. "But it has many features. Howard designed it as a perfect square. Through this door there's a washroom and a sink. Howard put in a large sink because that's the only source of running water.

You can fill your kettle, wash carrots, whatever. The shower is brand new and it doesn't leak. I know, I've tried it. This bed folds back into a couch so you have somewhere to sit when you're not lying down. Howard has one more coat to put on the kitchen chair. You'll get that tomorrow. Oh, and in here." She followed Louise through another door at the back of the room. "This is the laundry room which we enter from the other end. You're welcome to use both the washer and the dryer but you'll find it pretty busy on Saturdays. I like to do up the wash on Saturdays if I can. There's a small pond at the side of the yard, and Howard is working on a picnic table so when the weather warms up you can sit out there if you like. Other than the next door neighbours, it's very private. The hot plate is second hand, but both the elements work. That just about does it."

"I see," Marsha Hamilton said. She took a peek out the window to make sure the taxi driver was still waiting.

"Come on in and talk to Howard if you think you're interested. I leave the business end up to him."

When they walked back down the hall Marsha Hamilton slowed her pace over the heat vent. In the kitchen, Howard was looking something up in a huge dictionary.

"Ah ha, cheating again. He always cheats. It's the only way he can finish a whole puzzle," Louise said.

"So, what do you think?" Howard said. "If you don't mind a small room, it's pretty spiffy."

"How much are you asking?"

"Two hundred and seventy-five a month, payable in advance. That includes your power and your hot water too."

"I see."

"But we'll take two-fifty if you plan on staying a while."

"I don't have anywhere to go," she said.

❖❖❖

There were things she needed right away: bedding, a kettle, a toaster and something to make coffee. Good coffee. She would need to get in a supply of groceries as well, but that could wait. It was a Saturday and everything was open. Now that she'd found a place to stay she could do everything in stages. On her way back to the hardware store she'd seen earlier, she came upon a small family restaurant and decided to stop in for breakfast. She sat down at a table and was served by the same perky young man who had worked the night shift at the bus depot.

"Let me guess, lemon meringue pie and ice cream?"

"No, but that coffee sure smells good. Do you make cinnamon toast?"

"We make toast any way you want it. We make eggs any way you want them too. There are nineteen listed here on the menu but the cook is flexible."

"Cinnamon toast will be fine, thank you."

"White, whole grain or cracked wheat?"

"I'll try cracked wheat."

"That's my favourite. Here's your coffee. Fresh cream in the jigger. While I prepare your toast you might want to fill out this short questionnaire and answer the skill testing question. They go into the barrel and every week someone wins a free breakfast. You don't need to bother doing the calculations, the answer is 72. Doesn't this just feel like the beginning of a great day?"

She thought about it, and it did feel like a new beginning. She had no idea where she'd end up, but already this town seemed as good a place as any. The hills and mountains that surrounded the town made her feel safe.

"Here's your toast. I hope it suits you."

"You work here *and* at the bus depot?" she said.

"I sure do. I just work three or four hours here, though. Enough to help them through the breakfast rush. It's either work or sleep and I figure eight hours is enough for anyone. So, you're new in town. Did you find a place to stay?"

"I did. Over on Palmer Avenue. A couple called—"

"Howard and Louise," the boy said. "I know them. They've had that ad in the paper for more than a month. Not a lot of new people here. He's a first-aid man down at the mill. Well, I'll let you finish your breakfast. Brown's Bakery is the best in town. You'd find that out yourself eventually."

The restaurant walls were covered with slogans like "The bigger the wood pile, the better the chances of a cold winter," and "We never find time or suffer from lost time. We only fail to use it properly." She enjoyed her toast and coffee. She would come back again, and when she did she would choose a different booth and a new selection of slogans.

At the hardware store she bought a small coffee maker, a two-slice toaster and a kettle with an automatic shut off. "If anything doesn't work, just bring it back and we'll replace it, no questions asked," the man said and smiled warmly like a lot of bald men do. She took her purchases back to the room and headed out for linen and towels. She came home and made the bed and almost climbed into it. It was just past lunch time, and she was fading fast. She bought two bags of groceries and put them away but then decided she should get something to read. She'd always had a television set, even an old black and white, but she didn't have one now and didn't care. She liked to read and think and she'd have plenty of time for that.

She couldn't find the library but came across a second hand bookstore. There were two by Catherine Cookson she hadn't read in the bargain bin outside the door for fifty cents each. The image of lemon meringue pie wouldn't leave her and she stopped by the restaurant on the way home. The young man was there to greet her.

"I thought you said you only worked the breakfast shift."

"I do, but Brenda called in sick. I'm only on until six, then I'll have a chance to sleep."

"This is a friendly town," she said. "Wouldn't you say?"

"That I couldn't tell you. I've lived here all my life and I've only been to Calgary once for the stampede. I don't know what to compare it to."

By the time Marsha Hamilton got back to her room her legs felt like rubber. She realized the lack of sleep over the last forty-eight hours was catching up to her. She hadn't slept much for the last three weeks, with Bert crying through the night out on the porch and her watching his next move, which turned out to be no move at all. She made a pot of coffee, pulled down the plastic blinds and climbed into bed to read. Half way through page two she fell asleep for the night.

Marsha Hamilton was not sure where she was when she woke at ten the next morning. Then she remembered she'd run away from home and this was her room. There was a note under the door from Howard saying that the chair was finished and sitting in the hall, and she was welcome to it but that it might be a good idea not to sit on it for another twenty-four hours. She'd left the coffee maker on over night and the sludge left in the pot was like what she'd been served in bus depots and garages on the way.

Religion had never been a big thing in her world but something enticed her, while a fresh pot of coffee was brewing, to open one of her suitcases, find something formal and head out to church. On the street she could see a steeple up on a hill four blocks away. It was an Anglican church with an eleven o'clock service, and she found a seat in the third row of pews. The organist up at the front finished playing, and the shuffling of feet and squeaking of benches ceased as the minister made his way to the pulpit. The organist looked like the same young man who'd served her lemon meringue pie. She gave him a small wave, but he didn't wave back.

The minister's message was about the obligation to look out for those around us in need. She didn't follow his story line all the way through, but that seemed to be the gist of it. What she enjoyed was the peace and serenity, the feeling that she was part of something. The singing she hadn't experienced in years, the long drawn out lines found in the hymnbook, sung to match the droning organ. Because she didn't attend church regularly, it felt like she was attending a well-staged concert. The stained glass windows, ten of them in all, were different from one another, and the light that filtered into the church seemed surreal. She'd never given stained glass windows credit for anything other than ornamentation before. The collection in a Tupperware bowl, the only detail of the service out of tune.

The sun was shining. She couldn't remember if it was shining when she'd entered the church. It may have been the minister's message made her think of Bert. She found a phone booth on a street corner and tried again. The phone rang and rang but there was no answer. It was lunch time and he was likely eating his burger.

❖❖❖

Back home it was bridge club, volunteering at the hospital, cleaning a four-bedroom house, working Saturdays at the drugstore, cooking for Bert, gardening when the weather was good. Somehow she had managed to fit it all in, but now she had stepped out of the current, her days were as full as ever. She slept ten hours or more for one thing. It was hard to conceive of a body being so played out. She read. She walked down a new street every day. She spent most of her time in her room and the more she did the bigger the room became. It was all anyone really needed. Every afternoon she'd gotten into the habit of meditating, sitting on the bed. She knew nothing about meditation, had only seen pictures, so she sat in the lotus position, closed her eyes and tried to think of nothing. It wasn't easy to think of nothing. Things popped into her consciousness, and she reminded herself she wasn't supposed to be thinking, but thinking about putting thinking out of her mind was yet another thing to deal with. One afternoon she became totally relaxed and suddenly she saw a tiger, the face so close she could feel its breath on her cheeks.

Sitting in a room by herself made her a good listener. She heard Howard up early and in the shower. Louise never got up until he left for work and then her routine set in. She washed clothes on Saturdays, vacuumed Mondays, bowled Wednesdays and shopped on Fridays. She never saw Louise, unless they came home at the same time, she only heard her. It was an old house, and the sound carried. There wasn't much to listen for when Louise was home alone, but late at night after Howard was through playing handyman, strange sounds echoed through the house. She thought they likely had a TV and VCR in the bedroom, but if that was the case she was puzzled because they sounded like violent movies. Movies full of testosterone.

One day Louise drove up as Marsha Hamilton was arriving home from a walk.

"So, is Marsha Hamilton all settled in?"

"Yes, I am. Thank you."

"Have you managed to find a job yet?"

She hadn't looked for a job. Hadn't thought about working. The day before she left, she'd taken a certified cheque for the sum of her savings account and everything in this town seemed so reasonable, she could live for a year or more before she'd be destitute. Her life seemed full enough, and she tried to imagine fitting a job in.

"Are there jobs around?" she said.

"Not many. That's why I asked. Not much changes in this town. If someone dies there's an opening."

"I was wondering," Marsha Hamilton said, "about the cat. The ad in the paper mentioned a nosy cat. I haven't seen it."

"He ran away," Louise said. "The day after we put the ad in. I guess he was offended."

Every night when Howard came home from work he ate supper and puttered around the yard. Sometimes he'd be right outside her window working on the pond. The days were getting longer and if he wasn't fiddling with the pond he was out in his shed working on the picnic table. It became a pastime, watching him work. He did everything slowly. He would bring plants to the edge of the pond, then stare at the surface. Then he'd set one into the water and watch it float. Then he'd plant another. He was one of those men who would hold a finger up to his nose and snort a spray of mucus out onto the grass. She couldn't imagine him dealing with an emergency as a first-aid man.

With every passing day, she thought of Bert less often. She'd tried phoning several times but there was never an answer. One Saturday she felt the urge to take in a movie. She hadn't been to a matinee since she was a kid. The theatre had two screens that ran current movies in the evening, but the matinees always seemed to feature older, classic films. She saw *Who's Afraid of Virginia Woolf?* and walked out into the sunshine with mixed emotions. It felt like it should be pouring rain.

She had decided against getting a phone and stopped at a phone booth to try Bert one more time. The phone rang twice, and she was startled when a woman answered.

"Hello. Who is this?" Marsha Hamilton said.

"Well, if it isn't Marsha Hamilton. This is Dorothy Hammond. Where the hell are you?"

"What are you doing there? Is Bert okay?"

"Well, not really. He stopped taking care of himself. That's why John and I are here. We're trying to clean the place up a bit. He's staying with us for now, but John says it's only temporary. Here, I'll give you to John . . . it's Marsha Hamilton. I have no idea where she's phoning from."

"Hello?"

"Hi, Marsha Hamilton. Like Dorothy said, Bert's not up to much. He sleeps a lot and he cries a lot. Are you coming back home?"

"Did Bert ask if I was?"

"No, I was just wondering. He walks around the block when it's light out and then when it gets dark and he cries. I thought maybe if — "

"No, John, I'm not coming back. I'm happy where I am. Has anyone asked about me?"

"Not that I know of. We did get a call last night when we were in here doing the wash. Some guy phoned and said Marsha Hamilton had won a free breakfast. He started going on about eggs or something so I hung up. A lot of loose wheels out there if you ask me."

"Is Bert eating?"

"Hamburgers. Dorothy makes them every second day, but I'm getting tired of them myself. You sure you're not coming home?"

Before she hung up, she left John Hammond with a message for Bert. Anything she didn't have in her three suitcases he could keep. She didn't want any of it. Not the house, the car or the trouble. She thought about Elizabeth Taylor and Richard Burton and knew she could never go there.

❖❖❖

Marsha Hamilton had an alarm clock in the one suitcase she'd never unpacked, but there was no use for it with the life she was leading. Early one Saturday morning the birds woke her up. Their chorus drew her out of bed and out of the house. She headed down to the park and sat on a green bench in the corner of the park near a flower garden that looked promising for summer. The crows were having fun emptying a garbage can, and even though she knew putting the lid back on would be the responsible thing to do, she couldn't bear to spoil their fun. Over in the far corner of the park was a playground with coloured plastic tunnels and ladders and swings. There were about a dozen kids running around and shouting as loudly as they could, and at first she thought it might be the same young man who worked in the restaurant who was supervising them. The more she watched, the more she was certain. The sight of him reminded her she was hungry and that she had a free breakfast coming her way.

It felt like it was going to be the hottest day of the year, so she stopped off at home to shower and change into something lighter. On her way to the restaurant she noticed most of the stores were setting up tables and booths on the sidewalk. A town trying hard to take on a festive tone.

She sat at a different table and began reading the quaint sayings on the wall. "Wrinkle-free clothes are for those without a pressing need." "A bird in the hand is worth two in the bush until it craps all over you."

"Good morning. Cinnamon toast and coffee? Am I right?"

"Well, maybe. I got a call that I'd won a free breakfast. It might have been last week. I don't know if it's still good."

"You must be Marsha Hamilton. I know most of the names that go into the draw, and I thought it might have been you." The young man turned toward the kitchen. "*Hey, Mary. Marsha Hamilton is here for her free breakfast.* I just love it when people come in for their free breakfast. You might find this hard to believe, but we've had people win before who never show up to claim their prize. I'm not kidding."

"Didn't I just see you at the park with a group of children?"

"That was me all right. My sister runs a Saturday camp for kids but she has to go to Calgary twice a year to have chelation. Me and my brother pitch in for her when that happens. My brother has the kids at the pool right now."

"And you play the organ at church?"

"No, that's not me. That's my twin brother, Tony. The day you see me playing organ in church you know the Devil's won the election. But I can sing. God, I love to sing."

She looked around the restaurant. There were three other tables filled with people and no one had waited on them yet.

"Well, I'll take a minute to look the menu over. I think I'll order something I've never had before."

"Risk taker," the young man said. "Got to love that."

It wasn't until Marsha Hamilton had resided in their home for close to two months that Louise started knocking on her door in the evenings. If Howard was working on the pond, they'd sit at her small table and watch him go through the motions. Louise would press for details about just why a woman would move to such a static town on her own, unpack two of her three suitcases and seem content to sit and watch life go by. Had these inquiries come the day she arrived, they likely would have been answered with an autobiographical novel, but things were different now. She felt secure in her insularity. No one knew her, and while she was certain this didn't stop some from speculating, their speculations were bound to be hollow. She liked the idea of writing a new history.

"A man can just play himself out," Louise said. "They're there right before your eyes, solid as oak, then before you know it they're on their way out. It happens to all of us eventually. Women are the ones around long enough to see it, that's all."

"They slow down," Marsha Hamilton said. "Is that what you mean?"

"Slow down. Howard started to slow down when he turned sixteen, but these last few years . . . well look out there. See that wheelbarrow he's got? You haven't seem him use it, have you?"

"No. But I'm sure he has a plan for it."

"Oh, he has plans all right. Filed away where he can't find them. He hasn't used the wheelbarrow since he dug the pond out a year ago but he takes it with him wherever he goes. He worked on this room you're staying in for four years. There was a time he was a competent first-aid man but they find joe-jobs for him now. They feel sorry for him."

"That's too bad. I had no idea. I just thought he liked to take things slowly in the evening. His way of relaxing."

"There's nothing anyone can do," Louise said. "His license has expired is what it comes down to."

Then Louise stopped coming. Marsha Hamilton was puzzled but thought perhaps she was just a busybody and an unsuccessful one at that. The sounds in the house changed. A few days later, she wondered if Louise had fallen ill. She waited on the porch one afternoon until Howard came walking down the street.

"I haven't seen Louise for a few days. She's not sick is she?"

"She's gone to the store. How's that chair holding up?"

"The chair is fine. It's very solid."

"I made that chair," Howard said. "Made it with my own hands."

She waited and watched. There was no evidence that Louise was anywhere about. One night she saw Howard out beside the pond, staring at his wheelbarrow.

"This pond is looking great," she said.

"Thank you. It's my first pond. I want to get it right."

"I still haven't seen Louise. Is she inside?"

"She's gone to the store."

"But she hasn't come back."

"Then she'll be at her sister's."

"Where does her sister live?"

"Maine I think. Or Vermont. Five letter word for New England poet. Frost. That's where she is, where Robert Frost lived."

Howard always put the wheelbarrow back in the shed at night when he was finished.

❖❖❖

In the heat of summer, the town relaxed. There were more people downtown on Saturdays, but the rest of the week was pedestrian. Marsha Hamilton had a routine. She went to the library on Tuesdays, a small library with a friendly librarian, Miss Bennett, who always mentioned what the weather was doing to her arthritis. Miss Bennett was also in the habit of asking if she'd read Thomas Hardy, and Marsha Hamilton eventually found the best thing to say was, Yes, she'd read everything he'd written. She bowled on Wednesdays at two o'clock when a group of mentally challenged adults took up three of the six lanes, and she could bowl over to one side. There was a great deal of cheering and squealing when any of the pins fell down, but she preferred that to being around competitive bowlers. She wasn't a serious bowler, but started keeping track of her scores and imagined the local paper reporting on the Marsha Hamilton League. *Marsha Hamilton remains in first place. Her average this week was one eleven. Well done, Marsha Hamilton.* Friday mornings were perfect for visiting the New 2 You store. Once and a while she'd buy herself a pair of shoes for four dollars, but most of the time she liked to look at the bargains to be found, and just knowing that bargains existed was enough to reinforce her faith in the world. She returned to the movie theatre on Saturdays, but only if it was cloudy. Otherwise, she walked. Up and down the streets, out into the country, sometimes for three or four hours at a stretch. Howard mentioned he'd heard there was a part time job opening up at Brannigans Chocolates so she went in to inquire. It turned out there was an opening, Tuesday afternoons and the odd Saturday if the owner, Cleo, was out of town. This suited her perfectly. She'd worked there for a week before she found out the job used to belong to Louise.

The young man who worked at the bus depot and the restaurant, Marsha Hamilton found out, had latent acne for very good reason. He came into Brannigans to buy copious amounts of chocolate at least three times a week. Everyone who worked in the store knew him, called him Beamer, even though his name tag at the restaurant said Ernie and the one he wore at the bus depot said Giles. It was hard to go anywhere in town and not run into him, and she noticed he was equally friendly with everyone.

Fall season was beautiful in this little town. The deciduous trees wore their colours proudly. Winter came early and after the second snowfall, the ground remained covered for months. It never became hideously cold like it could in Swift Current, and that was a blessing by comparison. Howard's life source dried up. He never did finish the picnic table, and as the weather became colder he stopped making appearances in the yard. She hadn't seen him for three days leading up to Remembrance Day and after Louise left in August, none of her rent cheques had been cashed. She knocked on his door the morning of the Remembrance Day service, thinking he might want to join her at the cenotaph. He never answered and she assumed he was sleeping and carried on by herself. When she got back she tried again but with the same result, and she entered his part of the house, fearing the worst. She found him in the back bedroom, lying on a single bed beside a double bed, staring at the TV that was showing highlights of various Remembrance Day ceremonies from around the country. The sound was off, and he didn't seem to notice she'd entered the room. There were three doctors listed in the phone book, and when she called she got an answering service. Dr. Coleman was on call for the holiday and he was at the house in under twenty minutes.

"How's my Howard doing?" the doctor asked. Howard continued staring at the TV in the corner and didn't acknowledge him. After a brief examination, Dr. Coleman phoned for an ambulance and suggested that Howard had suffered a stroke. Occasionally they can recover some of their functions, he said, but more often than not they head downhill.

"His wife, Louise," she began to explain, " . . . she's not been around since the end of the summer."

"I know all about it," Dr. Coleman said. "Louise has done this before. She'd better not wait too long this time or she won't be coming back to a husband."

After the ambulance pulled away, Marsha Hamilton went back to her room, but it felt different. It didn't seem like her room. Even when she looked around and saw all the things that belonged to her, it didn't seem like her room. She lay down on her bed and thought about what had happened. It wasn't something she could connect with. A perfectly harmless man named Howard had just suffered a stroke and been taken to hospital, he'd been abandoned by his wife, and it all felt like something she might have read in the newspaper. She couldn't muster up sadness or sympathy for his plight. All she could sense was the experience of being hollow.

She decided to take a walk into town and eat supper at the restaurant. When she opened the door to leave, a marmalade cat brushed past her legs, sat by the door to the main part of the house and meowed in long, well-rounded vowels. She opened the door, and the cat went directly to the kitchen and sat beside a cupboard near the fridge and resumed meowing. She found some canned cat food. Wherever it had been, it hadn't gone hungry. Its coat looked sleek and healthy and it ate only half of what she put out. The cat cleaned itself briefly, jumped up on a sofa chair and curled itself into a purring sleep.

Howard didn't recognize her two days later when she visited him in the hospital. The nurse on duty said he'd lost his facility for speech and was too unsteady to be trusted on his feet. Plans were in the works, she said, to put him into an extended care facility on the outskirts of down. Marsha Hamilton asked if anyone had come to visit and was not entirely surprised to find out the answer was no.

For the next few weeks, she continued on with her routine as much as she could. She bowled, she worked, she read and she thought a lot. Most of her thinking never went anywhere in particular, never reached a conclusion. Her own room had seemed like a safe haven when Howard and Louise were living in the house, but now it felt like the eyes of the world were on her, which she knew was a ridiculous supposition. She fed the cat twice a day and let it out in the morning when she went out for a walk. It was always back around supper time and wouldn't leave her alone until it was fed. She left the door to the main part of the house open so she could hear the cat if it wanted out. The cat would take to meowing outside her own door and soon she left it open as well. The cat was nosy, just like the ad in the newspaper had mentioned, and it didn't hesitate to make itself at home in her room. She found herself going into the rest of the house to feed the cat and lingering, looking around out of curiosity. On the kitchen table were two stacks of crossword puzzle books. She started going through them and found they were all filled in, but that none of the answers made any sense, just letters filling squares for the sake of filling squares.

When she turned the calendar over to May, it occurred to her she'd been living in this town for one full year. Her rent cheques hadn't been cashed since August, and there was nothing to indicate that her situation wouldn't continue.

❖❖❖

It had been hot in the early part of May, but then it turned cool and rained in the mornings for three days in a row. It was the same taxi driver who came to pick her up, but it was late afternoon and there was no sign he hadn't brushed his teeth. It might have been her imagination, but Marsha Hamilton thought she could smell toothpaste on his breath.

She'd never heard of a bus leaving early, but she got down to the bus depot an hour ahead of time in any case. There were two lemon meringue pies in the display case that hadn't been cut into, and she knew she wouldn't be able to resist.

"There you go. Lemon meringue with ice cream on top. Not many people order lemon meringue with anything else but a fork."

"Thanks," Marsha Hamilton said. "It looks great."

"So, you're moving on. We don't get many new people in town, but then again not many leave either. We're going to miss you down at the restaurant. You won two free breakfasts, isn't that right?"

"Three," she said.

"Well, it's a good time to travel. Spring, I mean. No snow in the mountains. Life so full of hope. I might just do the same thing myself some day, but then again, I might not. Whenever I think about travelling it occurs to me I don't know where I would want to go."

Marsha Hamilton set her fork into the pointed end of her pie and thought about what the young man had said. She thought about it long after the pie was gone.

Horse Sense

I ONLY MET CHARLIE LITTLEJOHN BECAUSE I WAS LOOKING for work. When you're sixteen and want a job is when you're likely to meet someone like Charlie Littlejohn. I didn't know that at the time, but I do now. My brother-in-law was in the navy, and that's how he knew him. I was to meet Charlie at the gas station on the highway at six in the morning, and he was willing to drive me to Sooke so I could apply for a job at the sawmill, pulling on the green chain. Most sawmills don't have green chains any more, the lumber is sorted by machine, and that explains why if you drive by Sooke today you won't find a sawmill anywhere.

I was fit and strong enough for sixteen, and I wanted a union job that paid well. Charlie bid on logs for the company and said he had no idea if they were hiring, but I was welcome to ride out to Sooke and take a look. At six in the morning the only indication of life on the highway was a truck dropping off bundles of newspapers on the corner. The sign said the garage was opened twenty-four hours a day, but someone must have changed his mind and not the message.

I'd never met Charlie Littlejohn, I only knew he drove a truck. Just past six a GMC pulled into the gas station and sat idling, the man behind the wheel rolling a cigarette over the steering wheel. He took no notice of me watching the sunrise, so I walked up and opened the door.

"Charlie Littlejohn?"

"Speakin'."

"I'm Danny Wilkinson. I'm here to get a ride out to the mill."

"Seat's empty," he said. I climbed in and shut the door.

The first thing I noticed about Charlie was how meticulous he was with his tobacco. We must have sat there for three or four minutes while he rolled a cigarette that looked like it had come right out of a package. He took a box of wooden matches out of the glove box and tapped the loose ends of tobacco with a match until the ends were perfectly even. When he finally finished, he slid the cigarette into his shirt pocket and pulled the truck onto the highway.

"You don't smoke, I'm guessin'."

"No I don't. I had one behind the backstop in grade five but I didn't like it."

Charlie pulled a pair of glasses out of the same shirt pocket and put them on. He settled back in the bench seat and looked out the windshield like it was his first glimpse of the world that morning.

"Figures. Smokin's not what it used to be. Used to be someone your age learned to smoke as soon as they could. It had something to do with becoming a man. Nowadays it's whipping the pants off a girl. Am I right?"

When you're sixteen, half of what you say to adults is to play along. The strange thing is the other half is to tell them to bugger off. That doesn't leave much room for honesty.

"That's the way things are, all right. How long will it take to get to Sooke?"

"About thirty-five minutes from here. This time of day the cops are sleeping. Leave here at eight and it could take you an hour."

I started thinking that Charlie couldn't have met my brother-in-law in the navy. Navy people know how to talk to you, even if they do make everything sound like it's a fact and not an opinion. I'd never been in the navy, but that's what occurred to me.

It was cool out and he kept fiddling with the heat vent. One minute it would blow cold air and next it would be so hot he'd open the breezeway window. When we'd been driving a while, we came to a store out in the middle of nowhere. It had a huge tire sitting out near the road so people would know what they were selling, but I couldn't imagine anyone driving this far out to buy tires. That's when Charlie pulled the cigarette out of his pocket and lit it.

"By the time I'm finished this cigarette," he said, "we'll be there."

The mill was near the Sooke Harbour. From the top of the hill it looked big. Charlie geared the truck down toward the parking lot so that his prediction of finishing his cigarette on arrival turned out to be true.

"How old are you again?"

"Sixteen. Just turned."

"Well you look like you can handle the job. When they ask you if you're allergic to cedar say no. If you can't remember your social insurance number, make one up. Who knows, you might get lucky and start today. This truck heads back to Victoria at 3:32. If you're in it you're welcome to a ride."

He pointed to the personnel office and walked toward the building farthest from the parking lot. He was carrying an old fashioned briefcase that made him look like a man who knew how to bid on logs. There was no one in the office so I sat on the step, hauled out my wallet and memorized my social insurance number.

I walked into the office at five minutes past eight. I figured it would be wise to give them time to get settled. A lady came away from her typewriter and up to the counter and I told her why I was there.

"Well, we'll just have to get you to fill out an application form then, won't we?"

I don't know what it is about women, but they often figure out when you're vulnerable and treat you kindly. I filled out the application, a standard one from what I could tell, and she called to a man sitting at his own desk, twiddling his pen.

"Fred, Danny has an application filled out. Do you want to handle it?"

The lady smiled and went back to her typing. Fred never answered her, but got up from his desk like he was dragging an anchor. He read my application over as if he were looking for signs of a criminal background.

"Well, Mr. Wilkinson, the fact is there's nothing happening at the moment. There's a strike pending, I'm sure you've heard about that. The men aren't taking their holidays like they usually do. I'll keep your papers on file and call you if anything changes."

He took my application and threw it onto the secretary's desk, and I was out in the parking lot at twenty minutes past eight. A long way from 3:30. I sat on the steps for a while, then wandered down and watched the logs come out of the water and into the mill. There were lots of jobs down there I could do if they'd let me, I knew it. Around ten I walked up to the main road and tried hitchhiking back to town. A few cars slowed down, but no one stopped so I headed back to the parking lot. I sat inside Charlie's truck and started rolling cigarettes with what I found in the glove box. The first one was thin and pointy. I started again and it wasn't half bad. I had six of them rolled and sitting on the dash when I heard the driver's door open.

"No luck, eh?"

"No. They said they're not hiring because of the strike."

"Thought that might be the case. I'll tell you what, there's a logging operation a couple of miles up the road. And a mining office close by. I'll whip you up there on my lunch break."

"If it's no trouble."

"Hey, Charlie Littlejohn said he'd get you work and that's what he intends to do."

He pointed out the mining outfit on the way to the logging office. It seemed more like four miles back to the mill, but it would give me something to do.

Had I ever worked in the woods before? No. Had I ever planted trees? No. Did I know the whole industry could be shut down with a strike any day now? Yes. The man going through the motions looked mean, like if he had his way he'd invite me outside to settle things. He said there was no point filling out an application, then stared at a stack of papers on his desk.

The man sitting behind the counter at the mining office asked me my name and phone number and wrote both down on a scrap of paper. "Thanks," he said.

I didn't bother trying to hitchhike back to the mill. For long stretches there was shade and I stopped every now and again to suck the sweetness out of the honeysuckle flowers. When I got back to the mill there was a van selling coffee and snacks. I bought a jelly doughnut and sat in Charlie's truck. I didn't feel like rolling any more cigarettes. If I'd found any matches, I'd have tried smoking one.

❖❖❖

"It's not easy to get your first job. It's worse now than when I was your age."

Charlie was in a lighter mood going home. He had six cigarettes in his shirt pocket instead of one and a day's work behind him. He started telling me about how he got started. After grade ten he quit school and worked for a farmer in Alberta. He worked six days a week for two months before the farmer told him he didn't have any money to pay him.

"Whatever happens," Charlie said, "you don't want to end up with a job like that."

Nope, Yes and Really were the words I'd been using to keep Charlie happy. I was thinking of throwing in a No way, just for variety, when he slammed on the brakes and pulled into a driveway. He left the truck idling and sat hunched over the steering wheel. The radio was lit up, but there was no sound coming out of the speakers.

"My brother's not a bit like me," he said, staring straight ahead. "He's the kind of man who'd fart heading into the wind and turn his back on the less fortunate. The fact is he needs help and he'll pay for the work to be done. I'd see to it you got paid."

"Who's your brother?"

"Cecil. He owns this farm on your right. It's only forty acres, but it has promise. He'd work like a son-of-a-bitch from sun up to sun down if he could, but he can't because of his leg. Don't ask me how you can get arthritis in one leg, but that's what happens when it gets cloudy. He's falling behind. He told me so last week and I know he needs a hand. Fencing, haying, putting a roof on the barn. It won't pay like the sawmill, but it will give you a poke at something."

"That would be fine by me. I need work of some kind. I'm saving to buy a motorcycle."

Charlie pulled one of the cigarettes I'd rolled out of his pocket and eyed it like there was no mistaking its inferior quality. He lit it and said he'd introduce me to Cecil as soon as the cigarette was done.

"And one more thing before we go in. Cecil's cross-eyed, always has been. When you're talking to him, get into the habit of staring at his nose. He's sensitive if people stare at his shoulder."

The house stood on the lip of a hill and looked out over the rest of the property. Despite being a warm first day of summer, I could see smoke trailing out of the chimney. A black lab barked by the front porch, looking back at his owner from time to time. The place could use some care and attention, but it felt like a real farm.

"That's my brother. You wait here and let me talk to him first and don't worry about Randy. He barks because he thinks he has to."

The truck was only a stone's throw from the porch, but I couldn't make out what they were saying. They were sitting close together and paying attention to something in the newspaper. After ten minutes Charlie turned and waved me up to the porch.

"We're looking for a ten letter word for sad. Any ideas?"

Neither one of them looked my way, just kept staring at the paper as if patience would lead to a solution.

"Melancholy," I said.

"Does it end with a y?" Cecil asked, still staring at the puzzle. "That means yodel is right. I think that's it."

"Cecil, this is the young fella I was telling you about. Danny."

I stared straight at his nose when I shook his hand.

"So, you're a hard worker?"

"Oh, I can work all right."

"Well, I can pay you $2.00 an hour — "

"We agreed on $2.25, Cecil," Charlie said. "Paid every Friday."

"All right. $2.25. But that's only if you work out. I'll give you a week to show me what you can do."

In the middle of the driveway leading up to the house stood a huge maple tree. I could hear a branch break and someone yell, "Shit!"

"Noreen, get out of that tree, and watch that mouth. There's someone you need to meet. You'll break your bloody neck."

We watched a barefoot girl climb out of the tree. She jumped the last ten feet and sent a cloud of dust into the air.

"The devil's got hold of my daughter," Cecil said. "She'd a had ten kids by now if I didn't keep an eye on her."

She looked about my age, maybe younger. She had lipstick on and dirt on her cheeks. Her toenails were painted purple.

"Noreen, this is Danny. He's going to be working around the farm this summer. That means I'll be paying him to work and I don't want you getting in his way, you hear. It's after four and there's two cows down there waiting to be milked. Make sure you wash them first."

"Hi," Noreen said, looking me over before she sauntered off to the barn.

"The same goes for you, Danny. We castrate three or four calves here every spring and I'll do the same to you if you so much as touch Noreen."

I headed back to the truck and heard Cecil tell Charlie she was just like her mother at the same age, in heat seven days a week.

Charlie would pick me up on the highway in the morning and fetch me at the farm on his way home. He didn't want anything for it. He was doing two people a favour, he said, and he was going out everyday anyway. The next morning when I got into the truck there was a picture of a motorcycle sitting on the seat.

"Know what that is?"

"A motorcycle."

"Not just a motorcycle. An Indian. 1948. That picture is a sad reminder I could have retired early if I'd hung onto it. The suspension wasn't much, but it loved the highway."

"Is that you behind it?"

"That's me all right. People lose value as time goes on, not like machines. There's a lesson in that if you're smart enough to learn it."

He dropped me off out on the main road and reminded me to look at the nose, work like a bull and leave the daughter alone if I wanted work all summer.

I got to the front steps and heard a whistle from down by the barn. Cecil was waving a handkerchief in the air like he was surrendering.

"We've got to get that hay in," he said. "Around here you're best to haul it in as soon as it's dry, especially early in the summer. There's a pair of leather gloves in the back if you want them."

Noreen was already sitting in the back of the truck, a silly grin on her face.

"You ever hayed before?" she asked.

"No, never."

"It's not that bad unless you're allergic. We had a guy help us last year who didn't last a day. His face swelled up like a pumpkin, and he couldn't breathe. Then we had a guy come out who didn't weigh as much as a bale. He couldn't even lift one so we had to let him go. You look like you could lift a bale with one hand."

"Maybe."

"It gets hot out there. You can take your shirt off if you get hot. Most men do."

We started on the outside of the field and worked our way in. Noreen drove the truck only as fast as I could lift the bales up onto the flatbed where Cecil stacked them. When the truck was full, we all jammed into the cab and Cecil drove to the barn. There was a glass water jug on the floor and even though it was warm water, it was all I could do to wait my turn. It was an old barn with just the frame of the roof and we piled the bales onto a roller powered by a Briggs & Stratton engine. Noreen and I took turns throwing the bales on and Cecil stacked them in the loft.

"Two more trips like that one and it'll be lunch time," Cecil said. He looked pleased when he said it, so I assumed we were making good time. Noreen was shorter and smaller than I was, but the work didn't seem to phase her. The second trip out, her dad drove the truck and she stacked the bales on the back. She was barefoot, didn't wear gloves and was quicker than Cecil had been.

Noreen said, "Next week we'll be baling alfalfa. They're the heavy buggers." Then she smiled like she knew more than me.

Three days straight we hauled the hay in until the loft was nearly full. The third day it was just Cecil and me which made things a lot slower. He'd pull the truck ahead and we'd fire up as many bales as we could, then climb up and stack them. He taught me how to overlap them so they wouldn't fall off on the way to the barn.

"The first day she bleeds she gets cramps. I can't say for sure if it's all that bad, but her mother was the same way. I wouldn't put it past her to use it as an excuse to stay in her room and listen to the radio."

"I've never met her mother."

"Won't neither. She's gone. If you ever take up farming, don't marry a city woman. There's not enough noise in a place like this to keep them occupied."

The rest of the week I spent digging post holes for a fence. Cecil strung a line out for me to follow and gave me a fourteen foot two-by-four to measure the intervals. The first six inches came out easy, then there was a foot of clay. I managed to get a dozen holes dug when Noreen drove the truck down to where I was working.

"He wants to know if you plan on stopping for lunch or not."

"What time is it?"

"It's past twelve. We already ate. I've got your lunch with me. Hop in and I'll show you the creek."

She drove the truck to where the field ran into the woods and I followed her down a trail to a small creek that formed a large pool. I sat down against a cool rock and started in on my balogna and mustard sandwiches. Noreen waded into the water and seemed lost in thought.

"Cecil, your dad . . . do you think he's happy living out here?"

"Happier than most, I guess. Why do you ask?"

"He was telling me about your mom. How she left you both."

"You know nothing about my mom, so don't talk about her. My mom was different. I think she would have died here. It's not like she ran off with another man or anything. Some women need gossip all the time and there's not much to talk about around here. You eat like a horse, you know that. Once you start in you don't look up till you're done."

"I was hungry. Being hungry's not a sin around here, is it?"

Noreen came out of the creek and sat down in front of me. Her hair wasn't blond or brown or red but a strange combination. There were a few freckles on her nose and when she looked at me it was only for a moment before she looked

232

down again. Her dad, even with crossed eyes, stared with advantage. "Hey, now that you're finished, you want to go swimming?"

"I can't. I've got to get back to that fence line."

"You've already dug more than he could in a week with his bum leg. Come on."

"It's not much of a swimming hole," I said. "I've got work to do."

"It cools you off, though. You're not afraid to swim naked, are you? There's nothing to it. Here, watch this."

I'd already turned to head up the trail when I heard her whipping her dress off.

"My dad told you to stay away from me, didn't he? It's no use. I live here and I like being naked so you'd better get used to it."

Half way up the trail I turned around to take a peek, but Noreen was underwater by then and there was nothing but bubbles coming to the surface.

I was lucky to stay with my sister for the summer. She didn't charge room and board. There wasn't a shower, just a tub that I willingly slid into as soon as I got home. Her only rule was that I clean it every time — she was one of those meticulous people who couldn't stand a ring around the tub. Her husband was away on a navy junket for three months, so I suspect she was glad to have me around. I'd mow the lawn on weekends and help out where I could, but most nights it was have a bath, sit down to supper, then play with my niece and nephew for a while before I went to bed. It wasn't the most glamorous life for a sixteen year old, but I was sore and tired and usually asleep by 8:30.

"So how's the life of a farm hand?" she asked over dinner.

"Harder than I thought it would be, but it's okay. Cecil's not a bad guy to work for. He watches me all the time, but I guess that's his right."

One thing my sister had learned from our mother was how to fry pork chops until they were crisp and yet melted in your mouth. I had three of them on my plate and I was so happy I almost felt like singing. Good food can make a distant memory out of a day's work.

"After a while, when he sees what kind of worker you are, he'll probably leave you on your own."

"I don't think it's my work he's worried about," I said. I told her about Noreen. I told her that last winter Cecil had hired a guy to work on the weekends and that Noreen's dad caught her and the hired hand drinking beer in the hayloft and that was the end of him.

"He should have been fired," my sister said. "Giving liquor to a young girl like that."

"You'd have to meet Noreen to understand," I said. "She's kind of all over you before you know it. Most girls pretend to be shy even if they're not."

"So," she said, "that explains why you come home with slivers and bruises every night but are up and at'em first thing in the morning."

My sister started in on a story that happened to her when she worked as a waitress at The Fountain Ice Cream Palace, involving the owner's son. She loves to talk about the past, especially about when she was a teenager. People will do that, pick out a chunk of their lives and go on and on about it like it was a time when they were really alive, and everything after that pales in comparison. When I thought about my own life, there wasn't any one time that stood out from the rest.

Isn't that hilarious? she said, Isn't that almost exactly the same story? but my mind had wondered off to the chance I'd had to go swimming with Noreen.

❖❖❖

Every day I worked that summer, the dream of buying my own motorcycle never left me and Charlie did his part to see it never did. Every day he picked me up he had something to show me. "This here's my first motorcycle license plate," he told me one morning. "They made them in the penitentiary in the old days." He had quite a collection of motorcycle magazines, some dating back to the fifties. His basement housed a display of memorabilia, and even though I'd hinted he invite me over to see it, he never did. He preferred to feed me his passion slowly, a drug fed by intravenous.

"You love motorcycles so much, how come you don't own one?" I asked him one morning after he showed me a colour photo of a '64 B.S.A. he had framed and behind glass. When he brought one of his pictures they were always carefully wrapped in cardboard. I only got one good look at each picture because he re-wrapped them and tucked them under his seat before we headed out onto the highway. My question was followed by a long silence. I figured it had either stumped him or he had a hundred reasons, and he was trying to put them in some kind of order.

"It costs an awful lot of money to own a vintage motorcycle," he said.

"Probably does, but you could rebuild one. I watch the motorcycle ads every day and you see them sometimes. There was one last week in the paper, some guy on Saltspring Island had an old something or other and he only wanted five hundred bucks. It probably didn't run, but that would be half the fun, don't you think? You can get parts. There are clubs listed, I've seen them. It might take you a couple of years but then you'd have your own instead of just pictures."

I realized I might have made it sound like his collection was a stupid idea. "It's just that you seem to know a lot about them," I said.

I wasn't interested in an old motorcycle. I wanted a new one, and on weekends I went prowling around the shops downtown, dreaming. I started bringing my magazines to work so I'd have something to do while I ate my lunch on the front porch. Noreen and her dad ate inside.

"What is that?" Noreen asked one day after she'd bolted her lunch down and come out to watch me finish mine. She knew what it was, it was just her way of starting a conversation.

"*Motorcycle Showcase*. It's a special edition that shows all the new features coming out."

"I don't know why anyone would want a stupid machine like that. You'd be better off with a good horse. A horse is like a friend. A horse is smart and knows how to use every day to his advantage. What's a motorcycle ever going to do for you besides cost you money?"

I kept my mouth shut. Noreen was always trying to start little fires and I was just as willing to let them burn out.

After a reasonable amount of time had passed, I said, "One of these days I'll pull up to work on one and I'll give you a ride."

"I might ride. And I might not ride. It depends."

Cecil came limping out onto the porch. He seemed to be limping more lately and some afternoons he didn't do much. This turned out to be one of them and he told me to carry on with setting the posts in. "Make sure you tamp the shit out of them, Danny. Those posts have to stand up to more than the wind."

I was glad to be back fencing. I'd spent more than a week roofing the old barn. Cecil couldn't get up there with his sore

236

leg and he didn't want Noreen risking her limbs in the sky. The two of them hauled the cedar shakes up the ladder and I nailed them on. I'd never done a roof before but it wasn't too hard once I caught on. I was dreading the first big rain which would tell if I'd done the job properly.

Every fence post was dipped in creosote and left a day to dry, and that was Noreen's job. She'd bring the posts down with the tractor and drop them off where I was to set them. After every ten posts were set good and firm, I'd string three strands of barbed wire down the line, pull them tight with the crowbar and staple them like Cecil had taught me. He said the wires should be tight enough so you could pluck the same note on each one with your finger. At the end of every day I'd stare down the fence line with a sense of accomplishment.

Whatever jobs Cecil had set for Noreen each day she seemed to finish before me. She'd take her horse, Raider, for a ride in the late afternoon. He was a solid tan, slightly darker on the tail and mane, and she would gallop bareback up and down the field three or four times. Some days she'd trot him over to where I was working and ask how it was going. Other days she'd just sit off a hundred feet or so and watch me work. I had the habit of not wearing a shirt in the afternoons and my muscles were getting toned and tanned at the same time.

"My dad has to go into the hospital overnight for tests," she said one day at the end of her ride, then galloped to the barn before I could ask what for.

When I told my sister, Charlie and I would be staying overnight at Cecil's farm on Thursday night, she wore a smirk on her face but didn't say a thing. Cecil told Charlie he wouldn't go in for a doctor's probing unless someone would stay overnight to keep an eye on things. Since I wouldn't have a ride into town,

Charlie said I might as well sleep there too. Cecil was too preoccupied with the thought of spending a night in hospital to consider me. Charlie would have agreed to anything that week, because he'd found an old Indian motorcycle that needed refurbishing in the Vancouver Sun, and he was going over to Surrey to take a look at it on the weekend.

"He's asking a thousand bucks, but if I can get it up and running, it might be worth it," he said, and I could tell the way he said it the bike was as good as his.

Charlie said he could get time off work to drive his brother in, but Cecil would have none of it. He left by himself shortly after I got there in the morning and his face was pasty and full of fear. Noreen gave her dad a big hug and he patted her on the head like she was the one thing he had left in the world to care for.

Cecil had given me enough work for a week so I figured I wouldn't have any trouble filling the next two days. After she'd milked the cows, Noreen disappeared into the house and I never saw her all day. I sat on the steps at lunch time and could hear the sound of a vacuum cleaner, but she never showed her face. I stopped working at four o'clock, when Charlie came back, and the two of us sat out on the front porch and had a drink. He made me a rye and seven which I forced down while he drank three. He had a scrapbook of old Indian motorcycles with him and he was showing me what he hoped to accomplish. It's got to be original, he kept saying. I won't touch it if it's not original. We could hear Noreen preparing supper in the kitchen and the birds in the trees were singing their hearts out. I pulled off my work boots, swung my feet onto the railing, then looked out on the farm and imagined what it would be like if all of it were mine.

❖❖❖

"With cooking like that I'm surprised your dad doesn't have more fat on him," Charlie said after dinner. Noreen had made spaghetti, which is nothing special, but she'd layered it with cheese and baked it in the oven, and it was delicious. She seemed to be prepared to clean up after dinner was over, but Charlie insisted we do it. He carried his dishes to the sink, and I washed and dried. I found Charlie back out on the front porch when I'd done, singing out of tune to his rye bottle. Noreen had changed into a dress and was standing over him, massaging his shoulders. It seemed like a private moment so I went into the living room and turned on the TV.

"Do you mind if I hunt for something?" Noreen asked. She squatted down in front of the TV and kept flipping through the same three channels. What was I going to say? It wasn't my TV. She flipped around until she found a boxing match.

"You like boxing?" I asked.

"No, but Uncle Charlie does."

Noreen got Charlie settled in front of the two fly-weights going at it, his rye bottle, his 7-up, and a bowl of ice cubes, then signaled to meet her on the front porch.

"He doesn't get a chance to let loose like this very often. My aunt's not all there sometimes, and he tries not to upset her. Most of the time she doesn't even know he's around. So, do you want to learn how to ride a horse?"

There were three horses in the barn and I thought Noreen had in mind to saddle one for me. She was fascinated with riding bareback and said there was nothing like it. She got me up onto Raider and used the fence to climb in front of me.

"You sure he can handle two us us?"

"Don't worry about him. He needs the exercise. Besides, we won't be going fast."

As soon as we got out to the field she put him into a gallop. I'd only been on a horse twice before, both times in a saddle.

I started out with my hands politely clasped onto her waist, but when we got moving, I grabbed on for dear life.

"Isn't that the greatest?" she asked, after we slowed down to a trot and headed out onto the road.

"Yeah," I said. "The greatest. Where are we going?"

"There are some great trails up here in the hills. It belongs to the Johnsons but they just own it, they don't live here."

When you're on a horse going down a narrow trail on the edge of a cliff, you have to trust the horse knows what he's doing. Noreen seemed confident, but I envisioned all of us heading down to a gnarly death. The smell of being close to a girl on a horse was intoxicating, and when I felt brave enough to lift my head up to look around, the smell of the yellow broom at the end of the season was overpowering. We climbed slowly up to the top of a ridge where she tied Raider to a tree, and we walked along the edge of the rock face to the very top. You could see out over the valley for miles and to the farm house where Charlie was by now likely drunk in front of the TV.

"That's pretty impressive," I said.

"I knew you'd like it. Anyone I bring up here does."

"Weren't you scared we'd fall off the cliff?"

"Old Raider's got horse sense. He knows every situation he's in for what it's worth. That's something you won't get from a motorcycle."

When Noreen sat down beside me it didn't seem close or familiar after the ride of death up the hill. "I don't like school much, do you?" she asked.

"It's all right I guess. I've got two more years to go. How about you?"

"I'm going into grade twelve because I skipped a year, but I don't know if I'm going to go back. My dad would freak if he knew what I was thinking. I know what I want to do. I want to do just what I'm doing now. Some day I'll have this farm all to myself and when I do I'm going to work it my way and raise horses. No cows, chicken, sheep. No turkeys or pigs. My dad's tried everything, but I just want to raise thoroughbreds. As soon as I'm twenty-one I'm going to have kids. Four of them, two boys and two girls."

I imagined Noreen accomplishing everything she said she would. I had an image of Cecil sitting on the porch with his crossword puzzle and the maple tree decorated with four shoeless children.

"There's something else I'm going to tell you. In a minute I'm going to kiss you, and when I do I want you to kiss me back."

At first it was a gentle kiss. Then she held my head between her hands and her kiss became earnest, like she was searching for something. As if it was the most natural thing to do, I slid my hand under her dress and up her leg. I stopped when I realized she wasn't wearing underwear.

"I knew you were a good kisser," she said. "A man's not worth two cents stuck together if he doesn't know how to kiss."

On the way back, we didn't talk much. She asked me once if I was comfortable. I can't remember what I said back.

"I'll give Raider a brushing and put him back in his stall. You can take a shower if you like."

It was an old fashioned claw foot bathtub with a shower curtain you could pull around you inside the tub. It had been so long since I'd had a satisfying shower I went ahead and used it. There were three kinds of shampoo and four different conditioners to choose from.

I found her on the carpet in front of the TV, her head on one pillow, another pillow beside her. The TV was on and shed the only light into the room; the sound was turned down and racing cars were going around in silent circles. Cecil was lying awkwardly on the couch, his mouth open.

"Come here and I'll read your fortune. Get your head down on the pillow so you're nice and comfortable. I read palms and I'm deadly accurate. You have large hands, strong hands. I see a very prominent life line and your immediate future looks bright. You're going to live a long and healthy life. Your earlobes confirm that. It turns out you are about to embark on a very sensual experience. Someone who will make you very happy is going to remove your clothes and make you the center of the universe. You need to relax and release all of your tension."

When she got to her knees and pulled her dress over her head, her white nakedness was blinding. Her breasts smiled like miracles.

"What about your uncle?"

"Don't worry about him. He's gone to a world where nothing like this matters anymore."

Noreen was in no hurry. Her slow movements were measured, her exercising of them graceful and confident. When it seemed like I could hardly breathe enough to survive, she guided me inside her and I exploded. She said we would do it again in a few minutes and then began kissing me all over. It didn't take long before her second prophecy came true. I glanced up at the couch once, but Charlie hadn't moved a muscle.

"I'll get a large glass of orange juice to share. I put new sheets on the double bed. It's a wonderful experience to fall asleep with someone to hold on to."

When I woke up in the morning I was alone in bed. I didn't know what time it was, but I knew I'd slept in. When I got dressed and came into the living room, Charlie was still on the couch, covered with a Hudson's Bay blanket.

"Where'd you go?" I asked.

"Somebody has to milk the cows. I can teach you some day if you want."

She made me some toast and poured coffee. She'd already had hers. The whole time I was eating she stared at me, as if she'd never seen another human being eat breakfast before. Between my first and second piece, she walked around the table and kissed me, then sat down.

"My dad's coming back sometime this afternoon. His heart's irregular but they say they can monitor it with pills. He's not supposed to drive, but I know he will."

"Well, that's good news," I said. "At least it's not too serious."

I heard a car pull into the driveway and Randy started barking.

"There's also some bad news," she said. The look on her face was frantic all of a sudden. "Uncle Charlie is dead and what you and I know is that he died sometime in the night."

"What?"

"He's dead. I just told you."

Two ambulance attendants knocked on the screen door and Noreen followed them into the living room. "You can carry on with the fence," she said. "As soon as all this gets settled I'll come give you a hand." A few minutes later I watched them carry Charlie out on a stretcher. They had him covered, and I couldn't tell if his mouth was still open.

Noreen stood at the screen door until the ambulance pulled away.

"You need some more breakfast before you get started?"

"How could you do that?" I said. "How could you carry on knowing your uncle was lying there stone cold?"

Noreen grabbed a piece of dry toast from the toaster and headed out to the fields without another word. I realized, in her world, it would make sense for me to follow.

PHOTOGRAPH BY YVONNE PREST

BILL STENSON's debut collection is on the precipice of national recognition. Fifteen of the eighteen stories have been published in Canadian journals and magazines. In 2003, the *Malahat Review* nominated his story "Oil Paint" for the Journey Prize, as did Ottawa's *Storyteller Magazine* for "Simple". "Oil Paint" was also nominated for the Western Fiction Magazine Award and "No One Can Fish Forever", published in the *Antigonish Review*, was shortlisted for the CBC contest. In 2004, *Prairie Fire* has nominated "Horse Sense" for the Western Magazine Award.

Stenson writes and teaches in Victoria, BC. He is the co-founder and co-editor of the *Claremont Review*.